Ca[illegible] Historical Brides
Book 7 Manitoba

By Marie Rafter
with Margaret Kyle

Print ISBN 9781772998498
Amazon Print ISBN 978-1-77362-592-8

Copyright 2017 Marie Rafter and Margaret Kyle
Series Copyright 2017 Books We Love Ltd.
Cover art Michelle Lee

Library and Archives Canada Cataloguing in Publication

Rafter, Marie, author
Landmark roses / by Marie Rafter with Margaret Kyle.

(Canadian historical brides ; book 7)
Issued in print and electronic formats.
ISBN 978-1-77299-849-8 (softcover).--ISBN 978-1-77299-846-7 (EPUB).--
ISBN 978-1-77299-847-4 (Kindle).--ISBN 978-1-77299-848-1 (PDF)

I. Kyle, Margaret, 1961-, author II. Title. III. Series: Canadian historical brides ; bk. 7

PS8603.E4494L36 2017
C813'.6 C2017-905691-3

C2017-905692-1

Dedication

Books We Love Ltd. dedicates the Canadian Historical Brides series to the immigrants, male and female who left their homes and families, crossed oceans and endured unimaginable hardships in order to settle the Canadian wilderness and build new lives in a rough and untamed country.

Acknowledgement

Books We Love acknowledges the Government of Canada and the Canada Book Fund for its financial support in creating the Canadian Historical Brides series.

Chapter One

Silberfeld, Manitoba
Fall, 1946

Dust danced in the golden light slanting across the yard, falling warm on Elsie Neufeld's shoulders. Her fingers continued to shuck the pods from the sweet green peas in the bowl cradled on her lap. Bees droned in the rose bushes crowded against the south end of the wide roofed porch, almost drowned out by the shrieks of the *kjinja* playing hide and seek among the out buildings. It was nice to hear the young voices of her grandchildren playing with their cousins.

Porch boards creaked in time with the squeak of her old rocker. From the open window above, the voices of the young women working on quilting and sewing rose and fell with the rhythm of their conversation. Saturday afternoons were a constant source of pleasure for Elsie with preparations for the following day of rest being taken care of in anticipation of family and friends gathering to enjoy each other's company after Church on Sunday afternoon.

Dropping the last pea pod into the Rogers Golden Syrup pail at her side, she shook the large bowl of shelled peas, bending her head to survey the small round orbs, looking for any bits that might have fallen among them by mistake. Finding none, Elsie set the bowl on the small table by her side.

The tall figure of Ike Neufeld threw long shadows across the dusty yard as he skirted the galloping *kjinja*, playing and squealing with laughter, and made his way to her side. Heavy work boots shed chaff and bits of hay when he mounted the shallow steps and sank into the empty rocking chair on the opposite side of the small table.

"Warm day," Elsie said rising to step inside and fetch a glass of cold lemonade for her husband.

The screen door slapped shut behind her and she paused at the bottom of the stairs to listen to the laughter of the girls. Things hadn't changed much since she was a girl. There was something very comforting in that thought. Elsie continued into the big kitchen at the back of the house and took the jug of lemonade from the oak icebox. Before she set the glass on a tray along with some pickles and cheese for Ike, Elsie gave the huge vat of borscht a stir.

"Here you are, Ike. Could you move the peas, please?" Elsie pushed the screen door open with her hip and placed the refreshments on the small table, now emptied of the bowl of peas.

Ike straightened from placing the bowl by his feet, popping a handful of peas into his mouth as he did so.

"Ike!" Elsie scolded her husband good-naturedly. "Those are for supper."

He grinned at her, chewed and swallowed. "Now Elsie, nobody's going to miss a few peas." He took the water beaded glass of lemonade she handed him.

She settled back in her chair, smoothing her apron over the skirts of her dress. Never one to sit idle for long, Elsie pulled the sweater she was working on out of the basket under the small table. Forehead furrowed in thought, she worked the stitches of the intricate pattern, one foot pushing the rocker.

"What's troubling you, Elsie?" Ike chewed on a stalk of timothy hay he pulled from the long grass poking up through the rose bushes.

"Who says anything's troubling me?" She rocked a bit harder, needles flashing in the afternoon sun."

"We've been married more years than I have fingers and toes. I think by now I know when you're upset."

"It's little Anna. She came home from school on Friday in tears. The *kjinja* at school were teasing her again." Elsie's needles stilled in hands.

"That's Agnes and Walter's trouble to deal with, not ours. Did she tell them?"

"She didn't want to. Agnes says the child just needs to be the bigger person and ignore them. Walter believes it's just kids being kids and *dot woret aule woare*, it will all work out. Poor little thing feels all alone."

“What’s it all about? They’re not hurting her, are they?” Ike quit rocking.

Elsie shook her head. “Just name calling, at least that’s all Anna told me about.”

“What kind of names?” Ike’s knuckles whitened on the rocking chair arms.

“The same as always. Saying she’s thin as a rail, she’s so ugly no boy is ever going to want to marry her. She’s such a sweet child, it breaks my heart to see her so upset. I wish they’d pay more attention to what goes on in the school yard.”

“I suppose they try, but the teacher can’t be everywhere at once and those older children should know better.” Ike’s face darkened.

“I told her not to take it to heart. God loves all His children. We’re all beautiful in His eyes. I’m not too sure it was much comfort to her.”

Ike got to his feet. “I’ll just go have a word with Walter. This has been going on for far too long. He needs to speak to the school board. No point in talking to the parents, we already tried that.”

“Wait ’til tomorrow, Ike. No need to spoil a lovely afternoon with such unpleasantness.” She halted him with a hand on his arm.

“I suppose you’re right. It can wait ’til Monday.” He drained the last of his lemonade and sauntered off toward the men gathered by the threshing machine smoking and yarning.

Elsie tucked the sweater back into the basket, sticking the needles into the skein of bright wool. She pulled out the pattern for the pretty nightgown made of unbleached linen she was planning as part of her contribution to the hope chest for Leina's daughter, Sadie. When she was finished with a bit of intricate embroidery, she folded the garment and returned it to the basket. In passing, her fingers caressed the soft folds of the baby nightie she was knitting for Nettie's baby which was due in early December. Smiling, she pushed the pattern back inside, closed the lid and got to her feet.

Elsie carried the lemonade tray through the living room and into the kitchen. Sarah and Helena were already there, along with Ed's wife Betty and Hank's wife Frieda. She wound her way through the various preparations for the following day and set the tray on the immaculate side board, careful to be sure there was a runner under it.

"The peas are shelled, I'll just fetch them from the porch," she announced to the room in general.

"*Danksheen, Mutti*," Helena replied, busy setting out an array of pickles and Bothwell cheese on shiny plates. It would be time for supper soon enough.

Elsie sidestepped Frieda who was preparing dough for the buns. She paused in the living room to savour the laughter floating down the stairs from the rooms above. Unless she missed her guess there might be more than one wedding in the coming year. The youngest Hildebrand boy had been noted to be interested in Ed and Betty's third daughter, Ella.

In the stillness of the sunlit room, Elsie rested a hand on the crocheted pineapple antimacassar on the back of the sofa. *Where did the years go? It feels like only yesterday I was going to dances and spending Sunday afternoons playing cards with my friends and casting secret glances at Ike.* That was so long ago, now. A brilliant smile lit her features.

* * *

On an afternoon in September, much like this one, she'd been dancing with girlfriends to polkas on the windup gramophone. Oh, the fun they used to have. Her cousin, Anamarie teasing her about Henry Penner, saying how he was planning to ask her out. Elsie had snorted through her nose at the thought. Henry was nice enough, she supposed, but to go out with him…? Now if it was Ike Neufeld who was doing the asking…that was another story. He was tall and handsome with a shock of dark hair that persisted in hanging over his forehead. His broad shoulders and narrow hips struck a chord deep within her that Elsie hadn't fully understood at the time.

Her fingers stroked the top of the back of the sofa absently brushing off a speck of dust. She let her gaze roam over the polished mantlepiece where a small clock ticked off the time.

It was later that same long ago day, after they'd worn themselves thin dancing and laughing that Ike approached her. Elsie and Liz were gathering up the faspa remains and taking them to the kitchen. Ike held the door to the summer kitchen and to her surprise followed the two girls inside. She'd been further nonplused when he'd shooed Liz away to get the rest of the dishes.

Elsie pressed a hand to her breast in memory of the tumult that exploded in her chest that long ago day. She closed her eyes to better remember the deep timbre of his voice.

"Elsie, I've been thinking…" he'd paused and his ears had flamed red.

"Yes, Ike? What are you thinking?" Her pulse had thundered in her ears and she'd had to bury her hands in her apron to hide the trembling. Even her knees had gone weak.

"I was wondering if you'd like to go with me to the dance next Saturday. I mean, it's okay if you've got plans already…" his voice trailed off and his big booted feet shuffled on the clean-swept floor boards.

"Well, aren't we all going together? Fred's borrowing a car from a friend in Landmark and we can take the buggy…Why wouldn't you come with us?"

Ike blushed deeper and shoved his large hands into his trouser pockets, dropping his head so she couldn't see his face. "We always go together. But I didn't mean like that…I meant would you go with me, like just you and me, just the two of us? If you'd rather not, I understand. It's okay." He turned to leave as Liz returned with a basketful of table clothes and napkins, topped by the last of the dishes.

"Oh, you're still here, Ike?" She'd halted in the doorway, her gaze darting to Elsie's face.

Elsie had tried to shoo her away, but she must have misunderstood as she stepped past Ike and began to fill the enameled washbowl with water heated in a copper tub on the stove.

"I was just leaving." Ike stepped over the threshold into the bright evening sunlight.

"I'll be right back, Liz." Elsie dried her hands on her apron and hurried after him. "Ike. Wait."

The tall young man halted and half turned back toward her. "Yes?"

Taking her courage in her hands, Elsie swallowed hard against the sudden dryness in her mouth. "Ike, I would like very much to go to the dance with you. Not as part of the group, but just you and me, going with the rest of them." She laid a hand on his arm, the long muscles hard under her fingers.

"Really?" Ike had tipped his head back. Elsie could still see him as if he stood in front of her. The sun picking out the strong contours of his features, his blue eyes bright and intense on her face.

The memory still quickened her heart and brought a smile to her face.

"Yes, really," she'd answered him, a smile breaking across her face.

"Good." He cleared his throat. "That's good, then. I'll be by to meet you beforehand.

Before Fred gets here with the car. I can hitch the wagon for you."

Elsie had laughed, she remembered. "I think I can harness Polly. I've done it a hundred times..." she'd faltered at the expression chasing across his face. "But, if you'd like to do it for me, I'd appreciate it. Save me from worrying about getting my dress dirty. Thank you, Ike."

"That's set then. I...I...I gotta go." He strode across the short grass by the house, eschewing the path beaten in the dirt. If he'd gone any faster the poor boy would have been running.

* * *

"Grossmama, are you all right? I just came in to see if help was needed with anything." Sadie halted by her grossmama and studied her face.

"Yes, I'm fine. Just thinking." She shook her head to dispel the memories. "I was on my way to collect the peas from the front porch and got caught up in old memories." Elsie moved toward the front door.

"I'll get them, why don't you go back into the kitchen and supervise. I think the barley is roasted and just needs to be ground, the chicory is by the coffee grinder." Sadie patted Elsie's arm and skipped lightly out to get the bowl of peas, the screen door slapping closed behind her, before it opened again almost immediately and Sadie appeared with the bowl of peas tucked against her hip.

She hooked her arm through Elsie's when she caught up with her just outside the kitchen. Together, the two joined the rest of the women. Laughter and the warmth of family chatter didn't slow the work of busy hands.

* * *

Elsie straightened the new scarf, arranging it neatly on her head and smiled at her reflection. For a woman of fifty-five years she looked very well. The years may have etched fine lines at the corners of her eyes and around her mouth though the diffuse light filtering through the curtains softened them into nonexistence. She ran her hands over her still narrow waist and hips, smoothing the material of her best Sunday dress.

"Elsie, are you coming?" Ike's voice echoed up the staircase. "I've got the buggy waiting by the porch steps."

"Coming!" With one last appraising glance at her reflection, Elsie crossed the bedroom her heels clicking on the wood floor. No one could ever say Elsie Neufeld looked less than her best on a Sunday morning. The old house was quiet as she descended the stairs. Running her hand down the polished bannister, she smiled. The sunlit peace would soon be broken once the family arrived when Church was over. Her steps slowed momentarily when she entered the living room, ticking off the items prepared and waiting in the kitchen.

"Elsie…" Ike swung the screen door open and broke off abruptly when he caught sight of her standing in a golden beam of light.

"I'm right here, Ike. Come along, we're going to be late if we don't hurry."

Her husband came to her side in two long strides and tucked her hand into the crook of his elbow. "Standing there all bright and golden you're as beautiful as the day I married you."

"Thank you, Ike." Elsie giggled like a young girl and gave him a coquettish glance. "Sometimes it seems like only yesterday, doesn't it?"

"Somedays," he agreed moving toward the door and the waiting buggy.

Elsie went down the wide porch steps with her head high, pleased the long slender fingers of her hand looked elegant resting on her husband's arm. Her wrist peeking out from the sleeve of her dress was still thinner than her sister Agatha's. She patted at the strand of shining hair the prairie wind teased from under her hat, tucking it back safely where it belonged.

Ike handed her up into the buggy seat and waited until she was settled before going around to the driver's side. He ran a hand over Polly's hip as he passed and paused to straighten a strap on the bridle before joining his wife, the springs of the buggy squeaking in protest at the added weight.

"Giddup, mare." Ike slapped the lines lightly on the bay gelding's rump. The horse agreeably moved forward and obeyed the signals that sent her out of the yard and unto the dusty road. The September morning was warm with a slight edge to the air that said without a doubt that summer was fading. The breeze carried the scent of sun-ripened grain and last roses of summer nodding along the roadside. How she loved the smell of the wild roses that ran rampant over the rolling prairie. Overhead a pair of hawks circled in the autumn blue sky, bright in contrast to the golden prairie sweeping to the horizon. The creak and rumble of the buggy accompanied by the jingle of harness and the sound of the mare's hooves striking the soft surface of the road was comfortingly familiar. Elsie turned and smiled at her husband of thirty-five years. Time had been as kind to him as it had to her, she reflected.

Ike tipped his head and caught her eye. "Penny for your thoughts?" He raised an eyebrow.

She shook her head and patted his arm. "Just enjoying the morning. It's such a lovely day."

There was already a line of other horse and buggies outside the church along with a scattering of automobiles parked haphazardly anyplace they could find space. Ike brought the buggy to a halt, set the brake and stepped down. He tied the horse's lead to bracket in an open space on the hitching rail in the shade of a spreading tree. Elsie took his hand and disembarked the buggy, careful of her dress on the dusty wheel.

Together the couple joined the others entering the building, the white paint gleaming in the sun. Elsie nodded to acquaintances and scanned the gathering for her extended family. In such a small community it was impossible not to know everyone present and a hum of conversation buzzed around her. The men were handsome in their Sunday best and the women's bright dresses fluttered like brilliant butterflies as they moved toward the open doors.

Elsie blinked in the sudden dimness of the small area just inside the porch. She shook her head when Ike glanced down inquiringly at her. Satisfied she was fine, he led her into the nave and waited for her to precede him into the pew with the female members of her family. Ike carried on to where his sons Ed, Jake, and Hank and the young men of the family were already seated. Elsie settled herself beside Agnes and glanced over at her daughters and granddaughters. She smiled to see Agnes, Susan and Helena had separated the boys young enough to still sit with the women. Sarah hadn't arrived yet. Elsie frowned and turned to ask Agnes if she knew where her sister was. A stir at the back of the church distracted her and she turned to see Sarah entering leaning on her husband's arm. She smiled as she joined the rest of the women in the pew. Elsie kept her expression carefully schooled, but noted the pallor of her daughter's face and the faint sheen of perspiration on her brow. The building was warm and a bit stuffy, but she didn't think it could account for Sarah's pale face.

Perhaps it was just the pregnancy that was making the girl feel poorly. Elsie sent a silent prayer heavenward that it wasn't the malaria rearing its ugly head. Not again, she prayed. Not when the dear child was carrying again.

The pastor began the service and Elsie gave her full attention to the matter. The *Vorsängers* were in fine form, the choristers leading the congregation in responsive singing. They sat at the front of the church on the left side of the raised platform where they called out the number of the songs so the congregation could find the selection in their *Gesangbuch*.

Elsie joined her voice with the others at the appropriate times, giving herself over to the oneness of community the combined voices invoked. With all present singing mindfully and in the moment, offering the music to God with heartfelt love and praise, Elsie knew she was more than just one person. She was part of the soul of the congregation enraptured by the strength of their combined voices and purpose, praising and following the glory of the Almighty.

"I was so helpless, full of sin, nothing good in myself I find," she sang.

Somehow the hour long service always seemed to short, but Elsie never emerged from the church without feeling renewed and invigorated. Truly the love of God was a pure and powerful thing which she welcomed with all her heart.

Elsie rose with the rest of the congregation at the conclusion of the service and tucked her *Gesangbuch* into her purse. She joined the press of people crowding the aisle and heading for the door. Brilliant sunlight spilled into the small porch nearly blinding Elsie as she stepped from the shadowy interior of the building. Careful of where she put her feet until her eyes adjusted to the change in light, she descended the shallow steps. Her gaze raked the milling crowd for Sarah and Arnold, but she failed to see them.

"Come along, Elsie. Everyone will be at the house later. There'll be time to visit with the family then." Ike joined her and took her arm, heading toward the shade where Polly waited patiently.

By the time they arrived back at the farm, the sun was high in the sky and the temperature had soared from its earlier mildness. Even in September the air was humid and mosquitoes buzzed and hovered around Elsie's ears. She slapped at one and grimaced.

"I'm not looking forward to winter, but I will be glad when the weather cools enough for us to be rid of the biting insects," she remarked.

"The stock will be glad of the cooler weather too, but we must be thankful for the dry weather to get in the last of the barley." Ike halted the buggy by the front porch. He got down and came around to assist his wife.

She nodded her thanks and hesitated on the top step to watch him lead the horse across the yard. He was still a fine figure of man, she thought before going inside to freshen up before the rest of the family arrived.

Her fingers were busy adjusting the collar of her dress when the sound of voices drew her to the window. Below in the yard her sons and daughters were arriving with their families. Smiling, she turned from the happy scene and went lightly down the stairs. All the preparations for light noon repast and the faspa to follow later had been done the day before. There was nothing to do but set it out and enjoy having her family around her while they shared the meal.

After the general confusion of arrivals, everyone gathered in the dining room. Elsie glanced around the table at the bright smiling faces. How things had changed since they were young. At times it amazed her that these handsome and beautiful people had come from her union with Ike. She thanked the Lord for her good fortune and the abundance of her grandchildren.

When everyone was full Ike stood and offered the traditional blessing. '*Gesegnete Mahlzeit*,' which signified the end of the meal. The children left the table and dashed outside to play in the warm September sunshine. After the dishes were cleared, Elsie found time to draw Sarah aside.

"Are you well, Sarah? I missed speaking with you at church." She studied her daughter's face.

"I'm fine, Mome. Everything's just fine. I saw the doctor this week, you know that already. He said things are progressing as they should and I wasn't to worry. So I won't"

If Elsie thought the younger woman's smile was slightly forced, she forbade to mention it. "That's good then. You run along and find Arnold. Mind you seek out a nice spot for a bit of a nap." She patted her daughter's arm and watched her step onto the front porch. God willing, all would go well for her and the baby.

Chapter Two

Schweene Schlachte

“I’m going out to the barn now, Elsie.” Ike pushed back from the kitchen table and took his hat from the hook by the door. “I expect the boys will be showing up soon. I want to get the hogs separated and into the pen.”

“Be careful, Ike. Let the boys do the heavy work.” She flicked crumbs off the gaily printed oil cloth table covering after removing the coffee mugs to the counter by the sink.

“You do the same. Let the young ones do the scraping and carrying.” He shrugged into a jacket against the chill of the late September morning. The eastern sky was pearl gray with pre-dawn light, frost coated the boards of the porch when he opened the door and stepped out.

Elsie drew her hand knit sweater closer around her shoulders at the cool air sweeping across the kitchen. She stoked the big cook stove with more wood in preparation for the huge breakfast that would be needed once everyone arrived. In addition to their own children and their families, Ike had invited two other couples. Sarah and Arnold wouldn’t come until later. Elsie frowned. Poor Sarah was ill again with the malaria. A reminder of their time in Paraguay. Sarah was just a baby when they left the South American country after having moved there in the late 1920s, but not before she'd fallen victim to the mosquito carried disease. Elsie shook her head, she knew Sarah didn't look well after church last week, but the girl had insisted she was fine. *Please, don't let her pregnancy end badly again.* Elsie paused to say a fervent prayer and immediately asked God's forgiveness for the thought. Life and death were in His hands. Sarah and Arnold had already lost two babies due to Sarah having a relapse of the malaria while pregnant. Elsie shook her head and worried her bottom lip. How much could a body bear, she wondered. How many babies lost or still born before something died in a woman's heart?

"We can only hope for the best. It's in God's hands," she whispered to the silent room, hands busy filling the big kettle with water. She was surprised there wasn't a skim of ice on the top. She also filled the big cauldron reservoir on the side of the stove. It was handy to have the water warm all the time. Setting the kettle to boil, she went to check her supply of simples to be sure there was still Jesuit bark and Artemisia leaves. The nearest doctor was a fine man, but Elsie still put faith in the cures of the old woman in the Chaco area of Paraguay. The Mennonite community of Menno was established there in 1926-27. In exchange for religious freedom, exemption from military service, the right to speak German in schools and elsewhere, along with the right to administer their own education, medical, social and financial institutions, the Mennonites agreed to colonize the Chaco area which was at that time inhospitable and unproductive. The Paraguayan congress passed a law in 1921 which allowed the colonists to create a state within the state of Boqueron.

The Mennonite reputation of excellent farmers, hard workers and discipline made them perfect candidates to populate the area of western Paraguay and keep Bolivia from encroaching on the area.

Elsie and Ike, along with many others made the long arduous trek only to find themselves confronted with thorn forests, ponds and marshes. The area was hot and arid, but also prone to floods during the rainy season. The few thousand Mennonites hacked a community out of the wilderness. But not without loss of life to typhoid, which wiped out a good number of the colonists, snakes, and accidents incurred while clearing land and building shelter. Eventually, farms were established and the community thrived. Some enterprising soul even started a newspaper, the *Mennoblatt*, which to Elsie's knowledge was still a viable enterprise.

Her hand hovered over the jar of Artemisia leaves.

There had been good times in Menno, but the religious leaders were far stricter than the ones they left behind in Manitoba and Elsie had sometimes chaffed under the restrictions placed upon the women. In the end it was the death of the three babies, two from typhoid and one from some undiagnosed fever that had convinced Ike to bring his family back to Canada.

Satisfied there were enough leaves in the jar, Elsie returned to the kitchen. It was going to be a long day, but many hands made light work and the joy of the family gathering together brought a warm glow to her heart.

* * *

Sarah arrived with Arnold shortly after Hank and Frieda, coming through the door with bowl of potato salad in her arms.

"I'm fine, Mother," Sarah said before Elsie could speak. "It's just the baby, that's all."

"Even so, no heavy work for you. What does the doctor have to say about the malaria flare up?" Elsie took the heavy bowl from her daughter.

"He says to hope for the best, Mome. And pray." Sarah caught and held her mother's gaze. "It will be alright this time. I'm sure of it. I've been praying hard, and so has Arnold."

"I've prayed as well, Sarah. Why don't you set yourself down on the sofa and help watch the little ones. The older girls are fine with the toddlers, but I'd feel better if someone more responsible kept an eye on the babies."

"Sure, Mome." Sarah put a hand to her lower back and sank into one of the easy chairs, resting her feet on the ottoman. "Happy?" She smiled at her mother.

Elsie nodded and took the salad into the kitchen.

Not long after the children and babies were set up in the living room with Sarah and some of the older children to watch them, the men brought the first load of 'insides' from the hogs into the summer kitchen. A few late flies buzzed over the piles of intestines that would soon be sausage casings. Elsie pushed her sleeves up and moved a length of intestines from the pile. It was still partially filled with the animal's last feed. Beside her, Nettie and Susan were likewise engaged. Flushing the partially digested contents into a galvanized pail was tedious and hard work. All the material needed to be removed before the casing could be immersed in a huge vat of salted water. There they sat for several hours, during which time the women set about rendering the *schmalz* — the lard — and preparing the *yvreve* — the crackles. The *yvreve* and the *ripspeer* — the spare ribs — were put in a big cauldron and roasted until they were crisp. Once the spare ribs were cooked they came out of the cauldron and went into a pan where they were sprinkled with salt. The remaining lard was poured into large dish pans to cool and then placed in stone jugs for storage. The *yvreve* were especially tasty treats and Elsie grinned secretly when she caught her grown daughters sneaking bits from the pan of finished crackles, just as they had as young girls.

By lunch time the men had scraped the ears, feet, knees and head of meat. Once the lard was removed from the cauldron these pieces were thrown in and set to cooking.

Work paused momentarily while empty stomachs were filled and thirst assuaged. The lunch was prepared the day before and roasted with *bobatt* —stuffing. They set out *plumeoos*, faspa with buns, salt and *yevreschmalz*, this was the *yrevre* that came through the strainer in the *schmalz* jam. Coffee and tea was supplied in copious quantities.

By the time the lunch things were cleared away, the intestines were ready to be turned inside out and scraped. Elsie's shoulders ached and her fingers cramped by the time her portion of the task was finished.

Once the casings were cleaned and turned right-side out they were dredged in salt and put in a pan waiting for the sausage filling. The *formaworscht* —farmer sausage — was stuffed with ground meat and spices and taken to the smoke house to be hung. The *levaworscht* — liverwurst — was prepared a bit differently. One part liver was added to four parts meat trimmings, some neck meat and a bit of rind. Once ground, this was stuffed into the larger casing, when the casing was sufficiently full, the skin was pricked with a darning needle to keep it from bursting while the sausage was boiled in a huge cauldron.

Elsie and Frieda moved on to making the head cheese. They took the ground meat from the head along with some rind and salt and pepper. This was put in a cloth sack and flattened into the bottom of a flat pan. Elsie placed a board on top of the cloth sack and waited for Frieda to set a heavy crock of crackles on top. Left overnight it would squeeze out any excess fat. The older woman straightened up and wiped her forehead with the back of her wrist. Tomorrow the head cheese, feet, ears, heart and tongue would be covered with whey and stored in another stoneware jar.

Next she turned her attention to the side bacon — *siedefleisch*. It took some muscle to roll up the outer skin of the pig and tie it with binder twine. The older boys carried the sides to the smoke house to be cured along with farmer sausage. The big *schinkjes* — the hams — went into containers packed with salt to be cured. Once the weather turned colder the hams would be frozen in the uninsulated summer kitchen. The building served as a freezer and store house in the cold winter months. In spring the thawed meat would go into the smoke house to be smoked.

It pleased Elsie that no part of the pig went to waste. She set some of the pork hocks, legs and feet of the pigs aside to share with poorer members of the community. The rest would be boiled and pickled in *varick* — whey. Ears and tails were scraped and pickled the same way. Liver left over from the liverwurst was set on the counter to be fried for the evening meal.

By the end of the day everyone was exhausted but in a good way. A satisfied glow of comfort warmed Elsie's heart and eased the ache of tired muscles. There was a certain feeling of completion and connection with those who had gone before, keeping true to the traditional ways was a comfort to her soul. She thought of it as a bridge between the present and the past. A tribute in a way to the families who fled their home countries to avoid persecution but who brought their heritage with them.

She looked about the summer kitchen where everything was now neat and tidy. The hunger that could lurk in the long winter months ahead would be held at bay by the food put away after a long day of hard work. Along with the jars of preserves she and her daughters put up during the warm summer months and early fall, the abundance of food was a blessing. One she never forgot to thank God for.

No one in her family would go hungry if Elsie had anything to say about it.

Chapter Three

Bringing in the Sheaves

Elsie motioned the young girl from Bothwell she'd hired to help with meals for the harvesters to join the other girl already in the kitchen. What with the men come to help with harvesting the fields of wheat and barley, there was no way Elsie could manage on her own. Her girls were busy at their own places helping their men bring in their own crops. True, there was Agnes and Walter here, but many more hands were needed to ensure the crops were taken in before the frost could blight them.

"Take the coffee off the heat before it boils," Elsie cautioned Liz, the Bothwell girl.

"Yes, sorry." She flicked her long red braid of hair over her shoulder before moving the pot off the heat.

"The ham is in the icebox, Grace. Knives are in the drawer there. Start slicing the meat for sandwiches, if you would," Elsie directed the shorter of the two girls.

Grace's long blond hair was caught up in loose knot at the back of her neck. She hurried to do Elsie's bidding the strings of her apron swinging against her skirts.

The shouts of the harvesting crew carried on the still morning air where they gathered in the yard. Elsie glanced out the window and was surprised to see Sarah's husband Arnold among the men. She squinted against the slanting sunlight. Ike put a hand on the younger man's shoulder and shook his head. A knot twisted her stomach. Something was not right, not right at all. Arnold should be at home taking care of his own harvest, not standing here in the yard.

She swallowed hard. Her son in law shook Ike's hand and mounted the gelding he must have ridden over on. The man's demeanor gave away his dejected state of mind. Ike came toward the house with slow steps.

"I'll be right back. See that the coffee is ready for the men, and make up some fried eggs and ham on buns." Elsie smoothed her hair with nervous hands and went to meet her husband. Whatever it was he had to say to her, she didn't want other ears to hear. The practical part of her acknowledged something must be wrong at the Bertsch's. "It could be anything," she muttered. "Maybe that old equipment of his broke down again and he was over here looking for parts. Yes, that must be it."

The hinges on the door squeaked when she pulled it open and met Ike on the wide porch. The fresh scent of the late September morning was full of the pungent perfume of the pots of purple petunias set along the railing. Their sharpness softened by the heady sweetness of the late roses.

"Elsie…" Ike halted and wiped his mouth with his hand.

"What is it? I saw Arnold out here a minute ago." She paused and swallowed. "Did that old tractor break down again?" Elsie twisted her fingers together in the pocket of her apron, reminding herself to breath.

"Elsie, it's Sarah. She lost the baby. Arnold says he doesn't know what to do. She just sits holding the crib quilt she was working on and staring. He's scared."

"I'd best go over straight away." Her hands were already untying the long apron from around her waist. "Is her malaria bothering her? I'd best get some things together." Elsie turned back toward the house.

"I'll hitch the buggy for you." Ike stepped down off the porch.

"I'll call Helena and ask her to send Sadie over to take care of the lunch and give those girls in there some direction." She paused with her hand on the handle of the door and took a deep breath before straightening her shoulders and stepping inside.

While her mind calmly went about cataloguing what she needed to gather to take with her, her emotions churned wildly. Poor Sarah, and the poor child. This was the third pregnancy that had ended in sorrow. Sarah had always been the more delicate of the girls, there was no telling how she'd react to yet another disappointment. *It's worrying she isn't expressing any emotion, just sitting and staring.*

She's got to let that pain out, it does no good to hold onto grief like that.

Worry lent speed to her hands and in short order Elsie had gathered everything she felt would be useful. She stuffed it all into a covered basket and hurried to the door. The buggy waited at the bottom of the porch steps, Ike stood at Polly's head. The patient mare stoop hip shot, tail lazily swishing at the odd fly.

Elsie handed the basket to Ike who had come around to help her into the buggy. He swung the basket up onto the seat and then handed her up.

"You call if you need anything, okay?" Ike tipped his head back to see her better.

"Of course." Elsie picked up the lines and chirruped to the big mare. "I don't know when I'll be home, but Sadie will take things in hand."

The buggy swayed and bumped over the uneven ground of the yard. Once she turned onto the dirt road she urged the horse to a jog ignoring the pain in her hips the jolting caused. The sky was that pure blue so particular to early autumn. On either side of the road barley and wheat fields rolled to the horizon, some shorn of their crop already and some with heavy headed stalks rippling and shining in the strong sunlight. The sweet perfume of wild roses mingled with the dry scent of the dust disturbed by the horse's hooves. Elsie glanced at the full blown pink blooms nodding at the side of the road. Her mind on more pressing matters, she still took note of the bulbous bright red rose hips peeking out among the throng of dark green leaves of the bushes. She must remember to get the young ones to collect them. An excellent source of vitamin C, the hips also made a tasty jam.

"Heyup, horse," she urged the animal to a faster pace, slapping the reins on her rump. Snorting the mare hurried her pace to a trot, the buggy jouncing along behind me. Elsie held the lines in one hand and steadied herself with the other. Almost without having to be told the horse slowed marginally and turned into Sarah and Arnold's lane. "Slow down, you," Elsie muttered at the animal and shifted to a more secure position on the seat. Almost before the buggy halted, she dismounted from the buggy, wincing at the twinge in her knees when her feet hit the ground. One of the boys Arnold had around the place to help out took over care of the horse and buggy, Elsie tugged the basket down and hurried to the house. Bright red and white geraniums sat in pretty pots by the steps while multi-hued pansies lifted their tiny faces to the sun.

Arnold met her at the door, the screen door opening with a creak. "She's upstairs. I can't get her to even look at me." He ran a hand through his hair, leaving it sticking up in spikes.

Elsie resisted the urge to tell him to straighten his collar and comb his hair back into place. "I'll go on up and see what I can do, Arnold. Maybe have one of the girls helping in the kitchen to put the kettle on and make some tea." She spoke as she brushed by him and ascended the stairs. The poor man looked so helpless Elsie could hardly bear to look at him. At the top of the staircase she paused on the landing, took a deep breath and pulled her shoulders back. Taking another moment to compose herself, she used the hall mirror to pat her hair back into place and brush the dust from her skirt.

"Sarah?" Elsie rapped on the door with her knuckle before giving it a little push. It swung open smoothly without a sound and she stepped inside, setting the basket down at her feet. The woman in the chair was hunched over the material in her lap, fingers twisting the fabric into contortions. To Elsie's consternation, her daughter's face was dry, eyes wide and staring out the window in front of her. Sarah gave no sign she knew anyone had entered the room. "Sarah, look at me." Elsie moved to kneel at her daughter's side.

The bereft woman kept her gaze fixed blindly on the brilliant rectangle of sunlight spilling in through the window where the curtains fluttered in the prairie breeze. Her fingers tightened on the tiny quilt, knuckles whitening under the pressure. Elsie covered her daughter's fists with her hand and worked to loosen the fingers clenching the material.

"There now, just ease up, Sarah. That's a good girl." She eased the crumpled quilt away and tossed it on the end of the double bed. "Are you all right? Shall I have Arnold call the doctor? Sarah!" her voice sharpened in an attempt to elicit a reaction.

She was rewarded by an almost imperceptible shake of her daughter's head. A scuffle of boots on bare floorboards drew Elsie's attention to the doorway. Arnold hovered there uncertainly, anguish plain on his handsome face. She rose and crossed to speak with him.

"Call Agnes please, Arnold." She paused for a moment and frowned, glancing back at the unnaturally still woman in the chair. "And Doc Regehr as well. The poor child needs to be looked at and maybe something to ease the pain in her heart. Go now, man. She'll be fine," Elsie urged her son in law when he hesitated.

"I'm not so sure about that, Mother Elsie. I've never seen her like this. It scares me."

"All the more reason, then, to get a move a on and make those calls. Agnes first if you please. I'm going to need help cleaning things up before the doctor arrives."

Arnold took one last look at the shining blonde head of his wife drooping over her clasped hands before he fled into the shadows of the landing, his boots echoing on the stairs as he descended. Elsie caught her lower lip in her teeth. *I should have asked the boy to call Ike and let him know I'll be a while. What a time for this to happen. Right in the middle of harvest.* The deep timbre of Arnold's voice rumbled from the hall below. She nodded. *Good. I need*

Agnes to help me get Sarah tidied up and change the bed.

Flies were beginning to buzz lazily around the tossed bed clothes. Elsie moved to the open window and lifted the sill enough to shove the expanding screen into the opening.

"Light. The light is gone."

Elsie almost missed the desolate muttering. She spun around to find Sarah's unblinking gaze fixed on her. "What? What is it, Sarah?"

The muscles in the long neck rippled as Sarah swallowed hard before working her jaw, as if forcing words to emerge. "The light. It's gone." Her arms crossed over her belly and she bent forward over them. "Gone."

Elsie knelt and enfolded the slight figure in her arms. "Hush now. Hush. God has His reasons for what He does. There will be more children. Once you're healed and healthy again." She stroked the soft corn silk hair. Sarah's head rocked against her mother's shoulder.

"No, no more. I can't do this anymore. I can't." Finally, sobs shook the thin shoulders, a high pitched keening rose from Sarah's throat. "I can't keep doing this. Hoping this time will be different. That this time the baby will be healthy, and not gone before it's even born."

Elsie made soothing noises and rocked her daughter in her arms unable to make any sense of the now incoherent words punctuating the sobs.

"Mome, what can I do?" Agnes stopped in the doorway before entering and closing the door behind her. She dropped her sweater on the straight back chair by the wall. "What happened? Is it the same old trouble?" Sympathy and shared anguish darkened her blue eyes.

"Yes, the same trouble. I had so hoped this time would be different…" She shrugged helplessly. "She was just entering the fourth month…I prayed this wouldn't happen again."

"Oh dear, poor Sarah. It's God's will I suppose, and He must have His reasons. But still, it's hard." Agnes bustled over to strip the sheets from the bed as she spoke. With the bloody wet sheets, wrapped in the chenille bedspread, bundled in her arms she moved toward the door. "I'll be right back, I want to set these to soaking in cold water and salt. There should be fresh sheets in the linen press, I'll bring some back."

"Agnes, can you bring warm water and some clothes? I'm sure Sarah will feel better once we get these dirty things off her." Elsie lifted her head to catch her elder daughter's gaze.

"Of course, Mome. Be right back." She disappeared from the doorway, heels clicking briskly on the polished floor of the landing.

"Come now, Sarah. Let's get that hair brushed. You'll feel better once we get you set to rights." Elsie picked up the brush from the dresser and gently ran it through the tangled skein of golden strands. Her busy fingers plaited the long gossamer hair into one braid and tied it off with a ribbon from the tray in easy reach on the dresser. "There now, that's better."

"Here we are," Agnes returned laden down with fresh linens for the bed balanced precariously on a basin of water. Towels, hung over her arm, swung against the skirt of her dress. She hooked the straight chair over by her sister with her foot and set the basin of water down on it. Elsie pulled two of the towels and a wash cloth from Agnes' load and dropped the small cloth into the warm water. Agnes set the bedding on the end of the bare mattress and used a thick towel to blot the wet spot on the mattress. Thankfully, it wasn't large, the bunched up sheets must have caught the worst of it.

Elsie turned her attention to her younger daughter, easing the nightgown off her arms and over her head. Sarah sat like a wooden doll, stiff and unresponsive. By the time she was clean little beads of sweat were running down Elsie's spine. "Agnes, can you please pass me a clean nightgown."

"Of course." Agnes turned from her task and opened two drawers before finding the right one. She pulled out a linen night dress and handed it to her mother. "Do you need help with that?" A small frown furrowed her brow.

"I'll manage. Keep on with what you're doing. The sooner we get her into bed the better." Elsie gathered up the fabric and eased the night dress over Sarah's head. By the time she had the garment on correctly, Agnes was just turning back the covers of the newly made bed. Tires scrunched in the front yard. "That must be Doctor Regehr. Run down and let him in please, Agnes."

The sound of her light steps hurrying down the stairs resurrected Elsie's memories of her children racing and playing in the big house of their childhood.

"Sarah, Doctor Regehr is here. You need to talk to him, tell him what happened. You can do that, can't you?" Her hand stroked her daughter's hair.

"What happened?" Sarah finally focussed her gaze on her mother. "What do you mean what happened? I lost another child, another one…What have I done to deserve this?"

"You haven't done anything wrong, child. This isn't your fault—"

"How can it not be my fault?" Her voice rose in hysteria.

"Here's Doctor Regehr now. He can explain to you how it's not your fault." Elsie got gratefully to her feet and moved to stand by Agnes as the doctor came into the room.

"Agnes, Mrs. Neufeld." He stepped past them and stopped by Sarah. "Hello, Sarah. Let's take a look shall we?" The doctor picked up a limp wrist to take his patient's pulse. He glanced at the two women hovering in the doorway. "If we could have some privacy, ladies? I'll yell if I need anything."

"Of course. We'll just go down and see how Arnold is holding up," Elsie said.

"I could use a cup of tea," Agnes declared.

Reluctant to leave Sarah, Elsie hesitated in the hall even after Doctor Regehr closed the bedroom door. Agnes took her arm and led her down to the kitchen where Arnold sat at the table, head in his hands.

"How is she?" The man made a masterful attempt to hide his red rimmed eyes.

"As well as can be expected. Doctor Regehr is with her, he'll set things right." Agnes filled the kettle and set the water to boil as she spoke.

Elsie sank into the nearest chair, her knees suddenly unsteady. She glanced at the clock on the wall. Heavens the time was moving on. Her sense of loyalty to her daughter warred with the need to be at home helping with harvest.

"Here, Mother." Agnes startled her from her thoughts, setting a cup of tea on the table by her hand.

"Thanks, Agnes." Her hand trembled a little, setting the cup chiming against the saucer.

Arnold drank his tea in one gulp, set the cup back on the table and rubbed both hands briskly over his face. "Is there anything I can do here? I should be helping the men with the harvest. I was on my way out when…" He stood almost knocking the chair over backward as he did so.

"I can stay with Sarah. Why don't you go on? Might make you feel better to be busy," Agnes said.

"You'll call me if Sarah needs anything?"

Agnes nodded and began clearing the cups from the table. The scene was oddly blurred, as if Elsie looked through a narrowed lens that detached her from the reality of what she saw. A hand on her shoulder startled her and she blinked. Doctor Regehr stepped further into the kitchen.

"Sarah will be fine in time. I've given her something to help her sleep. Best thing for her right now." He washed his hands at the sink and dried them on a towel. "Someone needs to stay with her in case she wakes up. The medication makes some people confused."

"I'm staying," Agnes said. "I'll go up and sit with her." Agnes hurried from the room.

"Are you sure she's all right?" Elsie turned worried eyes on the doctor. "She was acting so…strange, I guess is the best word."

"Shock and grief will do that sometimes. This is the third pregnancy in a little over a year that has ended like this. But she's young and healthy, plenty of time to try again. God willing she'll be able to carry to term." He shrugged into his coat.

Elsie tightened her jaw and kept her thoughts to herself. Trust a man to think that it was that easy to get over losing a child. Like falling off a horse and getting back on, a woman was expected to just carry on. Elsie was all too aware how the loss of a child left a huge hole in a woman's heart. One that never went away. It wasn't something that was ever discussed, or even mentioned, but she was sure she wasn't the only one who grieved a lost child in the privacy of her heart.

"Well, I'll be off." Doctor Regehr took his leave.

"I'm going too. Can I catch a ride with you as far as the field at the end of the lane?" Arnold asked Elsie while he put his cap on.

"Of course. I do need to get back and keep an eye on things." She glanced at the stair case. "Agnes seems to have things well in hand here."

* * *

Polly stopped obligingly by the edge of the field where the binder was working. Arnold hopped down and went to join the stookers setting the sheaves of bound grain into stooks. Waving Elsie clucked to the horse and continued on her way. Turning into her own lane she found the men involved in the same pursuit. She leaned her elbows on her knees and rested her chin on her hands, needing a few moments of calm to compose herself before going back to the house. It was a pretty pastoral scene, the golden grain bound and standing upright, leaning on each other. How much quicker it would be if they could afford a combine, and easier on Ike to be sure. At least they had their own binder and enough family and neighbors to not have to hire too many men for this part of the harvest.

In the field the patient horses trudged along. A sickle knife in front of wide white denim belt of the binder and carrier platform flashed in the sunlight. The cut grain fell in a golden way onto the platform before being bound it into a sheave. The sheaves dropped onto the carrier from the belt before being dropped in rows for the stookers to set, dust danced golden in the air haloing the workers. The stooks reminded Elsie of rows of bushy tipis. They would stand and dry until they were ready for the thresher.

A shout caught her attention as she stirred herself to carry on for home. "What on earth? Whoa, mare." Elsie stood up to see better, shading her eyes with her hand. The men were gathering around something near the binder. She hitched the reins around the buggy brake and climbed down. Picking her way across the cut stubble as fast as she could, Elsie arrived at the binder out of breath. "Oh my goodness, what happened?" She dropped to her knees, mindless of the sharp stubble pricking her legs and the dust and chaff her skirt picked up. Hank, her second oldest son, lay senseless on his back.

"That gelding I borrowed from the Reimer's kicked him square in the chest when he was trying to fix one of the tugs on the harness." Ike bent down and peered at Hank's face. "Think we should move him?"

"Let me see." Elsie waved her husband back. "Is there something we can shade him with? Bring me some water."

Two of men provided some shade and Elsie wet her handkerchief from the dipper one of the men provided. Carefully, she wiped Hank's face, glad to see some colour returning even though his eyes remained closed. Suddenly, he took a deep shuddering breath and struggled to sit up.

"What? Where am I?" he managed to gasp out.

Ike put a hand on his shoulder. "Just take it easy, son. Darn horse kicked you in the chest. Sit up slow." He bent and slid an arm around Hank's shoulders.

Elsie sat back on her heels, wet cloth still dripping in her hand. "Why don't you come back to the house and rest a while?"

Hank got to his feet and stood wavering a bit. "No, Mome. I'm fine. Just take a minute to get my legs back under me."

"Really, Heinrich, I think you should come to the house." Elsie set her chin sternly.

"Using my proper name won't make any difference, Mome. I said I'm fine and I am. There's work to be done before the sun goes down."

Elsie looked at Ike with the hope he would side with her. He removed his dusty hat and wiped his forehead with the back of his sleeve. Jamming the hat back on his head he lifted one shoulder in apology.

"If he says he's all right, then the boy's all right. Time's a'wasting. This wheat isn't going to cut itself." Ike went to gather up the lines and set the binder in motion again. The others went back to work as well, leaving Elsie to make her way back to the patient Polly.

"See that you come up to the house in time for supper," she called after the men. Elsie climbed back into the buggy and set off for home. Harvest was a busy time and a happy time, but it could also be dangerous. The crop had to come off while the weather held hot and dry, which meant long days and tired people. Hank's accident brought back memories of Susan climbing up on the binder platform wanting to be with her brother Jake. She was a determined child, even at six years old. Ike had pulled the binder out of the shed to get it ready prior to starting the harvest. Jake was up on the platform helping, when Susan scrambled up too. Ike had been unaware she was even on the equipment. The child was standing too close to the sickle blade when Ike turned the crank to start the machine. She'd gotten a nasty slash on her leg, but both her and her brother learned a good lesson the hard way. Poor Ike, she'd thought he'd never get over hurting the child, wavering between anger at her for getting up there in the first place, and guilt for not looking before he turned the crank.

Elsie halted Polly and stepped out of the buggy. In short order she unhooked the buggy and striped the harness off the horse. Dragging the heavy leather straps into the barn she hung them where they belonged. She took a moment in the dark interior to release a sigh of tiredness.

One of the dairy cows lowed out in the pasture, reminding her they needed to be fed and milked. Patting her straggling hair back into place, Elsie walked into the sunlight and headed for the house. The clatter of dishes and murmur of conversation drifted into the living room from the kitchen. Helena's voice rose above the higher younger ones keeping things in order.

Satisfied all was moving along with the supper, Elsie ascended the stairs in order to freshen up and change into something clean. Feeling more like herself, she went down to join the activity in the kitchen.

"Mome! I'm glad you're back." Helena drew her mother aside and spoke in a low voice. "How is Sarah? Is she going to all right?"

"She's doing as well as can be expected. Doctor Regehr saw to her and gave her something to help her sleep. Agnes is sitting with her."

"That good, then. I'll pop over later and see if Aggie needs a break. Such a shame, I'm sure she's disappointed."

"How is the supper coming along?" Elsie glanced out the window at the sun sinking toward the golden brown hills.

"We seem to be out of a few things. Looks like a trip to Niverville is in order, but it's getting dark…"

"Harold has a car. Maybe we can use it. I'll go ring the bell in the yard, one of them will come to see what we want." Elsie headed back out to the yard. A dull ache lodged itself in her lower back. She didn't have long to wait before one of the older grandkids came loping across the field and up to the porch.

"What's wrong, Oma? It's not supper time already is it? We've still got a quarter of the field to go." His young face glowed in the slanting rays of the sun.

"We need to go into Niverville. Ask Harold if he'll come and drive us, please."

"Right away." The teenager raced off toward the cloud of dust thrown up by the binder.

Elsie went back into the house. "Have you made a list, Helena? Can you manage here until I get back?" She picked up her purse and pinned a hat to her hair.

"This is what we need." Helena came out of the kitchen with a list in her hand.

"Thanks, Leina. I'll make the trip as quick as I can. Oh, here's Harold now." Elsie hurried out to where Walter had drawn the car up to wait for her. It was a Model T Ford. The vehicle was a little worse for wear, but Harold's wife said he loved to fuss over restoring it to its former glory. Their neighbor held the door open for her and then closed it carefully behind her.

"I've brought Peter with me. He's asleep in the back, poor lad." Harold informed her

Elsie glanced at the ten year old curled up in the corner of the small area behind the front seat. He was small for his age, and his health was what Doctor Regehr referred to as 'delicate.'

It was still daylight, but the sun was sinking as they rolled out of the yard and turned south. Elsie allowed herself to relax against the seat, turning her head to gaze at the fall colours of the prairie highlighted by the low slanting rays of the sun. Her eyes must have drifted closed, the next thing she was aware of was the car braking sharply.

"What's wrong? Are we there?" Elsie blinked and pulled herself up further in the seat.

"No, it's getting dark and the darn headlamps aren't working. Again." Grumbling under his breath, Harold got out and stamped around to the front of the vehicle. Elsie jumped when he thumped his fist on the glass covering the lights. A few more thumps and he stood back glaring at the car. With a glance at the setting sun, he got back in and put the car in gear.

"I think we can make it to Niverville before it gets full dark. I should be able to buy new bulbs there."

Elsie nodded and tried not to worry about driving home in the dark without any way to see properly. Peter popped up from the back seat.

"Are we there yet? Can I have a licorice whip?" His blue eyes were sleep smudged under the shock of white-blonde hair that stuck up every which way.

"Not yet, Peter." Elsie smiled at him. The boy subsided into the back seat as the car moved forward.

Harold pulled up in front of the grocery story as the last light glowed in the sky. Bright pin points of lights appeared in the royal blue evening sky as the stars showed their faces. Peter scrambled out of the back seat to join his father who was opening Elsie's door for her.

"I'm off to find some bulbs for the headlamps. Peter, come with me." Harold and his son strode purposefully off.

Elsie followed them into the general store, turning toward the food stuffs rather than the side of the store that held the hardware. She wasted no time in collecting the items on her list. While she waited for her items to be rung up, Harold appeared at her shoulder.

"They don't have the right bulbs here. I'm going to nip over to Leppky's at the BA station. Bill should be around, he'll open up for me even if he's closed up. Do you need help carrying all that out to the car?"

"You go ahead over to Leppky's. Peter can help me carry the groceries out to the car." Elsie handed the correct amount of money over to Mrs. Bronstone. "Thank you." She smiled at the storeowner's wife.

"Nice to see you," Mrs. Bronstone packed the items into the string bags Elsie pulled from her purse.

"You, too. I don't get to Niverville as often as I'd like," Elsie replied.

The screen door swung shut behind Walter's tall figure. Elsie passed the lighter bag to her grandson and ushered him out of the store. The pair crossed the wooden boardwalk, feet echoing in the fast falling darkness. When they arrived at the car, the groceries went into the back and Peter tumbled in after them.

"What about my licorice whip? Pape promised." His lower lip trembled.

"Now Peter. Big a big boy. Your father is worried about finding the right bulbs for the headlamps so we can see to get home." She paused for effect, "And besides…" Elsie pulled a licorice whip out of her purse where she hid it after purchasing it along with the groceries. "I think I know a young man who deserves this." She held the whip where he could see it.

"Oh! Thank you!" Peter leaned forward to accept the treat from Elsie. He thumped back into the seat happily making the licorice disappear.

"Well, that's that." Harold opened the driver side door and stuck his head in. "Leppsky's has the bulbs but they're five cents more than the store in Chortitza. Five cents each," he clarified. "Highway robbery, that's what it is."

"But how will you see to drive home?" Elsie tipped her head to look at him.

"I've got an idea, but it will make slow going." The man disappeared and the trunk creaked open causing the vehicle to sag on its springs a bit. Muttering and muted banging reached her ears as Harold rummaged in the back. The trunk closed with a metallic crash and the tall frame moved to the front of the car.

Something clanked when he hung it on the radiator cap. A match flared, throwing his face into light and shadow. A small circle of light glowed at the front of the vehicle. Harold strode around and settled into the driver seat. “There, that should do it.”

“What have you done?” Elsie peered out the windscreen.

“It’s a lantern. We’ll have to drive slow, or the wind will blow it out, but it will get us home.” He slid the car into gear and eased out into the main street of town.

“We should have phoned Helena and let her know we’d be longer than we thought. She’ll have to make do and feed the men with what is there,” Elsie worried.

“It’s too late to turn back now. I want to be sure we have enough kerosene to make it home before it runs out.”

Elsie gritted her teeth and refrained from replying. It took a long time to get home, the journey made even longer for Elsie as she worried over Sarah and how Helena was faring with the men’s evening meal. The serenity of the broad night sky failed to soothe her as it usually did. She leaned her head against the side of the door, the wind from the open window cooling her face. Raspberry and rose bushes hunched at the sides of the road, throwing deep shadows over the surface that the wavering light of the lantern did little push back.

* * *

The week after the cutting of the crop was warm and dry with a good wind blowing across the stooks enabling the wheat to dry sufficiently for threshing to begin. Ike hired his brother-in-law Isaac's threshing outfit. It was another busy time on the farm. Elsie hired the same girls to help with the kitchen chores. Isaac arrived with his crew of ten men, the thresher pulled by a tractor, rather than the work horses. A long belt was attached to the thresher from the tractor to supply power to the machine. A box wagon was brought up to catch the straw that shot out of the thresher pipe. One wagon could hold approximately sixty bushels of grain. Once the dew burned off, the teams with the hayracks were out on the field loading the rows of sheaves to bring to the thresher. Once they had packed the hay rack with as many sheaves as possible, they brought them to the granary to be unloaded and wait their turn to be fed into the thresher.

Elsie brought some coffee and sandwiches out to the crew when they took a break. Suddenly, the thresher quit making its racket. Elsie looked up from pouring coffee, startled at the sudden silence. Isaac slid down from the top of the machine where he had been greasing it. He disappeared into the tool shed. She looked at Ike for an explanation. He lifted one shoulder in a shrug.

"Isaac, do you need help with anything?" Ike picked up his coffee mug and wandered over to the tool shed.

"No. I've got it under control." Isaac stomped back to the thresher and climbed back up the machine, a hacksaw in his hand with a look of grim determination on his face.

Ike stood for a moment looking up where his brother-in-law disappeared. The sound of the hacksaw grating on metal emerged from the innards of the thresher. When he was finished he climbed back down and started the thresher again. Leaving the machine thundering away, he returned the hacksaw to the toolshed.

"What happened?" Elsie queried when Isaac came to get his coffee.

"Nothing important," the man replied tersely and moved off to nurse his coffee away from the crew.

Later that night as they settled down to sleep Elsie brought the subject up with Ike. "What did Isaac need the saw for today? I've never seen him look so fed up and angry."

Her husband surprised her by laughing. "He didn't want to talk about it, but we plagued him until he did. A keyway was stuck out from the shaft further than it should have been. Caught his hat and a chunk of his hair and ripped it out. He was too mad to say anything at the time, just went and got something to cut the darn thing off with."

“How much hair did he lose? Was he cut?” Elsie propped herself up on an elbow to better see Ike’s face.

“Not too much. About the size of a quarter is all. He took his cap off to show us and the hole in his hat. Must have hurt like the dickens. Maybe that’s why he didn’t say anything at the time.”

The bed shook with silent laughter again. Elsie lay back down, puzzlement furrowed her brow. She would never understand how men could laugh off danger and potentially dangerous situations. Like they had to put up this brave front or something for their fellow males.

“Morning comes early, Elsie. Time to sleep.” Ike rolled over on his side and heaved a huge sigh.

“Good night, Ike.” Elsie folded her hands on top of the counterpane and closed her eyes. Sleep was slow in coming; her thoughts kept bouncing back to Sarah and Arnold. Her health was improving, but Sarah was so quiet, so detached from everything around her. She said another prayer for her youngest daughter. God would help her heal and bear the grief with fortitude.

Chapter Four

Canine Hero

Somehow September had slipped into October. Fall was in the air, the sun slanting across the wheat and barley stubble, raising a fine mist as the frost burnt off. The sharp edge to the wind was welcome after the heat of summer and it was a Godsend the number mosquitoes and flies were diminished by the change in seasons. A few hardy roses made bright pink counterpoints to the glossy rose leaves and bright rose hips.

She sighed and shifted in her chair, gaze roaming over some of the grandkids digging the last of the potatoes, onions and other root vegetables from the large garden. The feathery heads of the two straggly rows of carrots tossed in the breeze sweeping across the hills. Elsie pulled her jacket up tighter around her chin. Amusement pulled at her lips. The twins, Doris and Willy, raced across the yard accompanied by the yelping of Hund, the big black dog. Elsie shook her head, those two and that big hulk of a dog were inseparable. The twins and their older sister, Anna, called the animal Blackie rather than Hund.

Doris and Willy were Agnes and Walter's youngest children and lived on the home farm. It was nice to have the young ones close by. Even though the rest of her extended family lived nearby, it warmed her heart to have her oldest daughter and her family living with them. It made Elsie feel an integral part of their lives, part of the run of the mill everyday occurrences. Sometimes she missed the days when the children were all still living at home, the house full of their laughter and sometimes bickering.

The arguments over who had the prettiest hair, or the thinnest waist. The memory of the girls arguing over who would get to polish Ike's shoes for Sunday service brought a nostalgic smile to her face. Memories of those bygone days turned her thoughts to the more practical reminder that the family graveyard needed to be tidied before the snow came. She tipped her head back and watched a late red tailed hawk circling over the short grass prairie. Most of the big birds had already left the vicinity for warmer places in the south. Like clockwork they would return in the spring, as they always did.

Elsie found comfort in the yearly turn of the seasons, accompanied by the arrival and departure of the migrating birds. Nothing would stop the spring from turning to summer, or summer to fall and fall to winter. She loved watching the changing faces of the seasons reflected in the familiar landscape around her. The lengthening of days after the spring equinox, the warmer sun scouring the snow from the fields, then the first blush of spring appearing on the hills and high places while ice still skimmed the water in the ditches. The faint pink-green of early leaves bursting into brilliant green of new minted poplar and cottonwood trees. As spring rounded into summer, the wild roses nodded in the sun, perfuming the air and drawing the heavy bodied bumble and honey bees. The fields were stitched with springtime by horse and plow in the early years, plowing the furrows and sowing the seeds that would ripen into golden waves in time. Later, the work was less with the advent of tractors, but Elsie held dear to her heart the images of Ike and the patient draft horses turning the rich prairie soil, back lit by the slanting rays of the sun in early morning and evening.

But just as the seasons rolled across the prairie, so did the years roll across the people living there. Summer ripened into fall and the heavy headed crop of wheat and barley fell before the binder and gave up their precious grains. Some Ike stored for seeding the next spring, some went to the elevator in Niverville and was sold through the recently formed Canadian Wheat Board, and some went into the granary on the farm to feed stock. Sufficient wheat went to the mill to provide flour for household use.

Elsie massaged her fingers that were beginning to thicken with the bumps of arthritis. Her mother's hands had been stricken with the disease, by the time she died, her hands had been curled and painful. “Time waits for no man,” she said aloud misquoting Chaucer. There seemed no reason to mention tide along with time on the land locked prairie. Her thoughts turned again to those resting beneath the rustling grasses of the cemetery. She must take the youngsters there and tell them the stories of their family members lying beneath the headstones, old and new. It was so important for the young ones to remember the ancestors, remember them as real people, not just names in the family pages of the Bible, or letters inscribed on grave markers. A person needed to know where they came from in order to feel secure in where they were going.

The thought brought to mind a story her mother used to tell about the stripes on a chipmunk’s back. While the exact wording escaped her at the moment, the main message had been, the stripes were the paths from the eyes which saw now and tomorrow continuing to its tail which was always behind it and a part of yesterday. Those stories which were passed down from generation to generation were like the chipmunk’s tail, stitching the past to the present and giving the youngsters a rudder with which to steer through the troubled waters of the post-World War II era.

She got to her feet, shaking off the thoughts of the past. It was good to remember, but there was still work to be done. The diggers in the garden had reached the ends of the rows, somewhat untidy rows and random piles of overturned earth marked their progress. Elsie went down the wide porch steps and crossed the yard. The potatoes, onions, beets and carrots were piled in separate bushel baskets.

"Most of those need to go to the root cellar, but I could use some of the potatoes and beets in the house. Oh, and a few onions," Elsie addressed her grandkids, smiling inwardly at their grubby knees and dirt stained hands. "Once you've put those away get yourselves cleaned up, be sure to scrub those hands and don't be tracking mud and dirt into my clean house."

Anna, Agnes' eldest daughter, selected the vegetables Elsie asked for and trotted off around to the back door of the house. She'd leave them inside the door and not track up the pristine floor of the kitchen. The others headed off toward the root cellar laden down under the burden of the heavy bushel baskets. The younger ones were two to a bushel, each one heaving on the wire handle on their side of the basket.

"I wonder where Doris and Willy have gotten to? I can't even hear that silly dog barking." Elsie shoved her hands in the pockets of her apron and scanned the yard and surrounding fields. "Ike!" she called, seeing her husband emerge from the tool shed with a bug wrench in his hand.

He stopped and turned toward her. "What is it? It's not supper time yet." He glanced at the sky to check the position of the sun.

"Have you seen Doris and Willy lately?" She hurried toward him, one hand holding a wayward strand of hair in place that the wind insisted on pulling loose from the pins.

"Not recently. Last I saw they were headed down in the direction of the creek. Why don't you send Mary and Neil to look for them?" Ike nodded at the two grandchildren returning from the root cellar. Mary was busy wiping her earth stained hands on her apron, Neil strolled beside her, hands buried in his pockets. The two were Jake and Nettie's offspring.

Elsie hurried toward the pair intending to send them off on her errand. It wasn't like those two young ones to wander off so far on their own. She shook her head, not so little anymore, they were getting more independent every day.

"Oh my!" Elsie whirled and pressed her hand to her thundering heart.

Shrill cries pierced the late afternoon air. The frenzied barking of the dog added to her panic. "Ike! Something's wrong." She gathered her skirt in one hand and ran, wrenching the gate to the yard open, leaving it standing ajar behind her. Neil and Ike followed and soon passed her. Elsie gritted her teeth and ignored the uneven ground of the field that threatened to turn her ankle or shred her town shoes. Halfway across the broad expanse of wheat stubble Elsie stopped to catch her breath, holding a hand over the stitch in her side. A sense of urgency drove her forward.

Ike and Neil disappeared into the brush by the creek.

"Oma, what is it. What's going on?" Mary caught up with her and took Elsie's arm.

"I don't know. Something down by the creek. Listen to that dog howl."

"Let's hurry and see if we can help. Doris and Willy sound like they're being murdered." Mary let go of Elsie and strode ahead.

The screams suddenly stopped as well as the barking. Ike's voice carried across the distance between them, but Elsie couldn't make out the words. "Heavens above, what could possibly be wrong?"

Doris's small form burst out of the bushes running pell-mell toward Mary and Elsie. She reached Mary first, who scooped the child up into her arms, patting her on the back and trying to calm her tears.

"What is it? What happened? Are you hurt?" Mary set her down and ran her hands over the small sobbing child who buried her face in the older girl's skirts.

Elsie dropped to her knees, ignoring the sharp stubble that tore her stockings. "Doris, hush now and tell us what has upset you."

"Mome, I want my mome," Doris wailed.

"You take her, I'm going to go on and see where the others are." Mary pried the small hands from her skirt and transferred them to her grossmama.

Elsie squinted after her as she ran across the field her feet raising puffs of dust and chaff with each step. Turning her attention to the sobbing child, she gathered her close, stealing glances toward the creek over the child's head. "Hush, now, dear. Hush now. Tell Oma what happened."

The thin shoulders ceased shaking quite so hard and Doris turned a tear stained face upward. "Blackie…Blackie…" a sob shook her. "It's killing Blackie." Tears flooded her eyes.

"Blackie? The dog? Hund?" Elsie glanced toward the bushes by the creek. "What about the dog. Who's killing him?"

"Not who, Oma. The big kitty. We followed it 'cause it was so pretty. I wanted to…to…pet it…" The words came out between sobs and hiccups.

"A kitty?" Fear skittered down Elsie's spine. While not common, there were lynx in the area. Surely one wouldn't have come so close to the house. Unless it was a young one and hungry. The lambs were a few months old now, but still an easy kill for a big cat. "What colour was the kitty, Doris?"

The child sniffed and took a deep shuddering breath. Elsie handed her a clean handkerchief from her skirt pocket and waited while she blew her nose and wiped her cheeks. "Kind of brown, but sort of yellow, with a cute little tail. And Oma, it had these black pointy tufts on its ears. We only wanted to pat the kitty." Tears welled up in her blue eyes again.

"There, there, now Doris. You didn't touch the kitty did you?" Elsie got to her feet, hefted the five year old up onto her hip and started toward the creek. Doris shook her head, arms tightly twined around Elsie's neck. "Willy didn't touch it either, did he?" She held her breath and prayed while she waited for the answer. What was keeping Ike and Neil, and Mary? They be coming back by now. She quickened her pace. "Did Willy pat the kitty?" she repeated.

"No. he tried, but the kitty got mad. It…it…it growled at us." The little voice wavered.

Elsie halted to ease the pain in her back from carting the child on her hip and set her down for a moment.

"Oma! I need your apron," Mary cried, emerging from the bushes at the run.

When she got nearer Elsie caught her breath at the sight of fresh blood on her skirt. Shaking fingers untied the apron strings and she thrust it at the girl when she reached her. "Here, hurry. Who's bleeding? Is it Willy?" Elsie could hardly get the words past the tightness in her throat.

Mary shook her head and paused to catch her breath. "No. Not Willy. It's Blackie. The cat got him, but he protected the little ones. Neil and Opa chased the stupid thing off. Willy had the sense to climb a tree and the dog held the cat off at the bottom. I've got to go back. Neil's getting Willy down from the tree and Opa's seeing to the dog. We're going to have to carry him back to the house in your apron. I'll send

Willy back to you, and maybe you can get the little ones to house and send one of the boys or Onkel Walter with the cart for the dog. Let Taunte Agnes know what happened." Mary set off a run across the stubble.

Elsie picked Doris up again and wiped her face. "See now, it's all okay. Willy is coming and Opa is looking after Blackie. Everything will be okay. You musn't run off by yourself like that again. You understand?"

"Yes, Oma. I'm sorry, Oma," she mumbled. "Willy!" she shrieked at the sight of the boy making his way toward them.

He broke into a run when he got closer. "Oma! The kitty was mean. It tried to eat me!" he declared skidding to halt beside her. "Blackie was real brave. He saved me. That old cat was no match for Blackie!"

"Here take my hand, Willy. We need to get back to the house and send the cart back to your Grosspape so they can bring the dog up to the house." She clasped the grubby little hand in hers and hitched Doris higher on her hip. By the time she arrived at the house, her back ached, her stockings were ruined, and her shoes were filthy.

Agnes appeared on the porch, alerted by the shouts of the other children. She bustled down the steps and took Doris in her arms. "What happened, Mome?" Agnes pulled Willy close to her side.

"In a minute, Agnes. Paul, can you and a few of the boys get the cart hitched and take it across the south field toward the creek. Neil and Grosspape need help getting the dog back to the house."

The boys raced off to do her bidding and Elsie mounted the wide steps and sank thankfully into one of the big chairs.

"What happened? What's wrong with the dog?" Agnes sat down in the chair opposite, Doris in her lap, and Willy leaning against her knees.

"Those two decided to go exploring down by the creek and thankfully they took the dog with them."

"There was a big kitty," Willy interrupted. "With big ears and a short tail."

Agnes exchanged a look over the children's heads with her mother, eyes widened.

"The kitty was mean," Doris declared. "It growled at me."

"Bad kitty," Agnes smoothed her daughter's corn silk hair.

"It scared me, so I runned away," Doris said, nodding her head decisively.

Movement in the south field caught Elsie's attention. She stood up and looked meaningfully at Agnes. "Let's go get cleaned up, shall we? Oma needs to wash her hands and change her clothes, and I'm sure both of you will feel better with clean faces and clothes."

Agnes glanced in the direction Elsie indicated with a tilt of her head. "That sounds like a very good idea. Come on, little ones. Let's go wash." She got her feet and herded her two youngest into the house. Elsie followed, but not before she shot a worried glance at the cart making its slow way back to the house. *The children will be heartbroken if the dog doesn't make it. They love that silly thing. Anna especially.*After a quick wash she went upstairs to change her clothes and get a new pair of stockings. She peeled off the shredded ones and regarded them for an instant. There was no hope of mending them so she balled them up and reluctantly tossed them into the waste basket.

The high voices of the children echoed up the hallway from the kitchen, punctuated by the deeper tones of the older grandchildren. She caught the sound of Agnes' voice as well. Things seemed to be well in hand, so Elsie slipped out the front door and crossed the yard to the barn where the small cart was drawn up.

"How is he?" she asked when she was near enough.

Neil looked up and shook his head. Ike was bent over the animal holding a blood stained towel against one of the many wounds. Blackie thumped his tail at the sound of her voice, his breath coming in pants.

"He needs a vet, but I'm not sure he'll last until he gets here," Ike said.

"You called the vet for a dog?" her voice rose incredulously. Vets were an expense they tried to avoid. For Ike to summon the man for the dog was totally out of character for her husband.

"The dog saved those kids lives," Neil said, one hand stroking the tattered black ears.

"Was it really a lynx? I can't remember the last time one was seen around here." Elsie stepped nearer and looked down into the bed of the cart. Blood seeped into the rough boards and soaked the material of her apron that the dog lay on.

"Neil saw it," Ike said without removing his attention from the dog.

"It sure looked like a lynx to me. I don't know what else it could have been," Neil said. "Looked like a young one, pretty skinny, I could see its ribs before I managed to chase it off."

"Elsie, can you ask Walter to move the sheep closer up to the barns? He's over at the toolshed working on the binder. He should be told what happened to his children, too." Ike looked up from the dog. "And keep an eye out for the vet, send him over as soon as he gets here."

"Of course. What should I tell the children about the dog?" She regarded the animal dubiously. Blackie didn't look good to her at all.

"If they don't ask, don't mention it," Neil advised.

"If they ask, tell them it's in God's hands," Ike offered.

Pulling her sweater tighter around her shoulders, Elsie crossed the dirt yard. The clang of Walter's tools guided her to the interior of the tool shed unerringly. She stopped just inside the dim interior and waited for her eyes to adjust to the lack of light.

"Walter! Walter!" It was no use, the man apparently couldn't anything over the clang of his hammer as he straightened a piece of equipment. Carefully picking her way across the shed, she stopped where her son in law could see her when he looked up. She waited until he paused in his work.

"Walter!"

"Oh, I didn't see you come in. Is anything wrong? It's not supper time yet, is it?" Walter put his hammer down on the binder platform.

"Doris and Willy had a run in with what Neil claims was a lynx down by the river." She held up a hand to halt him when Walter made to move toward the door. "The children are fine, the dog took the brunt of it. Ike wants you to move the sheep up closer to the barns, we should probably put them in sheep fold at night for a while. Neil said the cat looked skinny and hungry. It must have been to go after people, even little one."

"Where are the children?" Walter wiped his hands on a greasy rag, a worried frown marring his handsome features.

"At the house with Agnes. She's giving them a snack and taking their minds off the poor dog," Elsie replied.

"How bad is Blackie? Sounds like he was a hero." Walter went to the shed door to stare across the yard to the group gathered around the cart.

Elsie trailed after him. "He's cut up pretty bad. I don't know what the children will do if he dies." She crossed her arms and gripped her elbows in her hands.

"They'll manage. It's only a dog, after all," Walter said brusquely.

Tires crunched on the bit of gravel by the gate. "That must be the vet." Elsie hurried out to direct the man to the cart by the barn.

Walter slapped his hat on his thigh and crammed it on his head. "Ike called the vet? Never thought I'd see the day. I'll go see to the sheep." He stamped off toward the pasture where the ewes and lambs were grazing, white cotton balls against the brown grasses.

"Good afternoon, Mrs. Neufeld. There's an emergency with your dog?" The vet put his truck in park and stepped out, reaching back in for his medical bag.

"Yes. He got in a fight with what appeared to be a lynx. He's over by the barn in the cart." Elsie pointed the man toward the front of the barn.

"A lynx? Are you sure? There aren't many around these parts that I've heard of." He shifted the bag to his other hand and slammed the truck door shut.

"Neil saw it before it got scared it off, and he said it looked like one, didn't know what else it could have been."

"No matter. I'll go see about patching up your dog." The vet strode off across the yard, leaving Elsie by the truck.

She really didn't want to go any closer. From what little she saw of the injuries, common sense told her it wouldn't be a good outcome. Turning on her heel, Elsie crossed the short distance to the house. Martin, Susan's husband sat on the porch steps whittling something, small curls of bright wood falling under his knife. Elsie stopped with one foot on the bottom step.

"Martin, would you go help Walter bring the sheep up closer to the barn?"

He set down the bit of wood and closed the jack knife, slipping it into his trouser pocket as he rose. "Sure. What's all the crying about in there?" He tipped his head toward the screen door through which the sound of sobbing could be heard plainly. Without waiting for her answer, he continued, "Something up with the sheep? Is Walter bringing them up for the vet?"

"The children had a run in with what we think was a lynx. The black dog got hurt keeping it from harming the children."

"A lynx?" Martin's eyebrows rose in disbelief.

"Neil says it was."

"How bad is the dog? The youngsters love that animal."

"I don't know, the vet is looking at him right now."

"I'd best go help Walter with those sheep." Martin strode off in the direction of the south pasture.

Elsie watched him go for a moment. Her gaze skipped over the huddle of men by the cart. She climbed the remaining two risers and stepped through the screen door holding it so it didn't bang shut behind her. The crying seemed to have subsided for the moment, at least it wasn't audible in the living room. She found Agnes and Susan in the kitchen with their brood of children at the table. The remains of jam sandwiches were smeared across tiny faces. The older children looked considerably more tidy. Agnes caught her eye and gave her mother a questioning look. Elsie shook her head and lifted one shoulder.

"All finished eating?" she asked brightly. "Let's get you all cleaned up, shall we?"

Between the three adults, and with help from the older girls, sticky faces and hands were soon spotless. Tragedy forgotten, the younger ones went off to play upstairs. Twelve year old Anna, Water and Agnes' oldest child, hovered in the doorway.

"Blackie's going to be all right, isn't he?" her voice wavered.

"I don't know," Elsie answered honestly.

Agnes went and put her arm around the girl's shoulders. "The vet is with him, he's doing all he can. Why don't you say a prayer for Blackie?"

"I want to go see him. I need to be with him," Anna insisted.

"That's not a good idea. You'd just be in the way," Elsie said.

"I don't care! I want to see him. I'll stay out of the way, I promise," she pleaded.

"You heard your grossmama. That's the last we'll hear of it, understand?" Agnes hardened her voice.

Anna twisted out from under her mother's arm and bolted out the back door. Agnes followed her to the door and pulled the screen shut.

"She's not headed for the barn," Agnes reported.

"She'll come around. Best let her be for a bit, I suppose," Elsie agreed.

* * *

Elsie set her unfinished cup of tea down on the kitchen table. Across from her, Agnes and Susan exchanged worried looks. Anna hadn't come back yet, but the girl had enough sense not to wander too far. A shadow flitted across the screen door a moment before the sound of footsteps announced the arrival of the men folks. Ike held the door for the vet to enter before him. Walter and Martin followed the pair. Susan got up to fill the coffee pot.

"Can I offer you a cup of coffee?" Elsie addressed the veterinarian.

"No, thank you, Mrs. Neufeld. I have to be running along, there's another call to make on my way back to town," he replied.

She waited until Ike had paid the bill and walked the man out to his truck. He came back into the kitchen rubbing his hands together.

"Getting chilly out there. There's a nip in the air," he declared.

"What happened with the dog?" Susan asked before Elsie could get a word in.

Ike shook his head. "Nothing much could be done. We did the kindest thing we could for him."

"Oh dear," Susan blinked hard, "The children will be sad, they love that old thing."

"It's Anna I'm concerned with. She's had that dog since he was a puppy. If he was anyone's dog, he was hers," Elsie worried.

"Anna will get over it," Walter declared. "The girl needs to grow up, animals come and go. It's part of life. She'd better get used to it." He sat down and took the cup of coffee his wife handed him.

"She is too soft hearted," Agnes agreed. "Why, she cries every time we slaughter the hogs or the steers, and her silly laying hens think they're pets, for goodness sake."

"Someone should go and find her, though. Let her know what happened," Susan suggested.

"I suppose." Agnes picked up her sweater from a hook by the door.

"Be gentle about it," Susan said.

"No sense beating around the bush. I'll just tell her right out." Agnes looked back with her hand on the latch.

“Wait, Agnes. Let me go. I think I know where she’s gone,” Elsie got to her feet. She laid a hand on Ike’s shoulder as she passed. Even though he was presenting a stoic front, she knew he was distressed over the dog’s death. He’d been a good stock dog and he had saved the children from injury.

Agnes shrugged and moved back to the table. “If you want, Mome. Be sure to take a cardigan, it’s getting cool out.”

“I’ll be fine.” Elsie pulled her sweater on and went out the back door. The wind was picking up as the sun sank toward the distant horizon. Magpies bickered in the Saskatoon bushes competing for last of the purple-blue berries. Elsie ignored their antics and pushed through a gap in the undergrowth. Her feet found the faint path worn in the twisted grasses and remaining wild flowers. *Anna has a secret hiding place on the far side of this mound.* She leaned forward, feeling the strain in the back of her calves as she mounted the incline. A few large boulders crowned the top, blocking the prevailing winds and offering a secluded place for a person to sit and think, or just be alone. Elsie was familiar with the location having used it many times herself when she needed to wrestle with a situation. *I wonder if Anna thinks she’s the only one who knows this place. Please God, let her be here.*

She reached the summit and rounded the hulking sandstone boulders. Pretending to ignore the girl sitting cross-legged in the grass at the base of the largest upright, Elsie pushed her hands into her pockets and gazed off across the prairie where it swept to the sky. The wind rippled the grasses, tossing them like waves on the sea.

"It's a pretty sight isn't it?" Elsie remarked without looking at her granddaughter.

"I guess." Anna shrugged and plucked a heavy headed piece of grass which she proceeded to shred.

"I figured I'd find you up here. It's one of my favourite spots too." Elsie settled on a convenient flat topped low boulder.

"Blackie's dead isn't he?" Anna's little girl voice vibrated with a tone too old for her tender years.

"I'm sorry, honey. Grosspape called the vet but there was nothing they could do." Elsie laid a hand on Anna's head and stroked her hair.

"Why wouldn't they let me see him? Why couldn't I say goodbye to him?" Tears made her voice ragged. "I needed to say goodbye. He needed me, and I wasn't there." The thin shoulders shook.

"He was hurt badly. It wasn't something for a child to see."

"I don't care! It was Blackie,.I needed to be with him. I'll never forgive them for not letting me go to him. He was my dog!" She scrambled to her feet and bunched her hands into fists on her thighs.

"That's pretty harsh talk for a little girl, Anna. God says we should forgive."

"I don't care," she repeated.

"Why don't we go back to the house? It's going to be dark soon," Elsie urged her, getting to her feet and going to stand beside her granddaughter.

"Where is he? I want to bury him. Dig a grave and put up a marker with his name on it." Anna set her chin stubbornly.

"He was only a dog, Anna. Dogs don't get grave markers. You know that," Elsie soothed her.

"He was a good dog! And he gave his life to save my brother and sister. Blackie deserves a grave. And a marker." She scuffed a toe in the loose dirt. "He was a good dog," she repeated.

Elsie sighed. "Let's go down to the house and I'll see what we can do about that."

"Honest?" Anna turned shimmering blue eyes up at Elsie.

"I promise I'll do what I can. We'll see what your parents and Grosspape have to say about, okay?"

"I'm gonna bury him, even if I have to dig the grave by myself." Anna set off down the back of the low hill, pushing through the underbrush.

Elsie followed at a slower pace. She had no idea where the dog's body was at the moment. She could only hope Ike or Walter hadn't taken care of it already. Or maybe, it would be better if they had? Anna was an odd little one, that was for sure. As unlike her siblings and cousins as a swan was from a duck. She hurried back to the house careful of the twisting roots and rocks underfoot.

She entered the kitchen slightly out of breath, expecting to find Anna there with the rest of the family. “Did Anna come in yet?”

“No, didn’t you find her?” Walter pushed his chair back ready to get to his feet.

“Sit down, Walter. I found her. She came back ahead of me. I was sure she’d be in the house,” Elsie replied.

“Then where is she?” Agnes got up and peered out the kitchen door.

“My guess is she went to find Blackie, if she’s not here.” Elsie sighed.

“Didn’t you tell her the dog is dead?” Ike demanded. “That’s what you went out there for.”

“Yes, I told her. We might as well have this conversation now, when she’s not here.”

“What conversation?” Walter frowned at his mother in law.

“She wants to give the dog a proper burial.”

“Out of the question!” Walter exploded.

“He’s a dog, not a person!” Ike agreed.

“You know that and I know that, but the child doesn’t see it like that,” Agnes said. “She loved that dog, all the kids did. Doris and Willy cried themselves to sleep tonight. They think it’s all their fault.”

“Maybe letting them bury the animal will help? Anna is distraught, and one of us should go out and find her before it gets any darker,” Elsie said. She moved toward the hall leading to the front door. "I'll go get her. I'm pretty sure I know where to find her."

* * *

Elsie sat bolt upright in bed, hand pressed to her thundering heart. A child's screams echoed through the house. She recognized Willy's voice, and the softer cries of Doris. "You go back to sleep, Ike. I'll go see if Agnes needs any help." She swung her legs out of the bed and pulled on her dressing gown. Feet stuffed into slippers she padded down the hall and poked her head into the children's room. Agnes was sitting in the old rocker both twins held in her arms.

"Mome, we're fine here now. Can you please go check on Anna?"

"Of course." Elsie withdrew and continued down the dark hall to Anna's room. The girl was sitting in a chair she'd pulled up by the window staring down at the barnyard. "Anna, you should be in bed. What are you doing?"

"Watching Blackie. I don't want any coyotes or something bothering him. He's out there all alone."

Elsie moved to stand beside her, looking down at the tear tracks glistening on her rounded cheeks in the faint light. "Remember, we pulled the cart into the barn and closed the door? He'll be all right until morning. You should be in bed. There's school in the morning."

“I’m staying here. Something might get into the barn,” she said stubbornly.

“Then I’ll stay here with you and watch.” Elsie sat on the end of the single bed near the window. It only took a matter of minutes before the small blonde head bobbed sharply and Anna smothered a yawn. Another ten minutes, and the girl rested her head on her crossed arms and closed her eyes. Elsie waited another few minutes before gathering her up and tucking her into bed. She left the door ajar and peeked into the twin’s room on her way back to bed. They were both snuggled in their beds, and Agnes and Walter’s door was closed. Elsie put her hand up to cover a yawn and went back to her own bed.

After the older children went off to school, Agnes and Elsie shared a cup of coffee at the kitchen table. A big pail of the last of the Saskatoon berries waited on the counter to made into jam. There was still some late rhubarb to be pulled, but for now it was nice to take a moment to rest after the broken sleep of the night before.

“What are we going to do about that dog?” Agnes rested her chin in her hand.

“I’m of a mind to let Anna do what she wants. It might help ease the little one’s minds too.” Elsie stirred sugar into her coffee.

“I just don’t know if that’s a good idea, Mome.” Agnes frowned.

“Let’s finish our coffee and get to work on those preserves.” Elsie finished her drink and rose to place the cup in the sink.

The day passed quicker than Elsie could give credit to. Before she knew it, the children were coming in the door. Tired from school and looking for a snack. Anna come through the door last, school books tucked under her arm.

"Do you want a snack?" Elsie halted her as she bypassed the kitchen door.

"No thank you, Oma. I'm going to get started on my homework." The girl paused with her foot on the bottom riser. "Did you talk to Grosspape about Blackie?" Her voice broke over the dog's name.

Elsie's heart twisted at the forlorn look on her granddaughter's face and she made a snap decision. Acting on it before she could have second thoughts, Elsie took the books from the girl's hands and set them on the second step. She took Anna's hand and with a finger to her lips for silence, the two slipped out the front door.

"Are you sure about this? Blackie doesn't look like himself anymore. It might be more upsetting than not doing this." Elsie cautioned as they crossed the barn yard.

"He's still my dog, and his soul is in heaven with God," Anna stated firmly with all the conviction of childhood.

"I don't think dogs go to heaven, Anna." Elsie wrestled with the need to comfort her granddaughter and to keep in line with the teachings of her religion.

"Blackie's in heaven. I know it. I want him to have a grave where I can go and visit him, like you do at the cemetery. You're always tell me how important it is to remember our ancestors, and to show our respect by keeping the graveyard neat and tidy. I want to do that for Blackie, he saved the twin's lives. It's the least I can do for him." Anna kept walking. Arriving at the barn she slid the door open and stepped inside.

Shaking her head, Elsie followed. For such a young child, the girl certainly had some strong opinions and strange ideas. Inside the barn, Anna stood by the cart, the burlap thrown over the dog pulled back from his head. Her small hand smoothed the rough hair over his eyes. Her fingers trembled only a little as she struggled to remove the collar from around his neck. Elsie bit her lip to hold back the tears when the blonde head leaned close to the big shaggy head and the girl whispered something to her friend. Wiping her eyes with the back of her hand, Anna straightened up and looked back at her grossmama.

"How are we going to move him?"

"Move him where?" Elsie had thought they could give him a place in the soft earth behind the tool shed. It seemed Anna had other ideas.

"Up the hill, by the stones," Anna stated as if it were the most obvious thing in the world.

"The hill?" Elsie said faintly.

"Yes. It's our special place. Blackie and me. That's where I want him to be. How are we going to get him there?" The girl was obviously not going to be swayed.

"It's not going to be easy, Anna." She glanced around the dim interior, her gaze landing on a small wagon the men used to haul calves in during calving season. It was only work of a few minutes to drag the conveyance over beside the larger pony cart. "Grab the apron he's lying on and help me shift him."

Between them they moved the animal into the wagon, which thankfully had side rails that fit into slots on the sides. Somehow the forty pound dog seemed to weigh eighty. Elsie's shoulders ached by the time they were ready to leave the barn.

"We'll go out the side door, it's closer to the path." Elsie motioned Anna to pull the door open. She took hold of the handle at the front and dragged the wagon toward the open door. Anna closed the door once they were clear and then got behind the wagon to push. By the time they reached the Saskatoon bushes Elsie's breath whistled in her chest. Every muscle was screaming for rest. Glancing back, Anna's little cheeks were bright red, the muscles in her forearms straining.

"Let's take a break. Do you think we should ask the other children to come with us?" Elsie suggested, thinking how welcome their added strength would be.

"Not until afterward." Anna leaned down and put her weight behind the wagon again.

Gritting her teeth, Elsie put her head down and plunged into the underbrush. Fortunately, the band of bushes was fairly narrow at the point where the path went through. Of course, once through, the trail led uphill.

When they finally crested the hill, Elsie sank down onto a handy boulder to catch her breath. She surveyed the area on the top of the mound. There wasn't much choice about where to bury the animal. *Bury! We forgot to bring a darn spade.* With all the worry about how to move the animal, a means to dig the hole totally escaped her notice.

"Anna, we forgot to bring a spade," she informed the girl.

"I thought of that already, Oma. I brought one up last night when I came. It's behind the bushes." The girl giggled at the expression on Elsie's face and went to fetch the item from its hiding place behind the thick brush. "I know where I want to dig." She indicated a spot just over the brow of the hill, on the south-west side. "That's where he liked to lie when we came up here. "I'll start." She stuck the spade into the clay soil and began to excavate the dirt. Once she had a good sized hole started, Anna stopped for a breather.

"Here, give me that. I'll take a turn." Elsie took the spade and sent her granddaughter to sit in the shade. A cool breeze whipped across the prairie, lifting the hair off her neck. It was easier digging into the side of the hill and before long she judged the cavity was deep enough. "What do you think, Anna? Will this do?" She leaned on the handle of the spade.

Anna got up and came over to inspect it. "I think so, I want to pile some stones on top too. To keep the coyotes and other things away from him."

Elsie clambered up out of the pit. "Okay, let's get Blackie over here and settled."

In short order the wagon was trundled over to the waiting hole. Anna insisted in lining the bottom with grasses and wild flowers. Solemnly making a pillow of autumn flowers for his head.

By the time the dog was safely covered with earth, and a sizable pile of big rocks and small boulders, Elsie was tired. The short October afternoon was waning, shadows lengthening and merging in the fading light. "There, that should keep him safe." Elsie dropped the spade into the bed of the small wagon.

"I just need to do one more thing, Oma." Anna scooped the spade back out of the wagon.

"Not today. The light's going and the family will be worried about us." Elsie picked up the handle of the wagon.

"It will only take a minute. I know exactly where it is." The girl scrambled down the slope, spade clutched in her hand.

"Anna, we really need to go," Elsie insisted, one fist planted on her hip.

"I'll be right there."

The scrape of the shovel accompanied small pants and grunts. "Anna!"

"Coming, Oma." She popped up over the top of the hill, a straggly bush in one hand, spade in the other. "Can you just move that one stone in the middle, please?"

Seeing it was no use to argue with the child, Elsie shifted the boulder and straightened up. "What in the world…?"

"It's Blackie's rose bush," Anna announced, placing the scraggly plant into the opening and carefully tamping the earth down around it. "There, now he's a Landmark Rose, and I can come here to visit with him and keep things neat." She turned and beamed up at Elsie. "Just like we do in the family plot. I even said a prayer for him while I was planting his rose bush."

"Oh…" Elsie was at a loss for words. Equating the dog with people and awarding him status equal with the members of the family who had gone to the Lord was stretching things, in her opinion. She couldn't find it in her heart to dim the light glowing in her granddaughter's face. "Let's keep that secret between you and me, all right?"

"Now, we can bring Doris and Willy, and the others, up here tomorrow so they can say goodbye. We can, can't we?"

"You'll need to ask your mother if she thinks it's a good idea." She hesitated and then plunged on. "But let's keep the bit about Blackie joining the Landmark Roses just between you and me."

Anna shrugged and nodded. She picked up the wagon handle with one hand and slipped her other into Elsie's. In the last glow of the sun before it sank all the way beneath the horizon, the pair made their way back to the barn yard.

Agnes was standing on the front porch when Elsie and Anna came out of the barn. "Where on earth have you been all this time?" She came down the steps and marched across the yard. "And what have you been doing? Anna, look at the mess of you! Go get washed up before your father sees you."

Anna ducked her head and scurried away. "Don't think this is over," Agnes called after her retreating back. "You've still got some explaining to do. Later."

Agnes fell into step beside her mother on the way back to the house. "You want to tell me what you two were doing? Where did you disappear to after the children got home from school?"

Elsie mounted the porch steps and sat in one of the big porch chairs and motioned Agnes to do the same. "Anna was out with the dog. She was determined to give him a proper burial."

"What nonsense! You didn't let her, did you? Sometimes that girl has the oddest ideas."

Elsie shrugged and slid her gaze away from her daughter.

"Mother! You helped her, didn't you?" She reached over and turned her mother's hand over. "Look at the dirt on your hands! How could you encourage her in such silliness?"

"The child was determined to bury the creature. I couldn't find it in my heart to deny her. You should have seen the look on her face."

Agnes sighed. "What's done is done, I suppose. Where exactly did the 'proper burial' take place?"

"Up on the hill behind the Saskatoon patch. She seems more resigned to his loss now." Elsie got to her feet. "I need to go get cleaned up and see about supper."

"I've got a start on it. You go ahead and get washed and changed. There's mud on your dress and leaves in your hair." Agnes held the door open for her mother to pass through ahead of her.

"Goodness, I can't let Ike see me like this." Elsie hurried across the living room and up the stairs, thankful to avoid seeing any of the men folks. In the privacy of the bedroom she shook her head while stripping off her muddy skirt. *Imagine the child thinking the dog was a Landmark Rose.* It was the name her own grossmama passed down to her, and that she had passed down to her own offspring and grandchildren. A wild rosebush bloomed by each headstone in the family plot. They grew in profusion over the prairie, perfuming the air and providing vitamin C rich rose hips in the fall. Offering life; even as the blooms lost their beauty and dropped their petals in the cold autumn winds. Elsie fancied it was symbolic of the beliefs and morals passing from one generation of the family to the next. "Landmark Roses," she whispered, pulling a clean dress over her head.

Chapter Five

A Matter of Beliefs

"I forbid it! Do you hear me?" John Bertsch's voice brooked no opposition.

Elsie paused in the doorway of the living room, drawn by the raised voices. The scene that met her eyes was perplexing. Helena stood beside her husband, face white and hands twisting together. Their youngest daughter, Ruth, sat on the sofa, head bowed.

"Whatever is going on here?" Elsie stepped into the room. Her gaze caught and held Leina's.

"Don't raise your voice in my house." Ike appeared at the foot of the stairs, tall and stern.

"I apologize," John replied. "It is important that Ruth realize what she has done, but I will moderate my voice in the future." His gaze never left his youngest daughter. "I said, Ruth, did you hear me?"

"Yes, Pape." Her voice was small and she didn't look up.

"See that you remember what I said. You can go now." John dismissed her.

Elsie followed her departure with her eyes. Something in the set of the girl's shoulders and tilt of the head warned her the subject might not be as closed as her son-in-law appeared to think.

"I don't know what we're going to do with that girl. You need to have a talk with her about what is right and wrong. Remind her what the Church's stand is on men like Fred Klassen." John frowned at Helena.

"I did talk to her when I first found out. She listened, and I thought she understood," Helena replied, sitting on the sofa.

"Apparently, you were mistaken." John perched on the edge of the easy chair.

"What has she done that's got you so upset?" Ike came down the last step entered the living room. He leaned on the mantle and surveyed his daughter and son-in-law. "You know I don't allow voices raised in anger in my house."

"Sorry, Pape," Helen said.

"Who is Fred Klassen?" Ike persisted.

Helen glanced at her husband and then looked away.

"A young man from Altona. He came up here looking for work," Helen began.

"Nothing wrong with that," Ike straightened up and hooked his thumbs in his suspenders.

"Oh, there's plenty wrong about the boy," John's voice was hard.

"Quit beating around the bush and tell me, then," Ike was losing patience with the whole affair.

"His home church took him off the church register. He's not welcome there. And he isn't welcome here either," John said, revulsion twisting his features. "He enlisted and fought overseas. There's no excuse for that. He had a choice like all of us. If he truly believed in the teachings he would never have gone. Murderer, our daughter thinks to be friends with a murderer." A muscle jumped in John's jaw. "We are pacifists! Thou shalt not kill. Where hate fails, love conquers. How can love conquer when a man has a gun in his hand? Look at the boy from Winkler, bragging about shooting down planes…and wearing his RAF uniform to church…" John's face purpled and he choked on the rest of his words.

Elsie clenched her hands into fists in her lap, nails biting into her palms. *Please don't let her be serious about this. Please God, give her the wisdom to see the error of her ways.* Helen's lips moved silent prayers as well. Elsie raised her gaze to meet her husband's eyes. Worry and controlled anger tightened his features.

"She understands how serious this is? If she continues to keep company with this person, his ostracism will extend to her as well. Does she understand this? Friends and neighbors will cross the street rather than walk by her. She will bring disgrace on this family. You must deal with this quickly and decisively," Ike declared, he thumped his fist on the mantle for emphasis.

"I can't agree more," John replied. "She is forbidden from even being in the same place as him, or any other man who chose to fight over beliefs."

"That's settled then," Ike declared. "Come give me and Walter a hand with the milking."

Elsie waited until the men went through to the kitchen and she heard the back door close. She scooted close to Leina and put an arm around her shaking shoulders. "There now, Leina. It's all handled now. Ruth understands what must be."

Leina raised her head to stare at her mother. "Does she? I'm not so sure. I'm afraid Ruth will do what she believes is right."

"She's a good girl. She won't go against the teachings of the church, and she won't risk bringing ridicule or worse down on our family," Elsie spoke with the utmost conviction.

"I hope you're right, Mome." Helena wiped her eyes and blew her nose with a handkerchief she pulled out of her pocket.

"Now let's talk about happier things. There's planning to be done for Sadie's wedding next spring."

"Before we get into that. How is Sarah lately? I haven't seen much of her, and she's really quiet when we all come over here for faspa on Sundays. I'm worried about her but I don't know what to say."

"Sarah is managing the best she can, I suspect. It's hard to lose child after child before they're even born." Elsie sighed and patted Leina's hand.

"But Mome, she won't even hold Ed and Betty's little one. Last Sunday afternoon Betty asked her to take little Katherina for a moment while she tended to Willy. I was shocked at her reaction and so was Betty," Leina said.

"What did she do? I must have been somewhere else when this happened," Elsie worried.

"You and Pape had already gone up for your nap after lunch. Sarah looked at the baby like Betty was trying to hand her a snake or something. Then she shook her head, mumbled something and bolted out of the room."

"Did you go after her?"

Leina nodded. "But not until after I helped Betty with the children. Then I went looking for her. John said Arnold took her home. Something about her not feeling well and needing to go home and lie down in the peace and quiet."

"I don't know what to do about her, I'm afraid." Elsie worried the fabric of her dress in her fingers. "It's like she's trying to shut herself off from anything to do with babies and children. Building a big wall to protect herself, maybe."

"It's going to be awfully hard to do that with all the babies and young ones in the family," Leina remarked. "Let's pray the pain will ease with time."

"Yes, I hope you're right and I will pray harder for the Lord to lighten her burden. Now, let's go find Agnes and talk about Sadie's wedding plans."

* * *

Elsie was under the impression the whole issue with Ruth and the boy from Altona was over and done with. At least until she went into New Bothwell with Ike to deliver raw milk to the cheese factory. Ike let her off on the main street of town near the general store and continued on toward the cheese factory. Elsie pulled the list out of her purse and moved toward the door of the establishment. From the corner of her eye a flash of colour caught her attention. Tina Goosen's bright dress reflected in the plate glass window of the hardware store across the way. She was a long-time friend and she belonged to the same quilting groups Elsie did.

"Tina!" She waved the hand holding the shopping list. A truck rolled by blocking her view until it rattled past. When the way was clear again, Tina was nowhere in sight. "How odd. I'm sure she saw me," Elsie mused out loud lowering her hand. "Perhaps she's in a hurry." Pushing the niggling feeling that something was wrong to the back of her mind, Elsie pushed the grocery store door open.

She paused just inside the door to let her eyes become accustomed to the dimly lit interior. Two women stood by the counter where Liz Rempel was totalling up their bill. Elsie smiled at Liz who raised her head, but gave no other sign another customer had entered her establishment. *Whatever is going on?* It wasn't like Liz to not welcome her customers. Elsie moved toward the area where sewing notions were displayed. She selected a few skeins of embroidery thread, a packet of needles and two spools of thread, one white, one black. In the remnants bin, a bit of material caught her attention. It was just the right weight and colour for a new blouse. Tucking it under her arm, Elsie went to the counter to leave her items there while she continued to shop.

"Good morning, Liz," Elsie greeted the shop keeper.

"Mrs. Neufeld," the woman replied without actually meeting Elsie's gaze.

The two women already there gathered up their purchases and left, making a point of not looking at the newcomer or greeting her. Uneasiness she could find no explanation for tightened Elsie's stomach. Liz's behaviour was out of the norm. In Elsie's memory the woman had never called her Mrs. Neufeld. She consulted her list and turned her attention to the woman behind the counter.

"I need a few things. Ten pounds of flour, five pounds of sugar, a pound of coffee…" her voice trailed off.

The shopkeeper produced the requested items without any attempt at small talk or pleasantries. "Liz, what is going on? Have I done something to make you angry? If so, I apologize, but I can't imagine what it might be."

The woman paused with the coffee in her hand, an audible sigh escaping her. "Elsie Neufeld, I've known you since we went to grade school together and I have to say I'm shocked you would allow such a thing." Her lips thinned into a straight line, her whole appearance radiating disapproval.

"What are you talking about? I haven't done anything wrong," Elsie protested. She glanced around but thankfully there were no other customers at the moment.

"Done nothing wrong?" Liz's voice and eyebrows rose in indignation. "How can you be so brazen? Do you mean to say you approve of your granddaughter walking out with that…that…"

"That what? I have no idea what you're going on about." A niggling thought crept into her head. Surely it couldn't be that, could it?

"That boy from Altona. He's as bad as that other one from Winkler, you know who I mean. Wore his RAF uniform right into church…"

Deciding ignorance was the best way to go Elsie plunged in, even though she was starting to have a sick feeling in her stomach she knew which granddaughter and which 'boy' Liz was referring to. "Who exactly are you saying my granddaughter is seeing, and while we're at it, which granddaughter are speaking of?"

"I can't believe you don't know." Liz pressed a hand to her throat. When Elsie remained silent, she continued. "Helen's girl, Ruth. She keeping company with that Altona boy who went to fight in Europe. Fred something or other."

Elsie tipped her head down to give herself a moment to think and compose herself. There was no point in denying the girl knew the man in question, honesty was the best policy, she decided. "I believe Ruth was friends with someone from Altona, but to the best of my knowledge that was over a while ago. Her parents spoke to her about it, and her grosspape too. There's nothing between them anymore." Elsie tapped her fingers on the counter. "Oh, and I'd like ten cents worth of licorice whips please. Ike loves those things." She smiled at the woman across from her.

Liz placed the coffee she was still holding on the counter and weighed out the candy with a bit more force than was necessary. She crimped the bag closed and dropped it on top of the rest of Elsie's purchases. The woman made a tiny noise in the back of her throat before giving a tiny nod and straightening her shoulders.

"Unless her parents spoke to her between this morning and last evening, there most certainly appears to be 'something between them'," Liz clipped the words off.

A wave of faintness swept over Elsie. *She couldn't. Surely she wouldn't.* The more pragmatic bit of her brain assured Elsie that Ruth probably would, and had done precisely what she had been ordered not to. "So that's why no one will look me in the eye, and Tina wouldn't cross the street to say hello. Guilty by association am I?" A small fire of anger ignited in her belly, tempered by the knowledge she would have behaved the same way if the situations were reversed. The men and boys who went to fight made a decision to ignore one of the pillars of their faith. They certainly couldn't have expected a hero's welcome when they returned home. A good man would have declared they were conscientious objectors and gone and served in one of the work camps with the rest of the Mennonite young men and objectors from other faiths. They made a choice, and now they were having to live with it. But, Elsie's family had made no such horrible choice. *Ruth must be made to see that what she does affects all of us. Just wait until I tell Ike about this.*

"Elsie, are you all right? Do you need to sit down?" Liz came around the counter and took Elsie's arm.

"No. No, I'm fine." She took a deep breath and forced herself to breath normally.

"You look awfully pale. Please sit down." Liz pulled a chair over. There were always a few chairs strewn about the store for elderly or infirm customers to rest in.

Elsie sat carefully on the wooden seat, fussing with her dress buying time to compose herself. She closed her eyes for a moment wishing to settle her racing thoughts. *Ike will be mortified if he gets the same treatment at the cheese factory I just received here. If he doesn't already know, I'll have to tell him. Oh, and I'm afraid how John will react to this news. Ruth has gone against his wishes and defied him. I can't even imagine...* "I beg your pardon, Liz? I'm sorry I didn't catch what you just said." She smoothed the material of her skirt and put a hand up to her hat.

"Would you like a glass of water?" Liz held out the drink she must have gone to get without Elsie realizing it.

"Yes, thank you." She took the glass, pleased to see her hand didn't tremble, although her heart was still racing. After taking a sip, Elsie got to her feet and moved to place the glass on the counter. "If you'd just be so kind as to ring up my items, please?" She stretched her mouth in a semblance of a smile.

"Of course. Right away." A bland expression slid over Liz's features. In a matter of minutes the transaction was completed.

Elsie looped the handles of the bag over her wrist and moved toward the door. She paused on the threshold, peering through the glass in the hope Ike was parked outside. The gravel road in front of the store was distressingly bare. Squaring her shoulders, Elsie stepped outside and took a seat on the bench against the front wall of the store. It took a great effort to put on an outward appearance of normality. It was a stroke of luck that the street wasn't busy and she wasn't forced to endure any uncomfortable encounters with friends and acquaintances.

The appearance of Ike's truck rumbling down Main Street brought her to her feet. She was already waiting at the curb before the vehicle came to a halt. Ike opened the door for her, took the bag of groceries and tucked them behind the seat. She stole a glance at his face when he assisted her up the high step into the cab. He must not know about Ruth yet. His handsome face was relaxed and he whistled on his way around to the driver side door. The springs creaked as he climbed aboard.

"Did they have everything on your list, or do we need to stop in Landmark on the way home?" Ike slid the truck into gear and drove out of New Bothwell toward home.

"Liz had everything I needed." She hesitated and then pushed on. "How are things at the cheese factory? Still busy as ever? Did you see Ruth? Leina mentioned she'd started working there."

"Same as always. I didn't see Ruth, she must have been busy somewhere else." He took his eyes off the road to glance at her. "Why do you ask?"

"Ike, I have to tell you something." Elsie stared unseeing out the wind shield.

"Some gossip you heard at the store? You know I don't hold with gossip." He frowned.

"About Ruth," she blurted before courage failed her.

"Ruth? What about her? It's good she's working, keeps the girl out of mischief."

"I only wish that were true."

Ike stiffened beside her, knuckles whitening where he gripped the steering wheel. "What nonsense is it this time?"

"It started when you dropped me off. I saw Tina and I know she saw me, but she refused to even look at me."

"Elsie, you've been friends for years. She probably didn't see you." Ike's grip relaxed on the wheel a bit.

"No, Ike. She saw me. I thought it was odd, and at the time I thought like you did, maybe she didn't see me. Then I went into the store, and two old friends I went to school with treated me like a leper. Liz was the one who finally told me." She stopped and bit her lower lip.

"Told you what?" Her husband's voice was stern.

"Ruth is still seeing that boy from Altona. They were seen together just last night. Here in town. I can't imagine that Leina and John have any idea it's still going on."

Ike cleared his throat in what sounded to Elsie very much like a growl. "We'll stop at their place on the way home. Get to the bottom of this once and for all. I won't stand for our good name to be dragged through the mud. How can she not understand the boy is a murderer? He took up arms and killed his fellow human beings. That's a choice he made, and now him, and all those like him, have to live with those choices."

Elsie nodded, too distraught by the seeming betrayal of faith and family loyalty by her granddaughter to think of anything sensible to say in response.

* * *

"She did what!" John slapped the table with the palm of his hand.

Both Leina and Elsie jumped at the staccato sound. Elsie kept herself from cringing at the controlled anger on her son-in-law's face.

"Liz Rempel told Elsie when she went in to buy some groceries. On top of that, people were rude to your mother." Ike fixed a glare on Leina.

"I didn't know anything about it," she replied.

John glanced at the clock. "Ruth should be home any minute now, she had the early shift this morning. We'll get to the bottom of this in a hurry once she gets here."

Leina got up and flitted around the kitchen making fresh coffee and setting out some biscuits on a plate. She brought them to the table and moved quickly to get cream and sugar. Elsie's eyes followed her daughter's restless movements, wishing she too had a reason to bustle around. Her nerves were jumping and it was a chore to sit quietly and appear calm.

"Leina, would you please sit down? You're making me jumpy with all your rushing around," John exclaimed.

"Oh, yes sorry." Leina returned to her seat, took up the coffee Elsie had poured for her and stirred sugar into it.

Elsie leaned forward to set her empty cup on the table, almost knocking it over when she jumped as the front door opened and closed. Light footsteps sounded in the hall.

"I'm home, Mome. Do you need help with supper?" Ruth's voice preceded her into the kitchen. "Hi Oma and Opa." She greeted her grandparents with a brilliant smile. "It's nice to see you." Ruth stooped to kiss Elsie's cheek. When she straightened up, the tense atmosphere in the room finally seemed to register with her. "Is there something wrong?"

"I believe you should be the one to answer that question," John addressed his daughter.

"Ruthie! You're home. Come see the house we made for our dolls." Maria and Doris, her two younger sisters burst into the kitchen. "We thought we heard you come home." Maria grabbed Ruth's hand and tried to drag her toward the hall door.

"Maria. Doris. Go back and play with your dolls. We're having a grownup conversation. Ruth can come and see your doll house later. Now!" John gave them both a stern look when the little girls hesitated.

They disappeared with a flurry of skirts and giggles. The patter of their running feet echoed overhead.

"Now, Ruth. Why don't you tell us again why you were late coming home after work yesterday?" John asked quietly.

The colour drained from her cheeks, although Elsie had to give the girl credit for not wilting under her father's stern regard.

"I told you, Sam asked me to work a bit later than usual." She clasped her hands behind her back.

"The truth, Ruth. I want the truth. No more lies," John's voice thundered in the small room.

The girl opened her mouth to speak.

"Think carefully before you say anything else," John warned her. "Lying is a sin."

She shut her mouth and swallowed. Her gaze sought her mother's across the table. Finding no support from that quarter, she looked at her grossmama. Elsie shook her head and deliberately turned her head.

"You've ignored my wishes and you're still seeing that boy from Altona." John lost all patience waiting for her to speak. He held up a hand to stop her when she appeared ready to speak. "Don't deny it. Your grossmama was treated to a rude reception in New Bothwell this afternoon because of your behavior. Do you not realize how your actions affect the rest of the family? And you're willing to lie about it on top of everything. That alone proves to me this relationship, if you can call it that, is a bad influence on you. I forbid you to have anything to do with him, and you deliberately went against my wishes. Do you care to explain to me how you met the boy in the first place?" John slapped the table with his open hand again. The sharp crack wiped all colour from Ruth's face and trembled. "Well?"

"I…I met Fred in New Bothwell," she paused and gave her mother a beseeching look.

"Go on," John demanded. "Where in New Bothwell, and how did you ever come into contact with someone like that?"

"He's not *someone like that*," she protested. "Fred's a good person, and he treats me nice—"

"He's a murderer," her father roared. "How did you meet him?"

"At the cheese factory," Ruth's voice was so low Elsie wasn't sure she had heard correctly.

"Where?" John was obviously making an effort to modulate his tones.

"At work. At the cheese factory." She raised her head and met her father's gaze.

"I can't believe they'd have someone like him working for them," he objected.

"He doesn't work there," she muttered.

"Then how did you come to be acquainted with him?" John raised an eyebrow in disbelief.

"At the factory," she repeated. "He delivers milk sometimes. He was polite, and we got to talking when he brought the paperwork in to get signed. I didn't know he was a soldier until later."

"And once you were aware you should have stopped the relationship immediately." John glowered at the girl. "Do the teachings of your faith mean nothing to you?"

"Of course they do! But I can't be rude either," Ruth defended herself. "I don't want to lose my job."

"Not being rude is a far cry from being seen having coffee with him in plain view of everyone in New Bothwell," her father countered.

Elsie was torn between sympathy for Ruth's obvious discomfort, and the knowledge that whatever was going on between her granddaughter and the ex-soldier had to be nipped in the bud. There could be no future, and nothing but heartbreak in such a relationship. Surely she couldn't want a man who had killed other human beings to be the father of her children. Elsie shuddered at the thought.

"Well, nothing to say?" John prompted his silent daughter.

"We aren't doing anything wrong," she began.

Leina's smothered sob was all but drowned out by John's snort of anger. "I can see there's no point in trying to talk any sense into you. As long as you live under my roof you will obey me, and if this behaviour continues you will no longer work at the cheese factory. Am I making myself clear?"

Ruth's head whipped up, eyes flashing with anger and frustration. She opened her mouth, but was forestalled by her grosspape. Elsie turned toward Ike.

"You're part of this family, Ruth. What you do reflects on all of us. Your grossmama was subjected to nasty comments and ridicule this morning. As head of this family I forbid you too have anything to do with this man. He has forsaken his faith, and I won't have you foolishly putting your own soul in danger as well. Hear me." Ike didn't wait for any response. He nodded at Elsie who got up from the couch and followed him out of the house.

Once they were in the truck, Ike looked over at her before starting the engine. "That should be the end of that," he said decisively. "Girl that age doesn't know what is good for her."

"I certainly hope she listened," Elsie spoke softly.

"She better have." Ike put the vehicle in gear and drove out of the yard.

Elsie was silent on the ride home. Something in Ruth's manner disturbed her. Where did that rebellious streak come from? Their arrival home pushed extraneous thoughts from her mind in favour of the things that needed to be attended to, which included putting the groceries away. Ruth was usually a sensible girl. Elsie was sure the girl would think over what was said and make the right choice.

* * *

The days grew shorter and the nights colder as October slid toward November. The plans for Sadie's spring wedding were coming together. Another bright spot as far as Elsie was concerned was the production at the cheese factory slowed during the winter months so Ruth was no longer working in New Bothwell. The topic of Fred Klassen from Altona was never mentioned in her hearing since the distressing incident earlier in the fall. Elsie glanced over at Ruth, her golden hair tinted red-gold by the sun slanting in the window behind her. The girl seemed happy enough, certainly not like she was pining away after an unrequited love. The older granddaughters and three of Elsie's daughters were gathered around a quilting frame holding the makings of a dachbiea. They were stitching the combed and carded sheep's wool between two cotton sheets to make a warm and long lasting blanket to stave off the winter's chill.

Sarah was the only one of her daughters who was absent. Her last miscarriage seemed to have broken something in her. Elsie couldn't recall the last time she'd heard Sarah laugh. When she'd pressed her about her apparent unhappiness, Sarah had only shrugged and remarked a woman could only bear so much sorrow. Shaking her head to dispel the melancholy thoughts, Elsie smiled at Anna, Agnes' daughter, who at twelve was old enough to join the quilting circle.

"How are you making out?" She bent closer to inspect the stitches. Pushing her own needle into the material for safekeeping she laid her hand over Anna's. "That's a good start, but take a look at your mome's stitches."

Anna dutifully leaned over to look at Agnes' handiwork.

"See how her stitches are all evenly spaced? And look how exactly they follow the lines from the pattern template." Elsie instructed her granddaughter. Agnes grinned at Elsie over her daughter's bent head, no doubt remembering her grossmama doing the same thing when she was that age.

Anna heaved a deep sigh, contemplated her somewhat uneven handiwork and looked up at Elsie with a rueful expression on her young face. "I suppose I must rip mine out and start over?"

"I think that would be a good idea, don't you? This quilt is part of Sadie's wedding present, and we want it look as perfect as possible. Besides, a woman needs to take pride in her needlework." She patted the young girl's hand.

"Are we ready for a break?" Leina secured her needle in the partially finished quilt and glanced around the gathering.

"I could use a break," Nettie agreed. She put down her needle and stood, stretching with a hand to her lower back. Her apron draping over the rounded bulge of her pregnancy. She moved to find a softer chair than the straight back wooden one pulled up to the quilt frame. Susan went to join her, the two talking softly amongst themselves. The younger children playing around their feet. Babies sleeping, wrapped in blankets on the floor, safely barricaded from the more rambunctious toddlers.

"Do you want some help in the kitchen?" Agnes left the quilt too.

"No, I think Leina and I can manage. Would you like some milk, Anna?" Elsie smoothed her hands down her skirts and moved toward the kitchen. "Coming, Leina?"

"Sure, Mome." Leina followed her into the kitchen, pausing in the doorway to glance back at Ruth now giggling with the others in the living room.

"How are things with Ruth?" Elsie poured coffee into a flowered pot.

"She seems settled…but I don't know…sometimes I think she's keeping secrets." Helena set out sugar and cream on a tray and reached up for the biscuit tin.

"Have you spoken to her about it?" A touch of unease twisted in Elsie's stomach.

"Of course, Mome. She swears everything's fine and insists she doesn't have anything to hide, secrets or otherwise."

"I suppose everything is okay, then. Perhaps you're just reading more into things than there is," Elsie suggested, lifting the tray with the coffee and setting it on the kitchen table.

"I certainly hope so," Leina didn't sound totally convinced. She placed the china tray of biscuits on the table as well.

"Coffee's on," Elsie called. She forgot about the conversation with Leina in the joy of the companionship of her family gathered together.

* * *

The dawn on the fifteenth of November was shrouded by a sheet of driven snow. Wind howled in the eaves and worked its way through every nook and tiny opening it could find, fluttering curtains where the window frames didn't fit quite snug.

"Looks like no school today." Elsie pulled the curtain back and rubbed the frost off the window pane to peer out. "It's a full blown blizzard, if I'm not mistaken."

"Be a good day to do some paperwork." Ike tossed back the quilts and put his wool stockinged feet on the cold floor. "Once Walter and I get the stock fed and milk the cows it'll be an indoors day."

"I'll go start the coffee if Agnes hasn't already. You'll want something warm in you before going out in this." Elsie dressed quickly in the chill air, pulling on an extra cardigan.

"I'll be down in a moment." Ike pulled on another pair of long johns and reached for a thick flannel shirt.

Agnes had the stove already stoked and the coffee on when Elsie entered the welcome warmth of the kitchen. "I let the children sleep. There'll be no use trying to go anywhere today. Walter will be down in a few minutes."

"Your Pape should be too." She set a pot of water on to boil in preparation to making porridge. "This will stick to their ribs." Elsie measured the rolled oats into the rolling water. "We can make a proper breakfast once they come back in from chores."

The shrill of the telephone startled Elsie so she almost dropped the spoon she was stirring the porridge with.

"I'll get it, Mome." Agnes crossed the room and picked up the black receiver. "Hello."

The long silence and the expression on her daughter's face prompted Elsie to give the pot a final stir and move it off the heat. Setting the spoon on the spoon rest, she moved to stand beside Agnes, wiping her hands on a dish cloth as she did so.

"She did what?" Agnes voice was faint and she sat down suddenly on a kitchen chair as if her legs would no longer hold her.

"Did what?" Elsie hissed at her.

Wordlessly, Agnes handed her the receiver and hurried to save the coffee which was threatening to boil over on the stove.

"Hello?" Elsie held the phone like a hot potato.

"Mome? Oh Mome. She's gone and done it now," Leina's voice broke off in a smothered sob. In the background Elsie heard John's voice and the stamp of his feet as if he were pacing and shouting at the same time. Maria and Doris were crying loudly, almost drowned out by their father's hollering.

"Leina, tell me what's wrong. Who has done what?" The receiver hurt her fingers where she gripped it, pressing into her palm. In her heart, a horrible sinking feeling turned her stomach, she knew exactly who had done what. Elsie prayed she was wrong.

"Is something wrong? Was there an accident?" Ike came into the kitchen.

Elsie waved him quiet with her free hand. "Helena, stop crying and tell me what we can do to help."

"It's Ruth," she said, confirming Elsie's suspicions.

"What about her?"

"She's run off."

"Are you sure about that? Maybe she just went out to get a start on the barn chores before the storm gets worse."

"I'm sure. Maria found a note this morning shoved under the girl's bedroom door. She's run off with that…that…boy!"

"Oh my heavens. Not in this storm." Elsie clutched her sweater closed at the throat as if she were fending off the blast of the blizzard.

"It sounds like they went last night, before the storm blew in. We have no idea where they've gone."

Ike reached out a hand for the phone. "Pape wants to talk to John." Elsie handed her husband the phone and went to sit beside Agnes.

"Leina, put John on the phone," Ike demanded, raising his eyebrows at the high pitched wailing Elsie could hear even over at the table. "Tell the children everything is going to all right." There was a short pause during which the sound of crying faded. "John. Do you have any idea where to start looking for Ruth?"

Elsie attempted to slow the racing of her heart and calm her fears. She studied Ike's face looking for comfort and some assurance of a positive outcome for the situation. His face alternated between flushed and pale. One work hardened hand scrubbed at his hair, mussing his carefully combed hair.

"Well, that's it then. There's nothing we can do until this blizzard blows itself out. The lane is already snowed in. There's no way to get a vehicle down it and the roads aren't likely any better. Let us know the minute you hear anything." Ike ended the call and joined the women at the table. Before he could relay any information Walter stuck his head in the door. "I thought I heard a commotion."

"Come sit and have some coffee," Agnes answered. "There's nothing to be done until the storm lets up."

"Nothing to be done about what?" Walter joined them and accepted the coffee Agnes handed him.

"John and Helena's oldest girl has run off with that soldier from Altona," Ike's voice was flat.

A shiver raced over Elsie, raising the hairs on her forearms, Ike's failure to use Ruth's name made the situation all too serious.

Whatever can Ruth be thinking? This isn't something that will be forgiven easily.

"When did this happen?" Walter leaned forward and rested his elbows on the table.

"Last night before the storm broke from what John said when he called," Ike spoke again.

"I don't imagine they'll get very far in this weather." Walter glanced at the snow encrusted window pane.

"That's a small blessing I suppose." Ike drained his coffee mug and stood up. "I'm going to go start chores."

Walter got up as well. "I'm coming. It's a good thing we can follow the fence line to the barn. A person could get turned around very easily in a storm like this."

"Be careful," Agnes called after the men.

"Mome, we're hungry!"

Agnes' twins came bursting into the kitchen. Any further conversation regarding Ruth was put on hold while breakfast was made. Anna wandered in not long after the twins, also looking for breakfast. By the time the men came back from the barn the children were fed and had gone off to amuse themselves. Elsie and Agnes laid places for Ike and Walter and set platters of pancakes and sausage on the table. The smell of fresh coffee filled the kitchen. Conversation over breakfast was limited to the weather and mundane things. Elsie's stomach roiled with worry. She pushed the food around her plate but actually ate very little. The ringing of the phone was a welcome distraction. She left the table to answer the call.

"Hello?"

"Mome, have you heard anything?"

"No, Helena. I would have let you know right away. I take it you've heard nothing there either?"

"Not a word. Just the note."

"Does she give you any indication of where they're planning to go?"

"Nothing. Just that we're not to worry and this is what she wants. It goes on a bit about how she doesn't want to hurt us and how much she loves us. Fine way she has of showing it. How am I ever to hold my head up in public again?"

"It's true, she doesn't seem to have thought this through very well. What she's done is not easily forgiven."

Helena lowered her voice. "I'm not sure John will ever be able to find it in his heart to forgive her transgression against the faith."

"Perhaps with time," Elsie suggested.

Leina made a non-committal sound. "I should let you go, Mome. In case Ruth is trying to call."

"Of course. Let us know the minute you know anything." Elsie rang off.

She'd no sooner replaced the receiver than the phone shrilled making her jump. "Hello." Elsie snatched up the receiver again.

"Oma?"

"Ruth? Is that you?" Elsie spoke loud enough for everyone in the kitchen to hear.

"Yes. Are you very angry with me?"

"Angry? No. disappointed yes. I'm not sure you fully realize the gravity of your actions," Elsie felt compelled to try and impress on the young woman the error of her ways.

"I have thought about it, Oma. A lot. I was studying my catechism and it suddenly dawned on me that none of it meant anything without Fred. Is that so horrid of me? I couldn't bring myself to pledge my heart to a faith that judges a good man for following his convictions and beliefs."

Elsie supressed her surprise at the decisiveness in her granddaughter's voice. "But Ruth, his convictions run counter to the teachings of the church. Thou shalt not kill. When hate fails, love conquers. It goes against everything we believe in to take up arms against another human being."

Ruth's sigh echoed over the phone lines. "What about all those Jewish people the Nazis murdered? Are we supposed to just stand by and let that happen? Fred felt he was doing God's work by helping to free those innocent people. Something more than staying here where it was safe and declaring himself a conscientious objector. He had to follow what he believed in."

"Ruth, are you saying you believe your pape and grosspape, and your onkels are afraid to face the Nazis? Are you calling them cowards?" Elsie's voice rose sharply.

"That's not what I'm saying at all, Oma. Opa and Pape, and the onkels had to do what they thought was right. They had the right to follow their beliefs, why are they so against Fred following his?"

"Ruth," Elsie tried again to get through to her. "What that boy did goes against God's teachings. Perhaps he isn't seeing things clearly. The church will never accept him, and if you continue to associate with him, it will reflect on you, and us."

"We've talked about it a lot, Oma. I think Fred has a right to his beliefs and he had the right to act on them."

"When are you coming home, Ruth. We can talk about this better in person. And you can speak to the pastor about it. He'll be able to help you see the error in your thinking."

"I'm not coming back, Oma. Fred and I are getting married in Brandon, and then we're heading west to make a fresh start."

"But, Ruth. This is your home. Surely you aren't intending to leave your family. You haven't joined the church yet, and you know you can't get married without doing that, and without being baptised. You must be married within the faith, Ruth. You must make your confession of your faith." Elsie's heart fluttered with agitation in her chest. She refused to believe what Ruth's words seemed to imply.

"I'm not coming back," Ruth insisted.

"This is your home," Elsie repeated.

"My home is where Fred is. Tomorrow, he'll be my husband."

"Does your father know what you're planning?" Elsie tried a different tact.

"No. That's partly why I called you. I'm tired of arguing with him and Mome over belief and faith. I love them, and I don't want them to worry about me, I just can't match words with them over this anymore. If you let them know I'm all right then they won't have cause to worry."

"Ruth, that's too simple. Of course your parents are going to worry about you, and about your soul. Getting married outside the church will break your mother's heart. They only want what's best for you."

"What about what I want? What about what I believe?"

"You're far too young to know what you want, Ruth. Stop this nonsense and come home where you belong," Elsie said.

"I am where I belong, Oma."

"How can you turn you back on your faith, the things you were brought up to believe in?" Exasperation gave her voice an edge.

"I think you hit the nail on the head, Oma. It's all a matter of belief, you're right about that."

"I'm relieved you're finally talking some sense. Now come home."

"You misunderstood me, Oma. It's a matter of belief and choosing what to believe in. I believe in Fred and the love we share. He's a good man, kind and gentle."

"He killed people, Ruth. Took up arms. He's a murderer," Elsie tried again to impress the seriousness of the situation on the girl.

"Fred is not a murderer. I don't believe that for a second. I have to go, Oma. I love you all, but I won't come back when the family won't accept Fred. It's all a matter of belief, Oma."

"Ruth! You listen to me…" The line clicked and went dead. Elsie held the receiver away from her ear staring at it in disbelief. "She hung up on me," her voice was incredulous. She looked from one astounded face to another around her kitchen table. Suddenly her safe secure world seemed shaken to its foundations.

"I need to call Leina." Elsie raised a trembling hand to dial the familiar number.

"Wait, Elsie. What did the girl say?" Ike demanded.

She turned to look at him. "She said, 'It's all a matter of belief.'"

Chapter Six

Christmas 1946

The news of the big November blizzard paled in comparison to the furor Ruth's abdication from the family caused. Elsie was relieved the upcoming holidays gave her family something more positive to concentrate on. The house always seemed full of the grandchildren whispering and planning what presents they wished to receive and even quieter whispers among the older children concerning presents for parents and each other.

Sadie was torn between plans for Christmas and plans for her May wedding. Even though it wouldn't be a huge affair, nothing like the pictures in some of the bridal magazines in the stores, Brides, Vogue and Modern Bride. Elsie sniffed. It was all a waste of time and money on such frivolous trappings. What really mattered was the love between husband and wife, not what flowers she carried or how expensive the dress was. She glanced across at Ike, who was staring at the flames in the fireplace, stockinged feet up on an ottoman.

Her own wedding day had been one of the most memorable days in her life. Second only to the birth of her children, all eight of them. The thought of Pida stilled her fingers on the knitting needles. Poor little man, he was only ten when he went to God. Such a sweet child. A bittersweet smile twisted her lips at the memory of his inordinate pride in keeping his Sunday shoes polished to a brilliant shiny black. She sent a silent prayer for the repose of his soul, safe in the arms of Jesus.

"Elsie, what's troubling you?" Ike's inquiry broke the train of her thoughts.

She shook her head and smiled at her husband. "Nothing, Ike. Just thinking."

He favoured her with a long look before picking up the Bible from the wide arm of the chair and opening it to the book marked place. Elsie resumed her knitting and let Pida's memory float back to the recesses of her mind. Better to concentrate on present. Sadie and Corny's wedding. With any luck Sarah would be feeling more herself by the time her namesake was married. Her daughter's detachment was a worry to Elsie, along with her refusal to have anything more to do with children and babies in particular than she could avoid. *We all deal with pain in our own ways. God will help her heal in His own time.*

There was also the new baby to brighten her thoughts. Nettie delivered a healthy baby boy on the fifth of December. Jake was thrilled to have another son, and Nettie doted on the child. While Sarah had congratulated her brother and sister-in-law, she refused to hold the infant, and couldn't seem to remain in the same room as Nettie and baby Isaiah.

Sadie and Cornelius Hildebrand planned to join their lives together after service on the first Sunday in June, 1947. She was still discussing with Susan if it would be better to have the lunch here or at the groom's home. Usually, the groom's family hosted a lunch after the marriage. But, there was another troubling thought. The Hildebrand's were thinking very seriously about joining the much talked about migration to Paraguay. Elsie suppressed a shudder. In the early 1920's she and Ike had joined the first migration to the South American country. Although the prospect had sounded promising, the reality had been far from it.

The religious leaders were far stricter than what Elsie had been used to in Canada. Women in particular had many restrictions placed on them. The heat was worse than she imagined along with the humidity. Each family purchased their own bit of land which had to be hacked out of the grassland upon arrival. Not to mention the bugs and biting insects, and snakes…and the tropical diseases the Mennonites seemed to have no resistance to. Diphtheria, typhoid, malaria…they had all taken their toll on the most vulnerable, the very young, the old and the pregnant women.

She must find a chance to speak with Sadie and see how serious Corny was on joining his parents and siblings in the migration. The threat of the government to take the Mennonite children during the week, returning them only on weekends was a disturbing notion and the bone of much contention among the community. With the end of the war the elder members of the community were also concerned the Mennonite youths would not be able to enjoy the same opportunities they had become used to during the course of the conflict. The returning soldiers were being given precedence in the job hiring process. All these things contributed to the interest in emigrating to either Mexico or Paraguay. The migration from the surrounding communities of southern Manitoba was headed to South America.

Goodness if the children weren't taught by someone of the Mennonite faith who would teach them their catechism and the German language? Although none of the teachers had any official schooling they were perfectly able to teach the young ones what they needed to know. The youngest students wrote their A-B-C's on slates or in notebooks and were taught from the *Fibel* — the ABC *Buch*. It was basically an illustrated beginner reading book especially for young children to read. The middle group were taught to read from the New Testament and the oldest children read from the Old Testament. They all learned to write by copying the Bible. The latter part of the school day was used to learn catechism and for lessons in German. She glanced over at Ike immersed in his study of God's Word. He had taught school during their time in Paraguay, and a good job he had done of it too. Such nonsense, the government thinking they could educate the Mennonite children better than their own community. On that point, she could understand why some of the younger families were eager to emigrate. Thankfully, none of her children were entertaining the notion.

Her thoughts turned to more immediate concerns. Onkel Jake would be arriving to stay over the holidays. And Taunte Mathilda. Mathilda could stay with Helena and John. They had extra room now Ruth had left. Jake would make out just fine here. The twins could move in with Anna. Or sleep on pallets in Agnes and Walter's room. She ticked off the things that needed to be attended to. Furniture to move, bedding to air. The turkey would be slaughtered on Christmas Eve, or maybe sooner if the weather held cold. She wrinkled her nose at the thought of dealing with de-feathering the bird along with all the other tasks which would need attention closer to the date.

There were hams aplenty hanging frozen in the summer kitchen. Potatoes, carrots and onions stored in straw filled bushel baskets in the cellar.

Elsie was looking forward to the German Bible conference, the *Bibelbesprechungen.* It was held between Christmas and New Year's Day each year down in Winkler. She loved the theme of the speakers, concentrating on a specific part of scripture or a portion of the Bible. The Pauline epistles were frequently a common choice. Agnes and Walter were staying home to take care of chores so Elsie and Ike could attend this year. Now if only the weather held. The trip would be impossible if it snowed or turned bitterly cold.

Finishing the cuff of the small sock she was working on, Elsie cast off the last stitches. Five pairs down, more to go. She selected a skein of pink wool from the basket and started on a small pair for one of Nettie and Jake's girls. Christmas gifts were simple and hand made. Offered from the heart and made with love. Elsie had glanced at the flashy pages of the Simpson-Sears and Eaton's catalogues in the Niverville general store last time she was there. So much money for such gaudy things. Her needles clicked faster, in time with the motion of her rocking chair. She hummed a snatch of hymn as she worked.

* * *

Christmas was drawing near. December 21st dawned bright and clear and bone-biting cold. Elsie wrapped her fingers around the coffee cup in her hand, welcoming the warm. Snow lay in drifts across the fields, pristine and reflecting the sunlight with an intensity that made her eyes water. The meandering trail of coyote tracks left blue shadows embroidering the otherwise unmarked expanse. Thank goodness the lynx that had frequented the creek earlier in the year was no longer a concern. After the incident with the twins and the dog, Walter and the boys hunted the cat down. The tawny pelt had been sold in Winnipeg for a good profit.

Such thoughts had no place in this holy season. Christmas was a time of joy and family fellowship, but Easter was the more highly regarded occasion. Christ's sacrifice and resurrection held more religious meaning than the date of His birth. Indeed, nowhere in the scriptures was the actual date of His birth recorded. But the events of Himmelfoat, the Ascension Day forty days after Easter Sunday when Christ rose from the dead, Easter Sunday itself, and Pentacost, a week after Easter, held the promise of everlasting life and a place in heaven for all those who gave their lives and hearts into God's hands.

School was over for the holidays, the patter of the twins' feet and the lilt of their excited voices sounded upstairs. Agnes was ironing the linen tablecloth readying it for the Christmas table. Ike and Walter were gone into St. Vital to the train station to pick up Onkel Jake and Taunte Mathilda. They weren't travelling together, but their trains arrived within a half hour of each other. One from Ontario in the east, and the other from Alberta in the west.

Elsie looked forward to seeing her father's brother and her mother's sister. Pape would arrive later in the day on the 23rd. Mome, God rest her soul, lay under the snow in the family plot. In the spring and summer the wild roses of Landmark drowsed over the grave markers and scented the air with their heady perfume. She pushed back the chair and got to her feet. Rinsing her coffee cup in the sink, she climbed the stairs to be sure everything was in order and ready for Onkel Jake in the twins' room.

Sun streamed in through the open curtains, a golden spill across the polished hardwood floor. The bed was made up with clean crisp sheets and a colourful quilt. A heavier Hudson Bay wool blanket was folded at the foot of the bed. Elsie leaned down and smoothed the pillowcase even though it was free of creases already. She straightened the braided rug by the bed and flicked a bit of imaginary dust from the bedside table. The door of the armoire was ajar. Elsie crossed the short distance and peeked inside. Agnes had cleared a space for Onkel Jake to hang his things. Elsie closed the door with a soft snick. Inspecting the tall dresser revealed the top drawer was also empty ready for their guest. Susan would have done the same at her home, in readiness for Taunte Mathilda's visit. She had planned to have Pape stay at Helena and John's, but he wouldn't hear of it after Ruth's departure in disgrace. Instead, Sarah and Arnold were putting him up. They had more than enough room in their house. Sarah hadn't conceived since the last miscarriage. Perhaps having her grosspape visiting her would help pull her out of the deep depression she seemed unable to rid herself of.

The crunch of tires on packed snow drew her to the window, Ike had borrowed a car as it was too cold for the buggy. Pushing back the curtain a bit Elsie watched the car coming to a halt by the front steps, letting the curtain drop back into place, Elsie hurried downstairs.

"Agnes, they're here!" she called reaching the bottom and stepping onto the hall floor.

"Who's here?" Doris and Willy appeared at the top of the stairs, high pitched voices raised in unison.

"Your Grootonkel Jake and Groottaunte Mathilda are here with Grosspape. Wash your hands and face and then come down to say hello." Agnes appeared tucking a stray strand of hair back into place and smoothing her long apron down over her dress. "Am I presentable?" she asked her mother.

"You'll do" Elsie smiled at her eldest daughter. "I've got fresh coffee on the stove and a light lunch prepared. Where's Anna?"

"Reading probably." Agnes gave an amused sigh. "She gets caught up in a book and forgets about everything else."

"Anna!" Elsie called up the stairs. "Come down, please. Company's here."

"Coming, Oma." A faint voice came from upstairs, followed by feet hitting the floor and a door opening and closing.

The clump of boots on the porch heralded the arrival of the guests. A blast of cold air swept through the open door. Taunte Mathilda's small figure preceded the taller one of Onkel

Jake. They crowded into the front hall to let Ike and Walter come in laden with their luggage. Elsie and Agnes hurried forward to take the coats and wraps and hang them up.

"Come in, come in." Elsie ushered Jake and Mathilda into the living room. She hugged the birdlike woman in welcome and was rewarded with a brilliant smile. "Please sit down. Here Taunte Mathilda, take the chair by the fire."

The elderly woman perched on the edge of the chair and held her hands out to the warmth.

Jake gave Elsie and Agnes a peck on the cheek before taking the chair on the other side of the fireplace. "It's good to be here. Travelling in this weather is hard on my old bones."

"Would you like some coffee?" Agnes offered from the kitchen door.

"That would be lovely, dear," Taunte Mathilda replied. "It's so nice to see you all."

"Coffee would hit the spot," Onkel Jake agreed.

"We have a light lunch prepared too. Susan and Martin should be here soon with their children. Sadie will be especially glad to see you. She's so excited about Corny coming home for Christmas, and can't wait for you to meet him."

"Where's the boy been?" Onkel Jake leaned forward and rested his elbows on his knees, hands clasped and hanging between his knees.

"There's not much work hereabouts in the winter. The lad's been in Dryden working in the pulp camps," Ike explained.

"Oh my, that sounds like hard work to be doing in the winter," Taunte Mathilda declared.

"Makes a man out of a boy, I'll say that," Ike agreed. "Felling trees with an axe, skidding them out with horses, it's hard work all right."

"Hilda Hildebrand worries over him, that's a fact," Agnes chimed in. "Frostbite is the least of her worries, she's terrified he's going to lose a hand or a foot to one of those big axes."

"Hello!" Susan and Martin, along with their children, crowded into the front hall in a swirl of snowflakes and wintry air.

Elsie went to welcome them and take their wraps. "Come in. Onkel Jake and Taunte Mathilda are in the living room."

Greetings were exchanged among the adults before the children were introduced to their relatives.

"Doris, Frank, come meet your Grootonkel Jake and Groottaunte Mathilda." Susan ushered her two youngest offspring forward. Solemnly, Frank shook hands with Jake and gave a little bow to Mathilda. Doris dimpled and smiled shyly at the strangers. "You know Sadie, of course."

"Hello, it's so nice to see you both again." Sadie smiled at her elder relatives. "Corny will be here this afternoon. His train doesn't get in until three o'clock. I can't wait for you to meet him."

"I'm sure he's a very nice young man, Sadie. Otherwise, you wouldn't have agreed to marry him. Besides I knew his grossmama, a lovely woman, so I'd not expect anything else from her grandson."

Elsie and Agnes repaired to the kitchen to bring the lunch into the dining room. A warm glow of pleasure filled Elsie's heart with joy. The knowledge that Helena and John, and the boys and their wives would be joining them later in the afternoon only added to the happiness. Having her family all together was always a source of pride and joy. Such beautiful children she and Ike had produced, and the lovely grandchildren as well. Now if only Sarah and Arnold would walk through the door, her world would be complete. It was Christmas, surely Sarah would find a way to sweep back the veil of depression she struggled under and join the family in celebration. Arnold was dealing with the whole situation well, she thought. No doubt he was also sad no babies had come of their union, and it seemed likely that wouldn't change in the future.

"There, I think that's everything," Agnes declared standing back to survey the table.

Elsie shook herself out of her thoughts. "The table looks very festive," she agreed mentally checking the exact placement of silverware and napkins. No fingerprints on the glassware or utensils. Places were set for the children with appropriate sized settings.

She moved to the living room door to call the family to the table. Sadie's voice stopped her cold in her tracks. Elsie only caught the end of the sentence.

"…Corny's family is planning to emigrate to Paraguay, but I haven't had a chance to ask him if he plans to go too," Sadie said.

Not today. Today is for family and joy. You can talk to Sadie about the reality of life in Paraguay later. And perhaps her young man won't want to emigrate. Hold that happy thought. Putting a smile on her face she stepped into the room. "Lunch is ready if you'd like to come through to the dining room."

Onkel Jake used the arms of the chair to push himself upright, and then gallantly offered Mathilda a hand up. It took a few minutes of organized chaos to get everyone settled at the table. Agnes and Susan served their little ones. Anna sat with her parents and was very solemn in appreciation of her inclusion with the grownups. Honestly, sometimes Elsie thought the girl was older than her years. They bowed their heads and folded their hands while Ike said the prayer of thanks for the food.

The phone rang partway through lunch. Elsie hurried to answer it in case it was Pape calling.

"Hello?"

"Hi, it's Arnold. I just wanted to let you know Sarah and I will be along a bit later. She's resting right now, but said she's looking forward to seeing Taunte Mathilda and Onkel Jake and her grosspape."

"Oh, I'm so glad to hear that, Arnold. It will be so nice to have the whole family together under the same roof. Please come whenever it suits you. Corny's train gets in at three and Ike is driving Sadie up to St. Vital to meet it. Pape will be here later today, too."

"Right, we'll see you later then. I'll tell Sarah her Opa will be there tonight."

Elsie hung up and went to share the news with the rest of the family at the table.

* * *

"Pape! It's so good to see you. Merry Christmas." Elsie went to the front hall when the door opened, accompanied by a waft of cold air. She looked around him while taking his coat to see the rear end of a car turning around in the yard. "Your friend didn't want to come in?"

"No, no. They have business in Winnipeg and just offered me a ride as it was on their way. It is nice to see you as well, Elsie." William Friesen gave his daughter a hug of welcome.

"I see. Well, come along into the dining room. Onkel Jake and Taunte Mathilda are here already. We're just finishing lunch, we didn't expect you until a bit later. Come sit down, there's plenty." Elsie ushered her father into the room and quickly set a place for him at the table beside his brother and sister.

When the light meal had satisfied everyone's hunger, Elsie and Agnes cleared up the dishes with help from Anna. They were just finishing the dishes when Arnold and Sarah arrived. Drying her hands on a tea towel before going to greet them, Elsie folded the cloth and placed it on the drying rack. She paused to smooth her hair and a run a hand over her skirt. Please let Sarah be happy, she prayed.

"Sarah, Arnold, how wonderful you could come. Merry Christmas!" She enfolded her daughter in her arms, alarmed at the sharpness of the bones beneath the material of her coat. "Come along, there's sweets and coffee in the living room. Have you eaten? I have plenty of leftovers from lunch if you'd like?" She gave Arnold a worried glance over Sarah's shoulder.

"I'm fine, Mome. I don't seem to have any appetite lately. Arnold might like something, though." Sarah slipped from her outer wear and let her mother take it from her. She hesitated as if not sure what to do next.

The lost expression on her thin face tore at Elsie's heart. She took the coat Arnold handed her and hung both garments on the hall coat tree. Sarah looked to her husband and moved toward the living room when he guided her with a hand on the small of her back. *Goodness, the girl looks frail. Surely, it can't all be from the malaria and losing the babies, can it?* She contemplated whether it would be better for Ike to speak to Arnold about the situation, or if she should. Elsie followed them down the hall to the living room.

"Would you like some lunch, Arnold?"

"No thanks, Mome. I ate a little something before we came over." He put a protective arm around his wife's shoulder.

“Some coffee then? And help yourself to the sweets.” Elsie busied herself getting the newcomers cups of coffee and refreshing those of her other guests. The conversation flowed around her, merriment and the joy of having her family together producing a happy glow in her heart. Finished with her hostess duties, Elsie took the chair beside Taunte Mathilda and was soon engaged in conversation catching up with everything the older woman had been occupied with since they last spoke. Pape was chatting happily with Ike and Walter, while Arnold and Onkel Jake appeared to be enjoying each other’s company. Sarah got up to take her cup and saucer into the kitchen and Agnes followed on her heels. Elsie followed them with her eyes, but refrained from joining them. Perhaps Sarah would speak with her older sister about things she didn’t feel she could share with her mother. Though she itched to be with them, she forced herself to focus on Taunte Mathilda’s story of her quilting group and the new project they were working on.

* * *

Agnes came into the kitchen with the last of the coffee cups from the living room. The quiet hum of conversation drifted in with her. She placed the china on the counter and picked up a tea towel to begin drying the items already washed and on the draining board.

Elsie stifled her curiosity and continued with the remaining plates in the soapy water. She shot her eldest daughter a sidelong glance and willed her to share whatever it was that Sarah and her had discussed earlier.

Agnes wiped an invisible spot from a saucer and set it on the table. Returning to the sideboard on the counter she paused before selecting another item to dry and met her mother's anxious gaze. "You're not going to like what I have to say." The words came out in a small sigh.

"Whatever it is, please just tell me." Elsie's busy hands stilled in the dish water, the task momentarily forgotten.

"Sarah wants Arnold to agree to move to Mexico." Agnes held up her hand to forestall the protest Elsie was about to make. "I tried to talk her out of it, but I don't know how much success I had."

Elsie pressed a hand to her chest as if that could quell her racing heart. "Why on earth would she want to do this? How can she possibly think it would be a good idea?"

"She's terribly depressed and upset over not being able to give Arnold the family he wants. Says there are too many sad memories here for her."

"But her family is here! Surely, you told her what it was like in Paraguay? You were old enough to remember some of it and why your father and I decided to come back to Canada."

Agnes nodded. "I did, and I tried to make her see that changing where she lived wouldn't get rid of her troubles." She shook her head. "Sarah wouldn't hear any of it. You know Mary, the girl she was friends with at school, moved down there with her family and they keep in touch. I think that's where she got the idea in the first place."

"Did she say what Arnold thinks of the notion?" Elsie resumed washing the dishes, needing to keep her hands busy in an effort to marshal her thoughts.

"She says he agrees it might be a good thing, but I'm not sure he's sold on the idea. He's desperate to do anything to make her happy again though, so he might just go along with it for her sake. Maybe Pape can talk to him? See if he can find out what Arnold really thinks."

Elsie nodded. "I'll mention it to him later. He won't be happy about them thinking of moving away."

"Neither am I, but Sarah seemed pretty set on the idea. She believes it's what God wants her to do. It's almost like she thinks if she goes to Colonia Manitoba, near someplace called Chihuahua, she'll be able to give Arnold the family he wants so badly and her malaria won't be a bother. She went on about that quite a bit."

"I suppose there's nothing to be done about it tonight and it's Christmastime. Let's not say anything to anyone, except your father and Walter, for the time being. I don't want to spoil the happy mood with talk of family leaving us. Bad enough that Corny's family is wanting to go to Paraguay. I do hope he doesn't decide that's a good idea." Elsie set the last clean dish on the draining board and dried her hands on a towel.

Agnes wiped the moisture from the china and put everything back in its place while Elsie drained the sink and tidied the kitchen. The two women linked arms companionably and returned to the living room where the lively conversation soon let her push the worries to the back of her mind.

Ike's chair was empty and Sadie was absent too. Elsie glanced at the small Kroeger clock on the mantel piece. It was family heirloom, brought from Russia with the first settlers. Ike and Sadie must have left to pick up Corny from the train at St Vital. *Please don't let him mention Paraguay today. I don't want to think about any of my family moving far away right now.*

* * *

Early twilight fell before the crunch of tires on the hard packed snow of the driveway announced the return from the train station. Agnes got up and went to put the coffee pot on again, while Elsie moved to the entranceway to greet her future son-in-law.

"Hello, Mrs. Neufeld. Happy Christmas." Cornelius, Corny for short, Hildebrand gave her a brief hug, the cold of the December night sending shivers over her where his hands touched.

"Welcome, and happy Christmas to you as well. Please, let me take your coat." She held out her hand.

Sadie hung her coat and scarf on the hall tree and then did the same for her father. The diamond on her left hand flashed in the light from the lamp. She took her fiancé's arm and drew him toward the living room.

"Everyone is in the living room. Come on, I want you to meet Taunte Mathilda and Onkel Jake. You already know Grosspape. Oh, it's so good to have you home." Sadie's laughing voice faded as she towed Corny down the hall.

"The girl is surely excited to have the boy home and in one piece," Ike remarked. "And not a word about Paraguay all the way home."

"That's a mercy. I've heard enough talk about moving away for one night," Elsie replied, forgetting for a moment Ike didn't know about Sarah's crazy idea.

He frowned down at her, bushy eyebrows beetling over those vivid blue eyes Elsie fell in love with so many years ago. Ike was still a fine looking man, she decided.

"Was there talk about the youngsters going to South America while we were gone?"

"No. Something else, I'm afraid. But I'll tell you later. This isn't the time, and it's far too complicated to try and explain right now. I'm hoping it will come to nothing, but you never know."

"Fine for now, but I want you tell me everything later when it's quiet," Ike agreed with marked reluctance.

"Come, let's go join the rest of the family. It's almost time for supper and Corny must be starved." Elsie linked her arm with Ike's and drew him down the hall into the living room.

* * *

Later, after those who were leaving had departed, and the others were safely bedded down, Elsie hugged her dressing gown tighter around her and stood by the bedroom window. The full moon's light reflected off the mantle of snow covering the fields, etching distinct black shadows on the surface where the bare branches of the cottonwoods blocked the silvery illumination. It was a frigid night, which only made the stars more diamond bright in the sable velvet of the sky. The snow that had fallen earlier was dry and the moon woke rainbow sparks from the tiny crystals as they shifted in the slight wind that sighed around the eaves of the house.

The scene was so beautiful, and yet so deadly. The intense cold could kill a body in short order, and if any of the ewes lambed early, Ike would have to be sure they were kept warm. The cows hadn't been with the bull until later, so there should be no early calves at least. The window of the chicken shed glowed a warm cherry red, colouring the nearby patch of snow a deep pink. The heat lamp Walter installed at Agnes' insistence seemed to be working out well.

She turned her head at the sound of the door opening and Ike's footsteps. The rustle and whisper of the bed clothes being turned back preceded the creak of the bedstead as he settled in.

"What are you looking at, Elsie." Ike's voice held the husky note of tiredness.

"The moon on the snow. It's a beautiful night." She smiled at him.

"It's cold enough to freeze the breath in your nose out there." He pulled the quilt up higher. "Come to bed, morning comes early."

Elsie removed her dressing gown and hung it on the hook by the door. With one last glance at the wintry scene outside she pulled the curtains closed to block out the cold. She snuggled into the bed with a sigh.

"What did you mean earlier when you said you didn't want to hear any more talk about people leaving?" Ike raised himself on an elbow and peered down at her in the dark. "I almost forgot to ask."

Elsie wriggled up so she was propped against the head board and studied her husband's face in the shadowy light. "Agnes and Sarah had a talk this afternoon." She paused.

“And?” Ike prompted her when she remained silent for a long moment.

“Apparently she keeps in touch with that school friend of hers, you remember Mary, don’t you?”

“Of course, pretty little thing she was.” Ike nodded.

“Well, Mary and her family moved to Mexico, and now Sarah wants Arnold and her to do the same.”

Ike was silent for a long moment. Elsie noted the deep furrows in his forehead, accentuated by the faint light. For the first time it struck her that his age was showing. She always saw the young man she’d married when she looked at him, never acknowledging the wear and tear of the weathering of the years between then and now. In her heart they would both be forever young. But now, with one of her daughters, and one of her grandchildren, talking about moving away, for the first time in her life she felt old. Not old like Pape of course, but older than she’d ever felt before. It was not a sensation she enjoyed, she decided.

“Is Sarah really serious about such a thing?” Ike finally broke his silence. “Is Arnold in agreement?”

“I haven’t had a chance to talk to her myself, but Agnes says it all has to do with them not being able to start a family. Somehow Sarah has gotten it into her head that God is punishing her for something, and if she moves to Mexico and devotes herself to His work everything will work out as she wants. I'll find time to speak with her in the next day or so, if you can have a word with Arnold and see what his thoughts are. I don't have a good feeling about the whole thing, Ike. I really don't."

"She's a woman grown, Elsie. Long past the time we can tell her what or what not to do." Ike heaved a sigh and settled back onto the mattress. "I will have a word with Arnold though. See if he can provide some enlightenment."

The bedstead creaked as he rolled over and the evenness of his breathing soon told Elsie her husband had managed to fall asleep. She wriggled down in the bed and pulled the quilt up to her chin. Try though she might it was a long time before she could compose herself to sleep.

* * *

With all the celebration and observances associated with the occasion, it was almost the new year before Elsie had a chance to speak with Sarah. The day was bitterly cold with a brisk north-west wind herding fleecy clouds across the brilliant blue fields of the skies. Even with the fire stoked in the stove and all the doors and windows prepared for the winter frigid fingers of ice snaked through unseen nooks and crannies wrapping around Elsie's ankles and nipping at her fingers.

"More tea, Sarah?" Elsie rinsed out the pot and refilled it with hot water, adding loose tea before fitting the lid into place and slipping a knitted cosy over the pottery. The heat of the pot warmed her hands a bit. Setting the refreshed vessel on the trivet resting on the table between them, Elsie returned to her seat.

"Please, Mome. The winters seem to get colder every year. Goes right through to my bones." Sarah gathered the woolen sweater closer around her thin shoulders. She glanced out the frost sparkled window toward the barn. "I don't know how the men do it, out there doing chores."

"God gives us the strength to do what we must." Elsie tested the tea strength before refilling the two empty cups on the table. "He might test us, but He will never give us more that we can endure."

Sarah's gaze swung back to her mother. "How can you be so sure?"

Elsie hid her startlement at the question by concentrating on pouring milk into her tea. "I'm sure because it is His word. Christ died for us and will rise again at Easter with the promise of Everlasting Life. Surely you must know that if you search your heart. He is our foundation and our comfort." She studied the younger woman's face, searching for what she wasn't sure. Acceptance of her words or at least the knowledge there were things that couldn't be changed and must be learned to live with. What she found instead, did nothing to calm her worries.

Sarah took a sip of tea setting the cup back into the saucer with deliberate clink. She raised her gaze to meet her mother's taking a deep breath before she spoke. "I know you don't agree, but Arnold and I are going to move to Mexico in the spring. I'd go now to get out of this cold and away from the memories, but Arnold is right, travel at this time of year is chancy at best. Can't you please try and understand how I feel? I just can't stay here any longer…I don't mean it like that Mome," she said in response to Elsie's hurt expression.

"How do you mean it then," her voice was stiff in spite of her efforts to appear unmoved.

"It's just…I don't know…" Sarah got up and moved to the window, tucking her hands under her folded arms for warmth. "I feel closed in here, like I have no place where I can go and not feel like I'm being judged a failure as a wife. All those girls I went to school with…I can't stand the pity in their eyes when I run into them in town trailing their brood of children behind them." She whirled around, eyes wide and shimmering with tears. "Some of them have four toddlers and another one on the way…" Sarah's voice faltered. "I can't even give Arnold one child. What's wrong with me, Mome? Why is God punishing me?"

"Sarah, I realize it must seem like that, but you know the doctor explained it's the malaria causing the miscarriages, not anything you've done or not done." Elsie attempted to soothe her.

"Why me?" Sarah cried, throwing herself back into the vacated chair. She put her head down on her crossed arms and sobbed.

Elsie moved around the table to sit beside her. She rubbed Sarah's back and murmured soothing words until the thin shoulders ceased shaking. Agnes appeared in the doorway and halted, a shocked expression on her face. Elsie waved her away with her free hand. The shock cleared from her face to be replaced by sympathy. She nodded and withdrew, taking the little ones with her. Elsie glanced at the clock; no doubt the young ones were looking for their supper.

"There now, Sarah. You need to pull yourself together. Taunte Mathilda and Onkel Jake will be up from their nap soon, and it's almost supper time. You don't want the others to see you like this, do you?"

Sarah raised her head and wiped her eyes with a handkerchief dug from her sweater pocket. "You know I don't. Pity is the last thing I want." She sniffed mightily and went to splash cold water on her face. Turning back toward her mother, she leaned on the counter. "Can you understand why I feel I just have to get away from here? It will be better in Mexico, I just know it. Why, even you and Pape went to Paraguay in the twenties."

"Which is where you caught malaria when you were just little. Do you not think I feel guilty about that when I watch you struggle with all this?" Elsie waved her hand at Sarah's tear stained face. "A mother is supposed to protect her children, care for her family. If we hadn't gone to South America would things have been different—"

"Or would God have arranged another trial for me? Is that what you're trying to say?" Sarah cut her off.

Elsie sighed. "No, that's not what I was going to say. I was only attempting to let you see that I feel responsible for your troubles, and it weighs on my heart. I pray to God every night to show me a way to make your load lighter, to help you find a way to be happy."

"I have found a way, Mome. Arnold and I must go to Mexico. I've dreamed about it, it's summer all the time, no snow, no wind, no freezing my nose off every time I stick it out the door. Mary says the community is strong and thriving." Her voice dropped to a whisper. "She told me in her last letter about a woman who hadn't been able to carry to term who emigrated last year, and now she has a healthy baby." Sarah looked up, a fervent light in her eyes. "That could be me by next fall. I know it. Don't you see we have to go?"

"Have you talked to the pastor about this?" Elsie tried a different tack.

"Yes, of course. Arnold insisted, and I wanted to, of course. He said it was a wonderful thing that we wanted to help those who were already in Mexico and he thought our addition to the community down there would be a great asset. Arnold has already been asked to teach at the school," she finished proudly.

Elsie's heart shrank in her chest at the pronouncement. She had no idea the plans had progressed so far. "Do you have a place to live down there? When we went to Paraguay there was nothing but arid grassland and thorny bushes, we had to hack out a clearing and build a shelter on the land we bought. Have you looked into things like that? What about a water supply?"

"Oh, yes. Arnold's taken care of all that. There's close to forty-five of our villages in the Manitoba Colony which is where Arnold and I are planning on going. And I think Mary said about another eight or ten in the Swift Current Colony. She also mentioned a smaller daughter colony at the north end of the settlement. It's a separate seventy-two-thousand acres they just purchased last year, so that landless young married couples from both colonies can settle there." She paused. "She sent some pictures too. Each village has between ten to thirty families. The farm yards are arranged on both sides of a main street with fields for crops behind them. Every family gets a hundred and sixty acres and there's a common pasture too." She stopped and looked at Elsie with eyes bright with expectation and excitement.

It was the first time in months Elsie has seen Sarah look excited about anything. "Do you own the land, then?" She said the first thing that popped into her head. There was no point criticizing the plan when it was plain her daughter had already made up her mind. Perhaps it would be a good move for Sarah and Arnold. Maybe God did have his hand on them. Elsie could only pray that was the case.

"I don't understand all the details, but I think the colony holds the paperwork. Every family purchases their land from the *Oberschulze.* He and another trusted man hold the documents for the large parcel and then the *Oberschulze* keeps a record of payments. When we've paid the agreed upon price, the land is ours." Sarah stopped and frowned. "It's not like here, where we have the papers that says the land is ours, in Mexico we won't get any legal documents, but everyone Arnold has corresponded with assures him that the *Oberschulze* is an honest and trustworthy man and there's nothing to worry about."

"If you decided to come home, would you be able to sell your land, or mortgage it to someone?" Elsie searched her brain for bits and pieces of legalities she recalled Ike ironing out when they bought the land in Silberfeld which they still lived on.

"I don't' think so. Arnold will know. Anyway, it won't matter," Sarah's declaration held a note of finality to it.

"What do you mean, it won't matter? Money is hard to come by, you want to be sure you won't lose everything."

"Mome!" Sarah laughed. "I'm not going to move all the way to Mexico to turn around and come home." Her voice softened, "I'm going to miss you and Pape, and everyone here. But I know in my heart this is the right thing for Arnold and me."

"I just want you to be happy, Sarah. That's all I ever wanted for all my children." Elsie reached across the table and covered her daughter's hands with hers.

"Good then, that's settled. Now let's get some supper on the table. The men will be coming in soon and no doubt they'll be freezing. I hope the weather breaks soon. Anna said some of the eggs were frozen this morning when she went to feed the hens."

Snow squeaking under heavy boots and the sound of male voices heralded the arrival of the men folks from the outside. The winter days were still short this soon after the equinox. The gradual lengthening of the daylight hours wouldn't be apparent for a few of weeks yet. Already the sky was full of fading light, the orange and gold of the sunset reflecting on the cold shadowed rolling fields of white. Soon, the world would be painted in colours of silver and black, as the stars lit their candles in the deep royal blue of the heavens. Starlight reflected from the snow always provided a faint argent illumination, black and grey shadows fading to blue on the crests of the surrounding fields. Twilight was a special time for Elsie. The interlude between the chores of the day and what needed to still be done before retiring. A time when family gathered around the table to break bread and share the news of the day.

Even while her thoughts were elsewhere, Elsie's hands moved swiftly to set the table in the dining room. With the extra company the kitchen table would be crowded and besides, it was still a time of celebration. Standing on the cusp with a new year stretching out before them, Elsie wondered what the coming months would bring.

Chapter Seven

Blizzard of 1947

Christmas celebrations were over and life settled into a comfortable rhythm for Elsie. The cold and snowy weather kept Ike in the house more than usual, and she enjoyed his company. The house often rang with the laughter of Agnes and Walter's youngsters confined to playing indoors. Sometimes, laughter changed to tears and cries of childish frustration.

Imperceptibly the daylight hours lengthened although the sky was obscured by clouds most days. Ike declared it was one of the snowiest winters he could remember. Knee high paths cut across the yard from the house to the wood shed and the out buildings. It required daily work to keep them open, the ever present wind sending snow to drift into the depressions at a regular rate.

Elsie was glad of Walter's presence to aid Ike with the never ending chore. Sarah was still a worry on her mind, always in the background even when she wasn't consciously thinking about the imminent departure. In some ways the brutal weather was a blessing. Anxious as the couple were to get on their way the inclement conditions precluded any notion of an early departure.

The house wrapped its warm arms around her family and kept them safe. The end of January was almost upon them and Elsie looked forward to the approaching spring. She would plant some oat seeds in a small pot in the kitchen toward the end of February so she would have some growing on Easter weekend. It was a custom she picked up from her mother, who had learned it from her mother. Over the years the significance of the origin of the tradition was lost, but to Elsie is always signified the promise of new life and plenty. And wasn't that what Easter promised as well? The Saviour's trials and sacrifices so that His children could look forward to everlasting life in his Father's House.

Her lips moved in the old familiar words. "Let not your heart be troubled. Ye believe in God, so believe also in me. *In my Father's house there are many mansions. If it were not so I would have told you. I go to prepare a place for you. And if I go and prepare a place for you, I will come again, and receive you unto myself, that where I am, there ye may be also."* She skipped forward to the bit she liked the best. *"Jesus saith unto him, I am the way, the truth, and the life. No man cometh unto the Father, but by me."* The passage always evoked a sense of security and comfort in her heart.

* * *

Thursday January 30th, 1947 dawned cold and overcast. The clouds were so low they seemed to touch the fields themselves, and the trees and shrubs shrank into themselves away from the touch. Ike and Walter came in from morning chores with cheeks chapped red from the wind. Elsie's husband knocked the smattering of snowflakes from his cap before hanging it up. Agnes shrieked with laughter when Walter kissed her cheek and rubbed his cold nose against her warm skin.

"Looks like a storm is brewing," Ike remarked settling at his place at the table and wrapping work worn hands around the large mug of coffee Elsie placed before him.

"Go on with you." Agnes swiped playfully at Walter with a dish towel.

He offered her an unrepentant grin and went to hang his coat up in the mud room. By the time he returned, Agnes was setting plates filled with bacon, waffles and vanilla sauce, black pudding and sausage on the table. Elsie added a platter of toast, and another with fried eggs on it. The waffles were a favorite of the young ones and they'd soon be coming in for their share.

"Do you think it will really storm?" Agnes glanced out the window at the pearl grey sky which was rapidly filling with wind driven clouds which scoured the landscape. The howl and whistle of its voice screeched around the eaves and rattled the window frames.

"It's going to snow, no doubt, but it won't last long. It rarely does," Walter assured her.

"Still, I should go and make sure there's plenty of wood inside the hen house to keep the stove going if it blows for too long. And check the feed bin too." Agnes pulled on a heavy sweater over the one she already wore, and stepped out into the mud room to gather coat, mitts and scarf.

"I'll come help, Mome." Anna came into the kitchen. "The chickens are my responsibility now, remember." She followed her mother into the mud room to swath herself in outwear. Only her blue eyes showed by the time she wrapped a long scarf around her face over her coat and pulled her knitted hat down low on her forehead.

"Let's go then, before it gets worse." Agnes led the way out the back door.

Elsie followed their progress across the yard, their bodies bent into the strong northwest wind, tails of their scarves whipping in the gale. Already flakes fell thicker than only half an hour ago. She sat down to finish her coffee before readying the children's breakfast. There would be no school today so Agnes had allowed them to sleep in. All except Anna, who was always up before the sun, even in the long days of summer.

When the men were finished eating, Elsie cleared the table and began the makings of pancakes for the youngsters to stretch the supply of perogies. A fist of wind rattled the windows and shook the frame house. Her heart jumped a bit in spite of herself. It's only a storm coming in, she reminded herself.

Anna and Agnes returned, a blast of snow and frigid air accompanying them. "My goodness, that wind cuts right to the bone," Agnes gasped while unwinding her snow encrusted scarf. "It's really starting to come down too." She gestured toward the window where snow stuck to the frosted panes in white blossoms.

Walter rose and went to put on his outer clothes again. "I'd best bring in some more wood before it gets worse out there. Looks like we're in for a blizzard if that sky is any indication." He turned his farmer's eye to the worsening storm.

Ike got his feet as well and went to join his son-in-law. "Best make sure the barn is shut tight and the livestock is well bedded."

"Throw them some extra feed just in case the storm gets worse by tonight. It will save you a trip out in the dark," Elsie suggested.

Ike turned to her with a smile, his coat half on one shoulder. "You trying to tell me how to care for the animals now, are you?"

"Go on with you, old man. I'm just trying to save you from being buried in some snowdrift. You wouldn't thaw out 'til spring."

His chuckle followed him out the door.

"I got a few more eggs," Anna announced, putting six brown eggs in the bowl on the counter. "The stove is pretty well stoked and the water isn't frozen. I already gave them extra straw this morning and filled the hopper with grain."

"You're a good girl, Anna." Elsie ruffled her granddaughter's hair.

The patter of feet in the upstairs hall announced the arrival of the rest of the family before their high pitched voices echoed in the stairwell. The phone shrilled over their excited chatter as the children burst into the room.

"Hello." Elsie answered the summons while Agnes shushed her brood.

"Mome? It's Susan. I just heard on the radio there's a blizzard coming. I wanted to be sure you knew so you could make preparations. They're saying it's going to be a bad one."

"We haven't had the radio on this morning, but it's snowing here now and the wind is picking up," Elsie replied. "Have you talked to Helen or Sarah yet?"

"Not yet, I called you first. I'll contact them as soon as I hang up. I don't trust the phone wires in this wind. The service might go down at any time."

"I'll let you go then. Thanks for the news. I'm going to call your brothers while the phone is still working. Stay safe." Elsie rang off. She turned to Agnes who was buttering toast for the twins. "That was Susan. The weatherman says there's a blizzard coming."

"I think it's already here." Agnes nodded at the snow covered window which was letting only a diffuse blue light now. "I hope the menfolk come in soon."

"It does look like it's going to be a bad one," Elsie agreed, casting a worried glance at the increasingly thick fall of snow and taking note of the different pitch in the wail of the wind. The screech of the telephone wires in the gale, clearly audible even in the house, sent a shiver down her spine.

"I'm going to call your sisters and the boys." Elsie lifted the receiver and began her calls. By the time she'd spoken to Helena and Sarah, the snow was already drifting across the drive and piling against the outbuildings. The phone connection crackled and cut out from time to time, but she managed reach Ed, Jake and Hank and reassure herself everyone was safely at home and not caught out somewhere in what was rapidly becoming a dangerous storm.

The last call she made was to Hank and Frieda who lived the farthest away, over by Niverville. Frieda assured her that they were fine and well prepared for the storm. It hadn't intensified at their place yet and Hank was out closing the livestock into the barn and pitching extra hay into the sheep pen and cattle mangers. She thought he would get the evening milking done before the blizzard hit. While it was now snowing heavily in Silberfeld, it was only beginning to fall outside Niverville. Elsie hung up the phone at the same time the tramp of boots stamping on the back steps, and an increase in the sound of the wind when the door opened, announced the return of the men from the barn.

With swift efficiency, she poured too large mugs of coffee and took the men's outerwear from them. Agnes came to help her beat the snow from the coats and scarves. She clapped the mitts together to knock what she could off. Rather than leave the garments in the mudroom, Elsie brought them into the kitchen and hung them over the backs of chairs near the wood stove. Agnes placed some large towels on the linoleum to catch the water than ran off as the snow melted.

"I don't like the looks of this storm," Walter remarked, wrapping his big hands around the pottery mug for warmth.

"It's just a blizzard. There's always at least one every winter," Agnes replied, although the furrows on her forehead belied her words.

"It's come up too fast, and there's an odd note in the voice of that wind…" Ike shook his head, years of farming and reading the weather patterns of the area putting lines of worry on his face.

"We've lots of food in the house, and feed in the barn for the animals. Anna has bedded up the chickens and there's plenty of dry wood for their stove. We'll just have to wait it out. These things never last more than a day or so," Elsie said, seeking to alleviate the tension in the room.

Anna and her younger siblings were playing hide and seek upstairs. Shrieks and laughter accompanied the patter of their feet. Elsie was thankful they weren't aware of their elder's concerns with the weather.

"Have you spoken to the boys?" Ike asked.

"Yes, every last one of them, and the girls too. Frieda said it hadn't really started to snow yet over by Niverville, but the others near here all said it was snowing hard. I made sure to call right away in case the lines go down in the storm."

"Ah, that's good then. One less thing to worry about." Ike leaned back in his chair, legs crossed at the ankles and outstretched under the table. He rested the coffee mug on his stomach, cradled in his hands. "The temperature is dropping fast. We'll have to make sure the fires stay lit during the night."

"I think we'll bring the twins into bed with us to keep them warm," Agnes said.

Walter nodded, head turned toward the kitchen window where the daylight was blotted out by the snow clinging to the single pane glass.

Elsie supressed a shudder when a particularly strong gust of wind hammered the north windows of the house. She hated the wind when it stormed like this. It always reminded her of the storms on the ship when they moved to Paraguay so many years ago. She'd been sure they were all going to drown beneath the great towering waves. The howl of a prairie storm somehow made everything come rushing back.

Anxious to do something to take her mind from the memories, she got to her feet and fetched the containers of coal oil and kerosene.

"Agnes, will you come and help me fill the lamps please? There's no telling how long it will be before the electricity goes out."

"Of course, Mome. I'll put some wood on the fire in the living room and start the little heaters upstairs in the bedrooms."

"Anna's room is on the north side, she might be better to sleep down here on the sofa near the fireplace. The wind will rip right through her room at the rate it's blowing."

"That's a good suggestion. I'll ask her if she would like to do that. You know how she can be, funny little thing." Agnes smiled.

"That's true. She does have a mind of her own," Elsie agreed.

The two women filled every oil lamp in the house but only lit the one in the living room. There was little to do for the rest of the day save listen to the radio when they could get reception and keep the children occupied. Elsie spent the afternoon by the fire in the living room knitting. She made sure there were plenty of batteries for the radio, if the power went out, as it surely would, they would need them.

The storm closed in around the prairie homestead and the winter twilight came early. Snow plastered the single pane windows and wind snaked through every crack it could find billowing the curtain when the gusts hit the building.

Elsie closed the door between the living and dining room as well as the kitchen. The cook stove would keep the kitchen warm, and the fireplace threw enough heat to make the living room cozy. The twins and Anna curled up before the fire on the braided rug Elsie made years ago. Agnes sat on the settee beside Elsie, while Ike and Walter huddled around the radio trying to get some news of the storm from the outside world. The tube radio crackled and gave off intermittent squeals while Ike fiddled with the dials. For brief moments the announcer's voice came through clear.

"It sounds like the storm is intensifying. They're warning against travel and advising people to prepare for at least three days of blizzard weather." The click of the switch was lost in the sound of the snow battering the house.

Elsie put down her knitting and moved to peer out the window. "Three days? That's more than usual for this time of year. Weather like this usually blows out in under forty-eight hours." She pushed the curtain back and scratched at the heavy frost coating the pane. "Oh my goodness!"

Her exclamation brought the other adults to the window. "Look at the height of the drift on the porch! It's up to the window sill already."

"Honest?" Anna popped up beside Elsie. "Let me see!" She dashed into the hall and pulled the front door open before Elsie realized her intention. "Oh! Come see all the snow!"

"Anna! Shut that door this instant," Walter snapped. He moved his daughter out of the way and pushed the door shut, but not before taking note of the piled snow against the screen door.

Elsie got a good look before the door slammed shut against the wind driven snow blasting into the front hall through the screen. The dry, hard packed snow was halfway up the door and covered the porch in an even, ever rising, blanket. If she didn't know there were four steps down to the yard she would have thought the door opened onto level ground.

She returned to the living room after sweeping up the snow from the hall floor. No sense in letting it melt and spoil the hardwood Ike so painstakingly laid when the house was built. With the abundance of oak trees, the hardwood had been easy to come by. Ike and Walter were standing by the door into the kitchen, while Agnes was calming a weeping Anna.

"I didn't mean any harm, Mome. I just wanted to see how much snow had fallen." The girl raised her tear stained face to her mother. "Do you think the chickens will be okay? The fire won't last for three days, will it? I can't let them freeze." She started to push away from her mother.

"Your father and grosspape will take care of them when they go out to milk the cows. Come along now, children. I think it's bedtime, and I believe I know just which Bible story will be a good fit for tonight." Agnes shepherded the children upstairs to the bedrooms where the small heaters were pushing back the ever increasing cold.

Elsie followed their progress until the shadows of the stair well swallowed them up. The reassuring tread of their feet on the floorboards overhead somehow offered comfort. She turned her attention to the men by the door.

"Where are you going?" she asked when they opened the door and started into the kitchen.

"You go ahead, Walt. I'll be there in a minute." Ike waved his son-in-law forward. "The way that snow is drifting we won't be able to get out of the house in a few hours. I've never seen a storm like this one in all my years. Walter and I are going to clear a path to the woodshed and the barn. It's gonna take some work to keep it clear I'm afraid."

"Wait, I can help," Elsie offered. "Just let me go change into something warmer."

"No. You stay here where it's warm. See if you can get one of the children on the phone, see how they're doing. Sarah and Arnold are alone, unless they've managed to make it over to Helen's. It will be safer if they can stay together and pool their resources." Ike moved into the kitchen and started to pull on his outer wear. Walter had already gone out into the lee of the house, protected by the mudroom projecting out from the house proper.

"Fine, I'll do that. But you be careful. The two of you stay together. Don't get separated, you know how easy it is to get lost in all that whirling snow. Don't be out there too long, either," she called after his retreating back. The kitchen door closed with a click of the latch, followed by the slam of the mud room door. Shaking her head, Elsie put more wood on the stove, almost dropping the last billet of oak when the lights flickered and died. She pushed the wood all the way in and slid the lid back into place with the cast iron lifter.

Feeling her way around the table in the sudden darkness, Elsie pushed open the door to the living room and stepped into the flickering glow of the kerosene lamp and the fireplace. She reached up and took the full lamp from the mantle where Agnes placed it earlier. She removed the chimney and lit it with a spill from the fireplace. Holding it in front of her she paused at the bottom of the stairs. Agnes seemed to have things well in hand, the soft illumination of an oil lamp shone onto the landing. The children were giggling about something, so the loss of electricity didn't appear to be bothering them.

Reassured, Elsie went back into the kitchen and placed the lamp in the middle of the table. It gave sufficient light for her to put on a fresh pot of coffee. Once the pot was on the heat, she lifted the receiver on the phone and tried Sarah's number. There was no answer and the line went dead after two rings. She glared at the phone as if it had done it on purpose just to vex her. Elsie tried Helen's next. Her knees almost gave out in relief when the call was answered.

"Helen?"

"Mome. How bad is it at your place?" Helen's voice came faintly over the crackling line.

"Bad enough. The snow is already halfway up the front door. Pape and Walter are out shovelling a path to the woodshed and the barn. How is it there? Are Sarah and Arnold with you?"

"Yes, Arnold brought Sarah over right after it really started to blow. About the same. Martin and Arnold are out shovelling too. The radio said we should expect at least three days of this. If that happens we'll be buried," Helen's voice took on a note of hysteria.

"Let's pray for the best. There's nothing else we can do, this is in the Lord's hands." Elsie paused. "How is Sarah managing? Is she all right?" She twisted the cord in her fingers, glancing every few seconds at the door.

"I think Sarah is taking this better than the rest of us. All she can talk about is going to Mexico. The only comment she's made about the storm is that it might postpone their departure if it takes too long to melt come spring." The faint hysteria faded to be replaced by exasperation.

"Did you get all the stock in? Thank the good Lord Ike got everything in before this began," Elsie changed the subject.

"Yes, Hank got word from the CPR that the storm was coming, so he called and let us know. Susan was supposed to call you and pass on the message."

"She did, thank you. Have you talked to your other brothers?" Elsie caught her bottom lip between her teeth. It was a worry when the family wasn't all under one roof, even though most of them lived nearby. Hank and Frieda, in Niverville, were the farthest away.

"Yes, Mome. Just after the snow started to fly. They were all ready and had the stock in," Helen's voice broke up and the line crackled and went dead.

Frowning, Elsie replaced the receiver. It was a comfort the line had stayed up long enough for her to reassure herself the family was safe and warm. She pulled the heavy iron frying pan from the drawer and set it on the stove top, putting a dollop of bacon grease into it to heat. The men would need something to eat after battling the cold and wind. She took the loaf pan of heavy porridge out of ice box and began to cut slices. It was more of a breakfast item, but it would surely stick their ribs when the men came in.

The drippings were sizzling in the pan now and she slid four slices into the fat. With one ear she listened for the mud room door. Ike and Walter had been out in the storm for over half an hour. Far too long in this weather. She could feel the temperature dropping by the minute, between the wind driving the snow and cold, it would scour the skin off your face in moments.

"Where are Pape and Walter?" Agnes came into the kitchen, a line of worry marring her fair forehead. She busied herself setting two places at the table and fetching cream and sugar for the coffee. "Do you think we should go look for them? What if something happened?" Agnes moved restlessly to the snow blocked window.

"They went out to clear a path to the wood shed and the barn. It must be taking longer than they anticipated." Elsie flipped the porridge slices in the pan making sure both sides were golden and crispy. "Can you please put the maple syrup on the table as well?" She snuck a worried glance toward the stubbornly closed mudroom door.

"Mome, I'm scared." Anna came into the kitchen and curled up on a chair, feet tucked up under her. "When is the snow going to stop?"

"It will stop when God wills it to," Elsie said. She set the flipper down and moved to give the girl a hug. "There's no need to be afraid. The Lord will watch over us."

"What are the twins up to?" Agnes addressed her daughter while casting a worried glance at the ceiling. All was quiet, which could be a good thing or a bad thing.

"You didn't leave a lamp lit up there did you? Not with the twins all on their own?" Agnes started for the door.

"No, Mome. I blew the lamp out and put it up where they can't reach it. They're asleep in your bed and I made sure the heater wasn't near the bed or the curtains," Anna spoke in an exact replica of her mother's tones.

Elsie hid a smile and turned back to remove the frying pan from the direct heat. She pushed it over to where it would keep warm, but not burn.

"When is Pape coming in?" Anna wanted to know.

"Pape and your grosspape will come in when they're done. Don't you worry your head about it. Both Pape and Grosspape are big strong men. A little storm isn't going to do them any harm," Agnes soothed the girl while exchanging a worried look with Elsie over the child's head.

"Oh, thank goodness. At last," Elsie exclaimed as the outside mudroom door slammed in the wind and the hollow sound of boots echoed on the wooden floor.

Moments later Ike and Walter shoved through the inner door.

"Pape, you look like a snowman!" Anna clapped her hands and laughed. "You too, Opa. It looks like fun. Can I go out and play in the snow?" She turned hopeful eyes on her mother.

"The wind would carry you away, Anna. Feel how cold it is." Walter drew off his thick knitted mitt and put his hand on her cheek. Snow dripped from the wool in his hand.

"Pape!" Anna shrieked and wriggled away from him.

"Anna, hush. You'll wake the twins," Agnes scolded her while hiding a smile.

Elsie went to help Ike out of his coat. The thing weighed three times what it should with the coating of snow. She hung it to dry near the stove and put the mitts of both men on the wire trees especially constructed for that purpose. Wrapping her sweater tighter around her Elsie scurried out to the mudroom to retrieve the frozen boots the men had stepped out of. Setting them on the drip pan near the stove she turned and gestured for Ike to remove his socks. The tops were frozen solid to his pant legs, small rivulets of melt water beginning to trickle down the material.

Agnes was busy doing the same for her husband. Anna watched in fascination as the storm's detritus became small puddles. At a word from her mother, she ran and got the men's slippers from the living room. By the time she came back Ike and Walter had coffee in front of them and were digging into the oatmeal pancakes swimming in syrup.

Elsie pulled the wet woolen stockings over the tall wire frames and placed them beside the drying mitts.

Anna stayed curled in her chair looking pleased to be included with the grown-ups. Before long her head began to nod and Agnes took her up to bed. Once she returned, the talk turned more serious.

"It's going to be a long night I'm afraid," Ike remarked with a pointed look at his son-in-law.

"What do you mean, Pape?" Agnes looked from one man to the other.

"With that wind and the amount of snow coming down, those paths aren't going to stay clear for long. One, or both of us, is going to have to go out every hour or so and keep clearing them," Walter replied.

"Pape?" Agnes looked to her father for confirmation.

"It's as Walter says." He got to his feet. "Let's set things right for the night here and get some sleep while we can," Ike said.

* * *

All through the night and into the next day the storm raged unabated. In the brief interludes when the radio would produce more than squawks and whistles they got news of the width and breadth of the blizzard.

"It doesn't seem possible that it's storming all the way from here to Alberta," Agnes declared.

"Maybe we heard wrong?" Elsie wondered.

"I don't know about that, Elsie. I've never seen anything like this blizzard." Ike shook his head.

"Has anyone been able to get through on the phone?" Walter asked glancing at the silent instrument.

‘Not since I talked to Helen yesterday. The line went dead right in the middle of the conversation,” Elsie replied.

“Line is probably down.” Ike scratched his head.

The lines of fatigue and worry etched on his handsome face worried Elsie. He and Walt were going non-stop trying to keep the path to the woodshed and the barn open. Agnes and Elsie talked about how to help when the men went out again into the teeth of the blizzard. The path they were clearing followed the fence line so at least there was little chance of going astray. The sides of the narrow alley were up to the men’s shoulders now. How much deeper can it get? Elsie worried.

Ike and Walter stumbled in the door, crusted in snow, ice coating their eyelashes and Ike’s mustache. White patches of frostbite covered both their noses and spread across their cheeks.

“That’s enough, Ike. You can’t keep going out there.” Elsie planted her hands on her hips and stared down at her exhausted husband slumped in the kitchen chair. “You’re too done in to even take off your coat. It’s time you let Agnes and I get out there and help.” She raised a hand to forestall his attempt to argue. “We’ve talked about it, and there’s no reason we can’t take it in turns to clear the snow.”

“Elsie, I’m too bone-tired to argue with you right now.” He got to his feet and shed his outer clothes before staggering off upstairs to fall into bed. Walter followed him up the stairs leaning heavily on the railing as he went. Agnes went after them armed with bed warmers and hot water bottles. When she came back down, she sank into a chair across from Elsie.

"I'm really worried, Mome. How long can we go on like this?" She rubbed a hand across her forehead. "They're both about wore out, and the snow just keeps coming." An especially hard gust of wind slammed the upper story of the building. It was a small mercy the drifted snow protected the lower floor. A small mercy, Elsie grimaced, protected yes, but so much snow piled against the house was frightening. She worried the pressure of the building snow would break the windows. The front door was firmly blocked now, the only way in and out of the house was by the mud room door which was in the lee of the building.

"Mome, I've been thinking. There must be something we can do to keep the darn snow from blowing down into the pathways." Agnes frowned and tapped her fingers on the table top.

"I don't know how." Elsie finished clearing the table before filling two mugs with coffee and joining her eldest daughter.

"There has to be a better way than what we're doing," Agnes insisted. "At least with the trenches getting so deep we have some protection from the wind, but it won't last long with the way the snow keeps drifting."

Chapter Eight

And The Snow Keeps Coming

Elsie paused to lean on her shovel and shake the fine snow from her head scarf. Just a foot above her head the wind howled and the blizzard snaked long fingers of white over the top of the trench. Agnes stopped as well, her lashes icy white, breath coming in great heaving gasps as she laboured to breathe in the freezing air.

"This is pointless, Mome," she shouted over the shriek of the storm. "By the time we get the one to the woodshed cleared, the one to the barn is already blown in."

"I just wish it would let up a bit." Elsie beat her hands on her arms to get the circulation flowing. Her mitts were frozen in a curve that fit around the shovel handle. Inside her fingers felt like wooden blocks, but at least she could still hold the shovel. "It's been snowing for three days." She glanced overhead at the invisible sky. "The last forecast we heard was for three days, but this doesn't show any signs of stopping."

"Three days. It feels more like three weeks." Agnes sighed and straightened up. "We should go in and get warmed up, or we'll end up like Pape and Walter with frostbite on our hands."

"I hate to give up just yet, but you're right."

They traipsed back to the house, knocking as much snow off their clothing as they could before going in. The men had been up all night fighting to keep the woodbins full and the paths clear. Last night they'd managed to get the cows milked and the other livestock fed. Now they were tucked up in bed sleeping the sleep of exhaustion.

Elsie held her hands as near the stove as she could bear, the returning feeling in her fingers and toes clenching her jaw and bringing tears to her eyes. "I don't know how long we can keep this up, Agnes. Maybe we should just let the tunnel to the barn blow in. There's feed out there and a few cases of mastitis isn't as bad as losing fingers or worse to frostbite."

"I know." Agnes pulled a chair close and drew warm woollen socks on her feet before propping them on the stove fender. "I'm worried about those silly chickens too. Anna is fretting over them. I managed to scrape the frost off the upstairs window and saw some smoke still coming from the hen house chimney, but they've got to be freezing in there. And the hopper only holds about four days' worth of grain."

"Losing a few chickens is better than losing one of us," Elsie said grimly. "Let's see if we can get the radio to work and get some news about when the blizzard is expected to end."

Hands curled around the warm pottery of the coffee mug, Elsie led the way into the living room. Agnes put more wood on the fire in there and the women drew their chairs closer to the flames. Elsie clicked the switch with cold fingers and was rewarded with a crackle and screech that resolved finally into intelligible words interspersed with crackles and sometimes drowned out by the howling wind.

It seemed the only programming was bulletins about the weather. When the reception degenerated into clicks and crackles Agnes leaned over and switched the machine off. Thank goodness the batteries were holding out so far. Elsie sat in stunned disbelief of what the announcer had relayed.

"It's far worse than we imagined," she whispered clutching the mug of coffee like a life line. "Winnipeg is shut down, the streets are plugged and people are running out of coal. At least we have lots of wood to keep us warm. The trains aren't running, or buses. Everything between here and Regina is snowed in."

"And they said they have no idea when it will end. The clouds just keep dumping snow, and the wind won't let up. I'm really starting to get scared, Mome. How long do you think we can hold out?"

Elsie reached over and patted her hand. "As long as we have to, Agnes. The Lord will look after us. His hand is over us all. We have lots of flour, meat in the summer kitchen if we can get there, jars of preserves and canned vegetables in the cellar."

"You're right. Water isn't a problem, we can just keep melting snow. There's enough of it." A laugh halfway between amusement and bitterness followed her statement.

"There, see. There's a bright side to every problem." Elsie smiled at her daughter and stretched her feet toward the fire, pulling a crocheted afghan over her shoulders.

Agnes reached for a striped Hudson Bay blanket lying over the back of the sofa. She stopped and then got to her feet. "I've got it, Mome!"

"What? Got what?" Elsie glanced wildly around her. "Is something on fire?" It was her worst fear. Fire was merciless and took no prisoners once released from its bonds of fireplace and stove.

"No, Mome. A way to keep the snow from blowing into the tunnels."

Elsie sat up straighter and set her mug down. "How?" The single word held her hopes and her prayers for a solution.

"This." Agnes shook the wool blanket with its traders' marks.

"A blanket?" It made no sense to her. "The wind will just blow it away."

"Not if we anchor it correctly," Agnes insisted.

"With what?"

"That snow is packed hard as cement. If we dig out at each corner, and then pack snow back in, it should hold. I hope. It's worth a try, I think." Agnes raised her eyebrows at her mother.

Elsie considered the proposition before mentally taking stock of the number of available blankets. "Even if it did work, and I'm saying *if,* there aren't enough blankets. We need them to keep warm and I don't want to risk losing them in the wind."

Agnes held the blanket to her chest and regarded her mother. Elsie knew that look; the determined thrust to the chin was pure Ike in one of his moods.

"Let's try it anyway with just one blanket."

"Try what?" Walter appeared in the doorway, wiping sleep from his eyes.

Agnes explained her idea to him.

"I don't know, Aggie. That wind is pretty stiff."

He studied her face for a moment and Elsie hid a smile at the look of resignation that flashed across his face.

"Let me have a cup of coffee and something to eat, then we can give it a try if you're determined to do this," Walter relented.

"Is Ike stirring?" Elsie glanced toward the ceiling, but couldn't discern any sign of movement above in their room.

“I don’t believe so. I’m pretty sure I heard him snoring when I went by your door.” Walter smiled.

“Let’s let him sleep then. This storm is putting a strain on him. Are the twins still playing in Anna’s room?” Elsie got up and moved to make a fresh pot of coffee.

“I’ll go check on them,” Agnes offered setting the blanket on the sofa back.

In moment she was back downstairs. “They’re still playing. Anna is such a great help with them. I feel like I ask too much of her sometimes. The heater in her room is keeping it bearable in there.”

Walter finished his coffee and started to put his coat on. Agnes joined him and soon the two were swathed in coats and scarves. Blanket firmly in her arms, she followed her husband into the mud room. Elsie fidgeted with things in the kitchen, anxious to know how Agnes’ idea would work out. It wasn’t long before the pair staggered back into the kitchen, half frozen and disappointed.

“It didn’t work,” Agnes said emerging from her snowbound outer clothes. “The wind catches it before we can get it anchored.”

“What didn’t work?” Ike came into the kitchen. “What have you been up to? Agnes, you shouldn’t be going out in the cold so often.”

“Here, Ike. Sit and have your coffee and let them explain.” Elsie set a steaming mug on the table.

Ike listened to the details of the failed plan, tapping a forefinger on the table, his brow furrowed. Walter ended his tale and leaned back, wrapping his cold hands around his mug of coffee.

"It's not a bad idea in theory," Ike began. "There's those two-by-fours in the corner of the shed, and some sheets of plywood I think we can still get to. We could build a frame inside the tunnel with the two-by-fours and nail the plywood to those to create a roof or at least a windbreak of sorts to hold the snow out."

Walter didn't reply at once, Elsie waited with bated breath. The idea seemed feasible to her, but then building and carpentry wasn't her strong suit either.

"You know, it just might work. Like what they do to shore up a mine shaft." Walter pushed back his chair and got up, reaching for his coat.

"Surely you don't mean to go out again so soon?" Agnes protested. "Your coat is still frozen, and your fingertips are still white. Please, wait a little while and get warm."

"The wind isn't letting up at all. In fact I think it's getting worse. If we don't do something soon it won't matter, because the tunnel will be all blown in." Walter pulled on his stiff coat and took the fresh scarf and mitts Agnes wordlessly handed him.

Ike drained his coffee and prepared to join his son-in-law. Elsie bit her tongue to stop from asking him not to go back out into the blizzard.

Even though he'd slept for a few hours, fatigue slowed his movements. Lines of exhaustion carved into his face.

"We need to bring more wood in at any rate." He took the mitts and extra socks Elsie handed him. "Don't worry. It won't take long to knock together the framework, after that it's only a small matter to get the plywood nailed on."

After the men departed, Agnes sank into the chair Walter just vacated. She rested her chin in her hand, elbow on the table and fiddled with a spoon. "I don't know how much longer we can do this, Mome. We've still got food, and milk from the cows. But I've never seen a storm last as long as this one, or be as fierce."

"I agree. It's only been a few days and it feels like months since the snow started. I hope the neighbors got their stock in the barns before it hit. Anyone who didn't will lose everything. The sheep will be buried, and unless they can find something to shelter them, cows and horses will freeze solid where they stand. Most everyone should have the swine inside for the winter, so at least the pigs won't freeze.

Running feet echoed upstairs followed by Anna's voice asking them to quiet down. Elsie glanced at Agnes and offered a tired grin. "At least the little ones don't appear to be worried."

"Thank goodness for small mercies," Agnes agreed. "Enough feeling sorry for myself." She got to her feet, "I have a roof over my head, food and warmth. It could be a lot worse."

"You're right, we have a lot to thank the good Lord for." Elsie patted her hand. "Now, I bet those young ones of yours are getting hungry." She glanced at the clock on the wall, it was hard to keep track of the time in the seemingly eternal darkness created by the storm. "Time to start supper. The men will be hungry when they come in." Elsie glanced at the window by habit and shook her head. Thick frost coated the panes on the inside, and on the outside a drift covered the bottom half of the window.

Forty-five minutes later, Agnes gave the borscht a last stir and replaced the cover. "If they don't come in soon, I'm going out to get them," she declared. "You don't think something happened, do you? They could be out there freezing to death…" The slam of the mud room door interrupted her. "Oh, thank God." She pressed a hand to her heart and hurried to open the inner mud room door.

Ike and Walter more fell than walked through the opening. Both men's faces were encrusted with snow and ice, as were their bodies. Elsie thought they resembled walking snow men. Frozen fingers fumbled unsuccessfully with buttons until Elsie and Agnes took over. Soon Ike and Walter were wrapped in warm blankets and sitting as close to the cook stove as they dared, drinking coffee laced with lots of sugar and cream. Although Elsie was itching to know if the scheme was successful, she was more worried about the two men. Ike in particular wasn't even shivering, though his hands shook. Not shivering was a bad sign when a person was as cold as Ike was. She cast around in her mind for any of Oma's's remedies that might help get his circulation flowing again.

"It worked," Walter finally managed to croak. "The tunnel to the barn and the woodshed are secure."

"Good then, Agnes and I can do the night milking and feed, you two need to get some rest and warm up right after we get some hot food into you," Elsie declared.

Ike's protest was pre-empted by a fit of hoarse coughing. He set the mug on the table to prevent it spilling. When the spell passed he leaned back in his chair, eyes closed, and in spite of the chill of his skin a thin sheen of sweat covered his forehead.

"I won't hear another word out of you, Ike Neufeld. It's up to bed with you. No arguments. Agnes, help me get your father upstairs, he's weak as a kitten," Elsie ordered.

To her surprise Ike offered no complaint. Pushing his body upright with his hands on the arms of the chair, he stood up and swayed alarmingly. Walter came around the table and took the older man's arm over his shoulder.

"You go get the bed ready, Mother Neufeld. I'll get Ike upstairs, he's too heavy for you two to handle."

Elsie filled two fleece covered waterproof bags with hot water from the big pot of melted snow kept simmering on the cook stove. Agnes ran to get more wool blankets from the storage chest while Walter and Ike made their slow way toward the bedroom.

"Mome, I'm worried about Pape," Agnes whispered after they passed the men in the hall. "That cough didn't sound good at all."

"I know. Silly old fool insisting on spending all that time out in the storm. I'll dose him good with cough syrup and a mustard plaster." Elsie bustled into the bedroom and flipped the quilts back. She slid the hot water bottles into the bed at the foot. The curtains bellied out slightly as the wind's frosty breath found its way around the frame.

"Here we are, Ike. I'll leave you to your wife's tender mercies." Walter helped Ike lower himself onto the edge of the bed and left the room.

"Do you need help getting him into bed, Mome?" Agnes set the folded blankets on top of the quilt at the foot of the bed.

"I can manage. You run along and get the supper ready for the rest of the family." Elsie knelt and pulled off Ike's two pairs of socks, now wet from melted snow that had found its way inside his winter boots. The feet her actions revealed his feet were white and wrinkled with cold. The little toe on his left foot caused her concern as it was pure white and very cold to the touch. With one hand on her husband's shoulder to steady him, she retrieved another pair of socks from the dresser and eased them over his feet. It was a bit of a struggle to wrestle Ike's clothes off and get his flannel nightshirt on. Grunting a bit with the effort, she eased him back onto the pillows and swung his legs up onto the mattress. Tucking his feet under the covers, she arranged the pigs so they would warm him, but not too quickly.

Ike's eyes fluttered closed, his chest barely rose with his breath. Elsie pulled the quilts up to his chin and then added the two Hudson Bay blankets as well. Ike's breath rattled a bit in his throat, so she added another pillow behind him to make it easier to breathe.

Satisfied she'd done everything she could for the moment, she went down to the kitchen where the children were just finishing their supper. Anna's food was barely touched and the child was pushing her potatoes around with her fork. The twins were eating quietly. Walter looked ready to drop where he sat, she caught Agnes giving him concerned looks, but wisely refraining from saying anything.

"Once the table is cleared, Agnes, you and I will go out and do the evening chores, if that suits you," Elsie said.

"You shouldn't be going out in this," Walter protested. His voice had a scratchy note to it.

"Is your throat sore?" Agnes picked up on the deviation in his tone.

"A bit. Just from yelling into the wind. Cuts right to the bone." He took a sip of coffee, and then coughed, holding a hand to his chest.

"Mome and I can manage just fine, Walter. If you can stay in the warm and just keep an eye on the children we'll do just fine, like I said."

"I can help," Anna piped up. "I want to check on the chickens. The stove must be out by now and they'll need to be fed."

"Absolutely not!" Agnes said. "Those hens will have to take care of themselves, Anna. It's far too dangerous out there, and there's no path shovelled to the hen house. None of us thought the blizzard would last this long."

"But they'll die, Mome! I can't let them die," Anna protested. "They're my responsibility, you even said that when we got the new chicks last spring."

"No, that's the end of it. No more discussion." Agnes slapped a dish cloth on the table and began to wipe up the crumbs.

"But Mome—"

"I said no more." Agnes' voice was steel.

Anna turned pleading eyes on her grossmama. Elsie was hard put not to intervene, but held firm.

Walter started to reprimand his daughter, but a spasm of coughing overcame him.

"You heard your mother. Respect your mother and obey her," he finally managed to croak.

The girl gave a curt nod, tears shimmering in her eyes. Rising from the table she took the last of the dishes to the sink before herding the twins from the room. "I'll read them their bedtime story and get the twins ready for bed."

"Let's get you into the living room into a more comfortable chair." Agnes directed Walter. "You go on in and I'll bring fresh coffee and a slice of cake I made with the last of the eggs today. All you need to do is listen for any commotion from upstairs. Anna is good with them, but sometimes they try and overrule her."

Walter got wearily to his feet and shuffled toward the living room door, blanket wrapped around his shoulders. "I'd argue with you, but I just can't find the energy. Be careful out there, this is a killing blizzard. I've never seen the like."

"We'll be extra careful, promise," Agnes assured him.

The newly protected tunnels made the trip to the barn and woodshed much easier and safer. The whistle of the storm and the fine sprinkle of drifting snow that found its way through the gaps between the plywood sent shivers down Elsie's spine. *Is it ever going to let up? How long can this possibly last? How long can we last?* She focussed on the bright red scarf wrapped around Agnes's head and shoulders, pushing defeatist thoughts to the back of her mind and prayed fervently as she shuffled along the narrow track. The flickering light of the lantern in her daughter's hand threw weird shifting shapes on the frozen walls. Rather than the orange-yellow glow warming and comforting Elsie, it evoked images of fire and brimstone. *Is God punishing us for something? Is this a sign Sarah and Arnold shouldn't emigrate to Mexico? Or Sadie to Paraguay?* She prayed harder and wrapped her faith around her in a blanket of protection.

"Finally!"

The barn door grated open, Elsie followed Agnes into the dark warmth. The interior was redolent with the heady odour of summer hay, urine and a mixture of animal smells. The strong scent of the swine over rode the less pungent attar of cow, and horse with underlying notes of the wet wool scent of sheep. It was blessedly warm after the cold trek from the house.

In short order the cows were milked and fresh hay thrown into the mangers. Agnes filled the feeder in the pig pen with chop and then threw more into a long feed trough they didn't usually use. The sheep had buried themselves deep in the straw bed and baaed softly at the two women. Agnes overfilled their feed trough as well.

"Just in case the tunnel closes in or something stupid happens," she remarked to her mother.

Elsie leaned the hay fork back where it belonged and checked the water pails one more time. The building was warm compared to the -29 degree weather outside, but wasn't enough to keep water from freezing. The women collected snow from outside the man door which was in a bit of a lee from the wind and filled the buckets with that. It would keep the animals from dehydrating, even it wasn't as good as drinking water, but it would briefly lower the animals' body temperature if they consumed too much. Elsie sighed and surveyed the animals one more time; it would have to do. Better a slightly cold animal than a dead one.

Taking the lantern and leaving the barn in darkness, the women wrestled the door shut behind them before beginning the journey back to the house. Elsie spared a thought for the chickens, thinking with regret about the loss of them and the eggs they produced. If all they lost to this storm was a few chickens it would be a miracle. Anna would be upset, but the girl was old enough to learn such things were a part of life.

* * *

Walter was asleep in the chair by the fireplace when they returned to the house. Elsie left Agnes in the kitchen brewing tea and went upstairs to check on Ike. He lay still on the pillows, mouth gaping and face pale. Even from the doorway, she could hear the breath rattling in his chest. Concern lent speed to her feet as she crossed the room to his side. His forehead was hot under her hand though he shivered enough to rustle the bed clothes.

Pulling back the sheets, Elsie opened his pyjama top and peeled the mustard plaster back. Bundling it up and recovering her husband, she went to re-join Agnes in the kitchen. The twins were asleep when she poked her head in the door on the way down the hall. A candle flickered in Anna's room. She was using a candle in order to ration the kerosene for the lamps.

"It's bedtime, Anna. Quit reading and put the candle out. No point wasting wax when we don't know how long this storm is going to last."

"I will, Oma." Anna closed the book. "Were you able to feed the chickens? I'm so worried about them."

"Anna, you know we couldn't get to them. The snow is just too deep. It's all we can do to keep the track to the barn and woodshed open."

"I think I could get there," Anna insisted. "I know I could."

"Don't even think about it, young lady," Elsie declared. "Now, bed."

"Yes, Oma."

She checked the small coal oil heater Walter had put in the room earlier to be sure it would last until morning. Satisfied, she closed the door, but left it ajar and descended the dark stairwell. Walter had wakened when she passed by the living room on the way to the kitchen. He huddled by the fire, thick woollen blanket over his shoulders.

"You should go on up to bed," Elsie encouraged him.

"I will, I'm just too tired to move." He offered her a weak smile. "How's Ike?"

"Sleeping, but I'm worried about his chest." She lifted the mustard plaster bundle in her arms. “I’m going to make a new plaster for him.”

Agnes looked up from setting the tea pot on the table when Elsie came through the door. “How’s Pape?” She eyed the plaster in her mother’s hands.

“He’s not well, I’m afraid. Sounds like an old man down a well. Hopefully another plaster will do the trick. When he wakes up I’ll try to get some tea and honey down him along with some of the cherry and willow cough medicine. Good thing we made up a big batch of it last fall.” The cough medicine consisted of camphorated oil, apple cider vinegar, cherry bark, lemon, willow bark, honey and crushed ginger. It tasted horrible but usually broke the back of the cold.

* * *

Elsie wiped sleep from her eyes and got up from the chair beside the bed in her room. Ike tossed and turned, radiating heat from the fever she couldn’t manage to break. She looked twice at the reading when she pulled the thermometer out from his arm pit. A flush of fear ran through her. Instead of going down the mercury now stood at a little over one-hundred and three.

“Ike.” She shook his shoulder. “Ike, open your eyes.”

There was no response, other than an odd twisting of his body and flutter of eyelids. Pulling the quilts back, Elsie opened his pyjama top and peeled off the used mustard plaster. Much good it had done, she thought wryly. Her fingers fumbled with controlled panic. Somehow, she had to bring the fever down.

Outside the blizzard howled incessantly, now into its seventh day. How long since Ike fell sick? Elsie mentally counted on her fingers. Three days? Maybe four? Far too long at any rate. His face was slack and slicked with sweat in spite of the frigid temperature of the room. She'd let the coal oil heater go out, hoping the drop in temperature would help cool his body. A weak cough wracked him, ribs standing out sharply against the exposed skin. The usual ruddy glow of good health was long since faded, the skin taking on a yellow grey tinge which sent chills down Elsie's spine. She laid a hand on his chest to assure herself he was still breathing. His respirations were shallow, the ribs rising almost imperceptibly under her touch. In some ways she'd give anything for the deep rasping gurgling sounds he made two days past. He was too still, and why didn't he hardly cough anymore? Pushing her panic away, Elsie pulled the curtains back from the window and pulled at the icy frost encrusted latch.

"If I can't bring that fever down I'm going to lose him. Dear God, give me the strength to do what I must. If it is Your will to take him, I will bend to Your will. But I'm asking you, please don't take him right now." Muttering more prayers while the metal latch burned her fingers with frostbite, Elsie struggled with the window. Finally it came free and she pulled the frame open. The wood screeched in protest but gave to her frenzied yanking.

An arctic blast of wind and snow swept over her, depositing sifting snow across the floor. Elsie pulled the window shut a bit but left it open enough to let in the cold air.

"Agnes," she called, leaving the room and hurrying down the stairs. "I need your help."

"What is it, Mome? Is it Pape?" Agnes appeared at the bottom of the stairs wiping her hands on her apron.

"I need some big towels and a couple of buckets. Now." Fear roughened her voice.

"I'll be up in a minute, Mome. I just need to get the buckets from the kitchen." Agnes joined her before Elsie was halfway back up the staircase. "How bad is it?" She met her mother's gaze, the question she didn't want the answer to clear in her expression.

"It's bad. If we can't bring his fever down I'm afraid, we're going to lose him. There's no way to get word to the doctor and no way for him to come even if we could reach him."

"What should we do? Oh my, it's freezing in here!" Agnes led the way into the sick room and then halted.

"It's the only thing I can think of that might break the fever. I want to wrap snow in the towels and pack it around him." Elsie took a bucket and wrenched the window open further, bending out to scoop drifted snow off the porch roof. The blizzard blown drifts covered the front of the house all the way up to the second story windows. “We’ll just have to watch that we don’t give your father frost bite.”

Agnes wasted no time in helping her mother fill the thick towels with snow and place them around the patient after putting a water proof canvas between him and the mattress.

“I wish I could get him to drink something, but he just spits it up, and I’m afraid I’ll choke him,” Elsie worried, wrapping her cold hands in the folds of her skirt.

“Why don’t you try and get some rest, I’ll stay with him for a while,” Agnes urged her.

“I’ll stay. You have the twins to worry about, and Walter.” She paused. “By the way, have you seen Anna in the last little while?”

Agnes frowned and shook her head. “Not since lunch time. She was worrying over those chickens again, but then she disappeared. Said she was going up to her room to read.”

“I haven’t heard her stir at all. Maybe you should check on her, she might have fallen asleep and if the heater has gone out…” Elsie lifted a shoulder. “I’ll watch your pape. If I need you, I’ll call.”

Agnes nodded and left, her footsteps soft on the floorboards of the hall. Elsie sank back into the chair pulling the quilt up against the brisk breeze coming in the window. Her eyes started to close, the jerk of her head nodding startled her awake.

“Mome!”

The near hysteria in Agnes voice brought Elsie to her feet, quilt sliding to pool on the floor. She glanced at Ike, but he appeared oblivious to the commotion. A new pang of fear spiked her heart.

"Mome!" The door burst open, narrowly missing bouncing off the wall. Agnes stood in the doorway, eyes wild.

"What is it? Is there a fire?" Elsie crossed to peer over the other woman's shoulder into the hall.

"No. It's Anna." She choked on a sob.

"What about Anna? Has she come down with something too?" Elsie made to push past her daughter.

Agnes shook her head, wiping tears from her cheeks. "It's worse. She's gone."

"What do you mean…gone? Where could the child go in this storm? The drifts are up to the windows…" Her voice trailed off as realization hit. "The chickens. She's gone to look after the chickens."

Agnes nodded and followed Elsie down the hall into Anna's room. The curtains were drawn, but belled in a slight draft. Elsie pulled the material back to reveal the window frame unlatched and slightly ajar. She yanked the window open and peered out. This part of the house was out of the direct blast of the storm but the drifts were still as high as the lower story eaves. Half closing her eyes against the sting of the wind driven snow, Elsie looked down. Small depressions, rapidly filling with snow, were still visible below the window and across the narrow overhang of the lower floor. Beyond the eaves of the house no tracks were obvious. She retreated back into the shelter of the bedroom and shoved the window closed.

"Don't latch it, Mome. She'll come back the way she left," Agnes said.

If she can come back. Elsie didn't voice the thought aloud.

"What can we do? I have to tell Walter." Agnes paced back and forth in the small room. "How could she be so stupid to go out in this weather? She's old enough to know how dangerous a blizzard can be."

"We should have paid more attention to her when she worried about the hens. Although I honestly would never have expected she would do anything like this."

"We have to go out and find her," Agnes declared, glaring at the window as if it was the inanimate object's fault.

"Go and tell Walter what's happened. Send the twins up to me. I can keep an eye on them while I watch your father."

Agnes ran from the room, steps echoing in the hallway and then clattering down the stairs. "Walter, Walter!" Her voice came faintly to Elsie's ears.

Elsie checked the heater in the twins' room and then went to sit by Ike. She moved the snow packs and replaced the ones that were growing too soft. There was a bit of water pooled on the canvas which she soaked up with another towel.

His forehead felt a bit cooler, but she couldn't be sure if was because the fever was less, or if his skin was just cold from the snow.

She glanced at the hand painted clock on the dresser. In another few minutes she needed to remove the snow packs and wait another ten minutes before taking his temperature again. Tiny shrill voices whispering announced the arrival of the twins. They poked their heads in the door, holding their finger to their lips.

"Mome said to be quiet," they whispered in unison.

Elsie smiled in spite of herself. She went to join them and drew them back into the hall. "Would you like to play in your room? There's that puzzle with the horse and cows you two haven't finished yet. Shall I set that up for you?"

"What's wrong with Opa?" Willy peered back into the room.

"How come he didn't say hi?" Doris asked.

"Opa isn't feeling well. He'll be better soon, but for now we need to be quiet and let him rest, okay?"

"Okay." Two blonde heads nodded seriously like little adults. "We can play puzzle. Maybe Anna can read to us?"

Elsie's heart jumped a bit before she managed to calm her expression. "Anna's busy right now."

"Doing what?" Willy wanted to know. "I don't see her?"

"She's doing something for your Mome. You'll see her later. C'mon, let's get that puzzle out. Then I have to go check and see how Opa is"

Elsie hustled the twins into their room and got out the puzzle. Leaving them happily sorting out the pieces she looked in on Ike. His breathing seemed a bit easier, though when she checked his temperature it still registered at one-hundred and three. She removed the snow packed towels and covered him again. The worry of frostbite overrode the attempt to bring his temperature down. It was up to the good Lord now, she'd done all she could.

On the stairs she met Agnes and Walter on the way up. Walter's face was grim, and tears stained Agnes' cheeks.

"I left the twins in their room playing."

"Thanks, Mome," Agnes replied.

"What are we going to do about Anna?" Elsie spoke quietly.

"I'm going to go out and see if I can find her." Walter's voice was rough with worry.

"You can't. The storm hasn't let up, and you'll only risk getting lost in it yourself," Elsie protested. "We can only hope she made it to the chicken house and managed to get the fire going in the stove."

"Anna's out there alone." Agnes wrung her hands and glanced at her husband.

"I'm going. This will help me find my way back." Walter held up a thick coil of rope Elise hadn't noticed he carried.

She followed them back up the stairs into Anna's room. Agnes pulled the door shut to keep the keening wind from swooping through the house. Walter dragged the single bed across to the window and tied the end of the rope to the bed post. He buttoned his coat and turned the collar up, wrapping a long scarf around his neck and over his lower face. Agnes handed him a knitted hat and mitts. He slung a bag over his shoulder containing extra mitts and warm clothes for Anna. Wrestling open the window he gingerly stepped out onto the packed drift, sat down and strapped on a pair of snow shoes.

"Be careful," Elsie urged him. "When the rope runs out, you be sure to come back."

"I'm going to find Anna," Walter replied. "Shut the window behind me."

A blast of wind whirled snow into the room, belling the curtains around Elsie. By the time she fought free and Agnes managed to close the window, Walter was engulfed in the storm and even his footprints were already filling in.

"I'll keep watch, Mome. You go see to Pape. Leave the door open a bit so I can hear if the twins need me."

With a last look at the snow encrusted window, Elsie slipped out the door and returned to Ike's bedside. The florid colour of his face was alarming, the man was burning up again. His body convulsed with a weak effort to cough before subsiding against the mattress. A blue tinge coloured his lips and deep purple circles pouched beneath his eyes.

Elsie knelt beside the bed and prayed with all her might. For Ike, and for Anna, and Walter, out in the blizzard trying to find his daughter. If only the snow would stop. She spared a thought for the rest of her family and prayed all was well with them. There had been no contact since the telephone lines went down and the radio batteries were running low. The last bit of news they'd heard was the blizzard reached all the way to Alberta, and Winnipeg was trapped in deep snow. The trains weren't running and all other ground transportation was at a halt. Even in the cities people were running out of food and fuel.

She was weary, so tired for fighting the storm and Ike's illness. Now Anna was lost too. Elsie laid her head on her arms and gave into a moment of weakness. Her tears wet the sleeves of her blouse while she prayed harder than she'd ever prayed in her life.

Needing to do something, she got to her feet and retrieved the towels she'd set to dry by the heater. Heedless of the driving wind, she opened the window enough to collect more snow to pack around her husband. Ike muttered and shifted weakly away from the compresses as she tucked them around him. Leaving him, Elsie looked in on the twins who were still playing quietly. There was no sound from Anna's room. She pushed open the door and crossed to stand beside Agnes at the window.

"How is Pape," Agnes asked. She laid a hand on her mother's tear streaked cheek.

“As well as can be expected, I suppose. There isn’t much change. How long has Walter been out there?” Elsie changed the subject, it was easier to worry about Walter than face the possible outcome of Ike’s sickness.

“Too long.” Agnes picked up the slack rope. “Either he hasn’t reached the end yet, or he’s untied it and gone on without it.”

“I’m sure he won’t do anything unwise,” Elsie said.

“I’ll wait another ten minutes and then I’m going to go find him. What if he’s fallen in a drift and hurt himself?” Agnes glanced at her watch.

“I don’t think you should.” Elsie shook her head.

“I can’t just keep sitting here and doing nothing.” Agnes paced to the door and back. “I’m going downstairs to get my coat and scarf.”

“If you’re determined I don’t suppose anything I say will stop you. I’ll keep watch here until you get back.” Agnes turned back to stare at the window, willing Walter to appear out of the swirling white world that beat on the glass panes.

Her daughter’s footsteps echoed hollowly in the stairwell. Agnes stopped to assure the twins everything was fine on her way back to Anna’s room. Elsie whipped around at the scrape of the window frame. Fine snow stung her face as the window swung inward and Walter all but fell into the room. Ice and snow clung to every inch of him, his eyebrows hoary with white frost. Agnes burst through the door with a cry of relief. Elsie peered out into the blizzard, but there was no sign of anyone following her son-in-law. She shoved the window closed with a heavy heart, and went to help Agnes divest Walter of his frozen outer garments. Elsie avoided her daughter's gaze. Somehow if Anna's absence wasn't spoken aloud, it kept the truth of the situation at bay for the moment.

"I couldn't find her," Walter croaked, collapsing onto the narrow bed. "The chicken house is buried up to the top of chimney. I tried to dig down but…"

"She must have got inside before the drift got that deep. There was smoke coming out the chimney, wasn't there?" Agnes pulled off his boots and then his socks. Snow had found its way into the boots and down the socks as well.

Walter met Elsie's gaze before answering his wife. "There was no smoke. I'm sorry."

"Still, Anna's a smart girl. She'll be fine. She's inside with those chickens of hers, keeping warm. The snow will act as insulation." Agnes clung to the belief her eldest child was safe and sound.

"It's always good to have hope," Elsie said. She picked up the clothes that were starting to spread melt water into a puddle on the floor. "I'll take these down to the kitchen and hang them to dry. Walter, you need to get something hot into you. I'll make some coffee."

Passing her own room she looked in on Ike. He lay unmoving on the pillows, mouth slightly agape as he struggled for breath. Moving swiftly, she continued down to the kitchen. The water was bubbling in the big cauldron attached to the stove. She set the coffee to brew and hung the dripping clothes to dry.

"Thanks, Mome." Agnes and Walter came into the kitchen. "I'm going to make a snack for the twins and get some food into Walter. Do you want anything?"

"I'm going to go sit with your father."

Experience told her the illness was approaching a turning point. Hadn't she seen it with the little ones with the diarrhea and fever in Paraguay? There was always a time when the sickness reached a crescendo, and then tipped either toward wellness or death. She refused to entertain thoughts of failure. Ike would get well again. He had too. Elsie pushed open the door and settled in the chair beside the bed.

The snow towels were finished and she removed them, dumping them in the pail she used to collect the snow. Taking Ike's hand in hers she closed her eyes and prayed. At some point she must have fallen asleep. There was a crick in her neck and she no longer held Ike's hand. Blinking in the dim light she focussed on the man in the bed. To her surprise, he'd turned on his side and was facing the wall. She put a hand on his shoulder to roll him onto his back. Ike's breathing was less laboured and when Elsie placed a hand on his forehead it felt cooler than before. He moved restlessly as she stuck the thermometer into his armpit. One-hundred and two! A wave of relief swept over her, it was almost too much to bear. While he wasn't out of the woods yet, it was a step in the right direction. Elsie took a moment to thank God for His mercy before going to give Agnes and Walter the good news. Now if only Anna would be found safe and sound.

* * *

The great blizzard of 1947 raged on for another three days. The only bright spot was Ike's continued improvement. Anna's absence ached in Elsie's heart like a boil waiting to be lanced. She wasn't sure what Agnes had told the twins, but they ceased to ask where their sister was. Walter went about the house like a ghost, pausing to stare at the closed curtains over the blocked windows. He and Agnes looked after the barn chores and bringing in the wood from the shed. Elsie spent the long days tending to Ike and knitting. Doing barn chores would have helped make the time go faster, but she knew Agnes and Walter needed the distraction much more than she did.

On February 8, 1947 the storm finally blew itself out. It left the three prairie provinces of Manitoba, Saskatchewan and Alberta buried under many feet of snow. The radio reception improved and stories of hardship and survival began to spill forth. Trains were trapped in deep drifts and had to be dug out by hand. Some lucky passengers had been dug out and taken to refuge in nearby houses. Those who were stranded in the middle of nowhere had to do the best they could with what was available on the train. It took some time before the tracks were cleared and the telephone service restored.

* * *

As soon as the snow stopped Walter, Agnes and Elsie began the task of digging out a path to the chicken house. Although Ike protested he was well able to help, he was relegated to the big chair in the living room. The temperature had risen from the minus 32 degrees of a few days ago, but it was still cold and windy. In spite of the weather a trickle of sweat ran down Elsie's spine inside her layers of coats and sweaters. She paused to wipe her eyes which were watering in the glare of sun reflected off miles of drifted snow. The harsh croak of a raven broke the silence seconds before the dark shadow flitted across the white canvas below. Ahead of her, Walter paused to follow the path of the bird, vivid sable against the brilliant clear blue sky.

"I've hit something!" Agnes called. She straightened and thrust her shovel into the snow. "I think it's the edge of the chicken house roof."

The blue eyes were bright in her pale face when Elsie met Agnes' strained gaze. Snow inched down her boots while she tramped along the path they'd dug. She needed to be with her daughter, beside her to face whatever God had decided. Walter reached his wife before Elsie, pausing to squeeze her mittened hand before he began clearing the area where Agnes made the strike.

"Let me help," Agnes offered. "I can't just stand here."

"Stay back until I get enough cleared to see what we're dealing with." Walter didn't pause in his work.

A white mist of dry snow flew up before being caught in the wind and showering down over the two women who stood with eyes closed, mouths moving silently in prayer.

"Now." Walter turned to them. "Hand me the axe, Agnes. I need to break through the roof."

Elsie released her daughter's hand so she could hand Walter the axe out of the bucket they'd dragged with them. She stood back while Walter tore a hole in the shingles and roof boards of the hen house.

"Anna?" He leaned down and peered into the dark interior. "Anna, it's Pape. Are you there? Can you answer me?"

There was no response except the whisper of the snow snaking before the prairie wind.

"Can you see anything?" Agnes's voice wavered and she clamped her bottom lip between her teeth.

"I'm going to drop in and see if she's in there."

Walter sat in the cleared space and shoved his feet into the hole. Elsie held her breath as he disappeared into the darkness. The two women moved closer to the gap, dark against the stark white landscape. The rustling of straw and then the scape of a match was the only sound.

"Is she there?" Agnes leaned over the opening. "Anna? It's Mome, can you hear me?"

"Wait, Agnes. Let Walter have a chance to get his bearing," Elsie said. Her heart sat heavy in her chest. Surely if Anna was there she would have said something by now. And if the girl wasn't there, then where was she? Not in the barn or the wood shed, so where?

"Anna? Anna?" Walter's voice echoed from below.

"Have you found her?" Agnes knelt at the edge of the hole.

There was a rustling of straw and silence before Walter's voice echoed out of the dark maw of the gap in the roof.

"She's here. I'm going to hand her up to you. Can you both manage to pull her out? Throw down the blanket."

"Oh yes, yes!" Agnes reached down. "Mome, I need your help."

Elsie kneeled by her daughter. Her hands trembled from more than the cold. Why didn't the child say anything? She must be unconscious. That was it. They just needed to get her warmed up. Frantic thoughts bounced in her mind, refusing to touch the knowledge of what she knew must be.

With Walter heaving from beneath, Agnes and Elsie pulled the unresponsive child out into the sunlight. Her fair hair splayed across her waxen face, the wind moving it slightly as if she breathed. Walter scrambled out of the opening the roof, face red with exertion, his lips tightened and grim. He caught Elsie's gaze over Agnes' back bent over her daughter and shook his head. Pain seized Elsie's chest and almost cut off her breath.

"Come, let's get Anna back to the house," Elsie urged Agnes.

"Maybe she's just cold, just sleeping." Agnes raised her face to look at Walter. "All because of the stupid chickens. Why couldn't she have stayed inside like we told her?"

"You go ahead and make sure the twins aren't near the window in her room. Tell Ike we found her," Elsie urged her daughter. "Walter and I will bring Anna."

Agnes set her chin and started to argue, but Elsie forestalled her.

"Think of the twins. They shouldn't see her like this. Go, take care of your babies."

Nodding, Agnes gathered up the bundle of extra blankets and warm clothes they'd brought with them along with the bucket of tools. The small axe had fallen into the chicken house and she decided it could just stay there for now. With one last look at the still blanket wrapped form she stumbled through the snow toward the upper story window which was the closest way in to the house from this point.

Elsie watched her go before helping Walter get the stiff figure into his arms. The burden was so small and empty, vivacity and life fled with the blizzard. Such a waste, she thought. God must have a plan for her, for all of them. Elsie bowed her head to His will and followed Walter's slow progress through the brilliant white and blue landscape. So much beauty did little to ease the bleak sorrow in her heart.

Elsie went in the window before Walter and held the curtains back as he clambered into the room with his burden. He moved slowly across the floor and stood by the bed for a long moment, as if reluctant to set his daughter down. Elsie shoved the window closed and came to stand beside him.

"Set her down, Walter. There's nothing to be done." She laid a hand on his stiff shoulder.

"I know. It's just hard…" His voice broke and a shudder ran through him.

"I know, son. I know." Tears were thick in her throat.

Kneeling, Walter set his daughter on the bed with gentle hands. He smoothed the pale hair back from her waxen face. Her eyes were closed and her face serene. If Elsie hadn't known better she could almost convince herself the girl was sleeping. Walter staggered to his feet when Agnes came back into the room, shutting the door firmly behind her. He folded his wife in his arms as they stood beside the bed. Elsie busied herself tidying up the snow that had tracked in, keeping her own grief at bay and not wanting to intrude on the private moment of parents and child.

"Why don't you go change, Walter? You too, Agnes. I can take care of what needs to be done here," Elsie urged them.

"I'll go change, but I'm coming right back. You shouldn't have to do this on your own. Besides, it's something I need to do."

Elsie nodded and waited until they'd left the room before going to the still figure on the bed. She removed the boots and socks before starting to pull the outer garments free. The heater in the room had gone out and Elsie toyed with the idea of lighting it to warm her freezing fingers. Common sense stopped her, the room needed to stay cold until they could clear the snow and hack a grave in the frozen earth.

"Here, Mome. Let me help with that." Agnes appeared at Elsie's side and helped removed the frozen coat and scarf. She had brought a basin of warm water and clothes back with her. Once the girl's body was naked the two women silently washed her and combed her hair. Agnes went to the clothes press and took out Anna's Sunday dress and underthings. Tears flooded Elsie's eyes so badly she could barely see well enough to help dress her granddaughter one last time.

"What are we going to do, Mome? We can't bury her with all this snow." Agnes swallowed a sob.

"For now, we'll keep this room cold, which won't be an issue in this weather, and keep the children out of here. Which won't be as easy. Once the weather clears enough, your father and your brothers will dig down to the turf in the family plot and then light some slow burning fires to thaw the earth enough to dig. When they've got it deep enough, we'll bring Anna."

"Oh, God." Agnes sank to her knees and gave into her grief.

Elsie kneeled beside her and gathered her in her arms, her own shoulders shaking with sorrow. "It's hard, Agnes. It's hard. But the Lord wouldn't ask more of us than we can bear."

Agnes shook her head and sobbed all the harder. When the storm of grief eased, she sat back on her heels and leaned her head on her mother's shoulder.

"What about the pastor? We'll need to be able to get him here to say the words over her."

"Walter will manage that, I'm sure. The roads should be somewhat passable in a few days, Walter can take the horse and sleigh into Landmark and bring the pastor out."

"A few days..." Fresh tears filled Agnes' eyes and she reached out to touch her daughter's cold cheek.

* * *

It was in fact, three days before Walter managed to clear a narrow lane with the tractor. The phone lines came back on line around the same time. Elsie took on the responsibility of calling the family and informing them of the tragedy.

Anna's onkels met Walter at the small cemetery behind the orchard and helped prepare the grave. It was hard, cold work. Agnes couldn't bring herself to go near the place. Elsie often found her sitting in the freezing bedroom with Anna. The preternatural calm of her demeanor worried Elsie. Agnes shook her head when Elsie encouraged her eat or get some rest.

"I only have a few hours left to be with her, Mome. I need to be here for her, and for me."

Walter got in touch with the pastor and arranged for him to come out once the grave was ready. It was a sombre procession that left the house. Walter carried Anna from her room wrapped in a quilt. He laid her in the small oak coffin he'd laboured over in the work shop. Agnes lined it with padding covered in Anna's favourite colour of blue. The twins seemed to understand the seriousness of the occasion and were uncharacteristically quiet. Agnes had explained to Anna's death to them as best she could, in terms Elsie hoped they understood.

The family gathered around the coffin in the living room to say a final farewell before Walter closed the lid. Doris and Willy shyly approached the casket and placed a picture of Anna and Blackie coloured in bright crayon on top of the still hands folded on Anna's stomach.

Elsie choked back a sob and blinked hard. She ushered the young children out of the living room and into the kitchen before Walter placed the lid over his daughter and drove the nails home. Ike was well enough to be down stairs and Elsie knew nothing would keep him from accompanying his granddaughter to the cemetery.

The sun was shining and the sky stretched in a blue cup over the prairie as the little procession left the house, led by the pastor, and made the short trip to the dark scar like a blight on the white landscape. Elsie stood with Ike, numb, and almost glad of the cold that kept her from truly acknowledging what was happening. It must be shock, she thought, this detached, horrible emptiness that refused to allow her to cry. Martin and Sarah had stayed away and Elsie was grateful for that. Sarah was finally starting to feel better, standing by the open grave of her niece wasn't something that would help her depression.

Only Walter and Agnes stayed behind, while Anna's Onkel Ed and Onkel Jake filled in the grave. Elsie was worried about Ike being out in the cold for too long, and truth be told, she didn't think she could stand the sound of the hard clods dropping onto the small coffin that held her granddaughter. Wrapped in a blanket of numbness, she went through the motions for the rest of the day, and it wasn't until she collapsed into bed that night that she let herself feel. Ike held her until she wept herself to sleep.

Chapter Nine

Spring Comes Every Year

After the long nights and short days of winter, the gradual warming of the late March weather was welcome. The house was unnaturally silent without Anna popping up at every turn. Even the twins were subdued. Elsie prepared for the yearly trip to Winnipeg for new Easter clothing. Her heart was sore with missing Anna, but for the rest of the family she must not let it show. Another sore spot to worry about was Sarah and Arnold's impending departure for Mexico. Usually, the arrival of spring mud and the departure of the snow was a cause for rejoicing. Indeed, it still was, she supposed. It seemed that the year of 1947 was to present a series of challenges for Elsie's extended family.

Plans for Sadie's wedding were going ahead. The girl could hardly wait for June to come around, and Elsie wished she could hold time in her hand for a moment. Turn back the clock and keep a close eye on Anna during the blizzard, pay more attention to the child's anxiety over the chickens. In addition it would postpone Sarah's departure, which would be followed soon after by Sadie's. Holding time in abeyance for a while would be most pleasing. She sighed at the foolish thought, things would transpire as God willed it, regardless of what one woman wished. The pastor spoke of giving yourself up to God's will during Anna's service. Elsie shook her head. Sometimes it was just so hard to do what she knew was right. Offering up a small prayer that all would be well with her family, she made a supreme effort to accept His plan and carry on as best she could.

The sun was shining on the prairie, sparkling in the creeks and the Seine River as Ike drove toward Winnipeg. Behind them in a small convoy came Helen and John, sharing a vehicle with Susan and Martin. Sarah and Arnold stayed behind to mind the stock on the family farms. Sarah said she had everything she needed for Mexico so there really was no point in them going. Ed and Berry, Jake and Nettie and Hank and Frieda were planning to meet them at Eaton's in downtown Winnipeg. Portage and Hargrave was quite near The Forks where the natives came to trade in the early days. Now there was the railroad, the immigration sheds, the Union stockyards and holding pens for the livestock. The sharp smell of manure and cattle could be detected on the street by Eaton's if the wind was right. The drive up to Winnipeg was longer than Elsie remembered, perhaps she felt that way from the constant need to answer questions from the twins in the back seat.

Elsie and Ike offered to take the youngsters with them and give Walter and Agnes a chance to have a break. Anna was a constant presence in Elsie's mind, and she could only imagine what Agnes was thinking. The Easter trip to Winnipeg had always been Anna's favourite outing.

Once inside the Winnipeg city limits the traffic was thicker, and although Elsie trusted Ike, it was hard not to grip the door frame and flinch when a truck came too close.

When they finally arrived at the T. Eaton store, she breathed a sigh of relief. It took a while to find a parking spot, but Ike managed to get one that was fairly close. They'd arranged to meet at the Timothy Eaton statue on the main floor. Elsie thought it was silly, but harmless fun, to rub the statue's left foot for good luck. The space was crowded as the statue was a popular meeting place. It was presented to the Eaton family in 1919 by store employees as a tribute to the store's fiftieth anniversary. It was in gratitude for the generosity extended by the Eaton store to those who served in World War 1. They pledged to all the employees serving overseas that they would have their jobs, or jobs of equal value, back when they returned home. For married men who enlisted voluntarily the company gave them full pay for the duration of the conflict, while single men received half pay. The soldiers also received regular parcels from Eaton's containing coffee, chocolate, socks and other items stocked by the store. The company also donated all the profits from government war contracts back to the war drive.

Ivor Lewis, an employee of the Eaton's advertising department created the statues. Two were cast, one for the main Toronto store which was unveiled December 8, 1919. The Eaton Choral Society sang 'O Canada' and Margaret Eaton and John Eaton accepted the tribute. A similar event took place in Winnipeg on December 11, 1919.

Personally, Elsie didn't approve of the war effort in either of the two world wars, but she could appreciate the generosity that prompted the company's actions.

Soon the family gathered and the women and children headed off to explore the delights waiting for them in the large store with nine whole stories of merchandise. The men dispersed to the main floor to make their purchases, and then to the foodeteria in the basement to await the end of the shopping party. By the time Elsie had traipsed from the second floor to the fourth and fifth floor, she was close to exhaustion. The youngsters were full of excitement, laughing and admiring their new clothes. Her daughters and daughters-in-law were just as happy with their new finery, if a trifle less exuberant than the children. Elsie caught herself more than once reaching for an item in Anna's favourite colour, thinking how much she would like it. From the corner of her eye, she caught Agnes doing the same thing, pausing to turn away and blow her nose on a handkerchief. Her heart ached for her, but nothing would ease the pain but time and the faith that Anna rested in the loving arms, of Jesus.

At last all the purchases were complete, and after joining the men for a quick late lunch in the basement foodeteria, the group made their way back to the parked cars. Waving goodbye to the rest of the family, she bundled Doris and Willy into the back of the car, surrounded by the myriad of packages. Agnes and Walter would drop Susan and Martin off at their place before returning home. By the time they got there Elsie hoped to have the twins safely tucked into bed and asleep. She was sure she wasn't the only one to be tired after such an eventful day.

The evening sun slanted across the Assiniboine River colouring the rippling water orange and gold. The water level was up, she noted with a farmer's eye, hopefully there would be no flooding this spring. It was always a possibility and not a welcome one. The Red was more of a concern than the Assiniboine, but both could be troublesome. Elsie pushed the thought away as Ike left the outskirts of Winnipeg behind. The prairie was brilliantly backlit by the setting sun, the remaining pockets of snow stained red as blood in some places by the rays, in others shadows lay like blue bruises in the hollows. Bruised as her heart was when she thought of Anna. How much worse it must be for Agnes.

Walter had burned the old chicken house down once the snow melted enough. Ike mentioned it seemed a waste, as the building could have been repaired, but he seemed to understand why Agnes couldn't bear to look at it. The thought of clearing out the poor frozen birds and replacing them with new chicks was more than any of them wanted to think about.

Ike and Walter cleared out a space in the big barn and fashioned a chicken coop there. While Elsie doubted they would ever see a storm like the blizzard of '47 again, it seemed prudent to take precautions just in case. The area was now populated by 100 tiny yellow chicks. Dorisnie and Willy were already learning to take care of them under Ike's careful eye.

* * *

Easter was a blessing with its promise of renewal and everlasting life. In many ways Elsie loved Easter more than Christmas. The joy of Christ's resurrection on Easter Sunday was a welcome counter point to the solemnity of Maundy Thursday and Good Friday. The sun always seemed brighter when it rose on that particular Sunday morning, haloing the folds of undulating prairie in saffron and rose. April 4, 1947 was just such a holy morning. Elsie leaned a shoulder on the kitchen door frame, standing with a cup of coffee in her hands and watching the grey gloom of pre-dawn gently change into soft gold and shades of pink and coral. Then the sudden burst of the brilliant orange orb flashing over the distant prairie horizon brought joy and a sense of healing to her heart. Last year, she and Anna stood in this very spot to welcome the dawn of another Easter morning. In some odd way Elsie felt Anna's presence at her side. With the dawn came the morning breeze, it brushed her cheek like a soft kiss and she held a hand to her cheek as if to capture the caress.

It was the last quiet moment she had that day, except for church service. It was a heartfelt celebration of the promise of new and everlasting life given to them by the death and resurrection of Christ. Elsie loved singing the Easter morning songs of Alleluia, along with *Rollt ab den Stein, Jesis Lebt* and *In Joseph's Lovely Garden*. She left the service with a profound sense of peace and a quietness of heart she'd hadn't felt since the blizzard.

The house was soon full to bursting with the whole extended family. Everyone brought something that had been prepared beforehand, paska bread, potato salad, *plummi mooss*, baked ham, cabbage rolls, potatoes, cheese, pickles, cinnamon buns, Zweiback buns made special for the occasion, and cookies. The table groaned under the weight of the banquet.

This Easter was especially dear to Elsie as it was the last one where all the family would be together. Sarah and Arnold were planning to leave for Mexico on the 15th of April. Elsie wished they would wait for June after Sadie's wedding, but there was a group of other families leaving in the middle of April and Sarah wanted to travel with them. Elsie pushed unpleasant thoughts to the back of her mind to be dealt with at a later date. Today was for enjoying the company of family and community and rejoicing in Christ's gift and promise of renewal. The wonder of spring came every year and each time it was a miracle after the harsh winter months.

* * *

The whole family turned out to see Sarah and Arnold on their way. Elsie blinked back tears and hugged her daughter one last time.

"It's going to be okay, Mome. I know this is what God has planned for Arnold and me. A new start and a new life." Sarah squeezed her mother close. "I'm going to miss all of you, though. You, especially." She sniffed and released Elsie to pat her nose with a handkerchief. "Now, I said I wasn't going to cry."

"Don't you dare, it will start me off, too," Elsie declared biting the inside of her cheek to halt the sting of tears at the back of her nose. "Go say your goodbyes to your father."

"Arnold." Elsie gave him a swift hug. "You take care of my girl, now. Mexico is a long way from here, but you know there'll always be a place kept here for you if you want to come home."

"Thanks, Mother Neufeld. We've got our faces turned to the south-west now. Mexico is going to be home for us from now on."

"Be sure to write and let us know when you arrive." Elsie squeezed his arm.

In a chorus of farewells and wishes for a safe journey the emigrating families prepared to take their leave. Rather than have everyone travel all the way into the train station in Winnipeg the families of the emigrating Mennonites had gathered at the church for a going-away picnic. Only those who were driving the departing families and their luggage into the city were making the trip. There were only so many vehicles to convey everything.

Most families were travelling with as little as possible, but some, Elsie noted, seemed to have packed everything they owned.

Bittersweet memories of her own journey to Paraguay over twenty years ago flashed through Elsie's mind. It had all been so exciting, right up to the point when they got on the train and headed for Montreal. But the promise of a new unrestricted life and land set aside for them buoyed her spirits, even during the long ship passage. The world had seemed so rosy and full of promise, standing at the rail watching the waves rush by with Ike at her side.

She recalled the reality of the Paraguay paradise they'd been promised, it still tasted like bitter ashes on her tongue. Her nails bit into her palm, if they hadn't made the move Sarah would never had contracted malaria and she wouldn't be on her way to Mexico at this moment.

"God works in strange ways," she muttered. "Who am I to question?" Elsie waved until even the last bits of golden dust settled back to the prairie road.

Chapter Ten

A Rose of Landmark

The snow had departed, hopefully for good and the early May morning was pleasantly warm. The day promised to be humid later on in the afternoon, but the morning was a good one for tidying up the family plot. It was a job Elsie both loved and disliked at the same time. There was something comforting about being surrounded by her ancestors, souls who had given her family life. Blood of her blood, bone of her bone, spirit of her spirit. It was important for the young ones to appreciate the sacrifices of the ones who went before them. Some of the names on the stones were those of people she knew personally, some were older still. She missed her mother and father, her tauntes and onkels who lay beneath the prairie soil. The small family plot was surrounded by wild rose bushes which were just starting to bud with the odd early bloom unfurling delicate pink petals and sending a waft of sweet scent to perfume the air.

All the women of the family met Elsie and Agnes at the gate to the cemetery. Agnes carried a small rose bush in a bushel basket that Walter had dug up earlier in the morning. Elsie was sharply reminded of Anna doing the same on Blackie's grave last summer. The irony twisted her heart.

Elsie set down her basket and pulled out the trowel. She attacked the weeds and grasses growing close to the markers with a vengeance. Though she tried to avoid it, her gaze invariably wandered toward the newest grave, so small surrounded by the pale green of new grass. Walter and Ike had set the headstone only a few days ago, the freshly turned earth gleamed darkly in the slanting rays of light. Tiny motes of dust and a few tiny orange and black Painted Lady butterflies danced in the air over the turned soil. The Monarchs were coming back too, flocking to the milkweed plants beginning to bloom in the verge by the road. She spared a moment to wonder how the delicate creatures could find their way to wherever they went for the winter and then made their way back.

She sat back on her heels to survey her work. One plot done, a dozen or more to go. She put her hands on her knees and pushed upright, bending to retrieve the trowel from the grass. The rose bush sat forlornly in its basket, small leaves glossy and new. *Such promise of new life*. Elsie pressed a hand to chest to ease the pain, of course it did no good. It wasn't a physical ache that could be eased by medicines. It was an ache that would only become duller with the passage of time, but Elsie knew it would never disappear.

Shading her eyes with her hand, Elsie looked over the small cemetery where her family toiled in a labour of love. She knew the story of every person who lay beneath the prairie sod surrounded by blooming roses. Landmark Roses she always thought of them. Their memories lingering like the faint perfume of roses left in a room after the flowers themselves were removed. It was important that at least one member of the family knew the stories and repeated them to future generations. As long as those who were gone ahead were kept alive in the collective family memory and their stories told, they would never fade away. It brought to mind the faded petals pressed in her grossmama's *gesangbuch*, a faint ashes of roses fragrance still perceptible when Elsie opened the fragile pages. The young ones would remember Anna's story and pass it on, they would remember because they knew her when she was alive. She was a real person to them. It was important the people they hadn't known were remembered as well. The stories kept them as an integral part of the family and the tales of their trials in Europe before they came to Canada was essential as well. It would never do to forget the persecution of their faith and the need to keep it pure.

Shaking her head, she moved on to the next grave, laying her hand in gratitude on the headstone she had just finished clearing. Some of the lettering was worn with the weather, but Elsie knew them all by heart, when she learned the names and stories from her grossmama she'd repeated them over and over in her head at night while she lay in bed. She sighed. Who was she to pass the responsibility on to? Anna had been her first choice, but as that was no longer possible, she cast about in her mind for another candidate. Perhaps Jake or Nettie's Mary? The girl was bright as a new penny. Elsie glanced around the small area until she spotted Mary squatting by a grave near the rose hedge. The girl seemed to be in earnest conversation with someone, but she was alone. Elsie rose and made her way across the grass toward the child.

"Who are you talking to?" Elsie knelt beside her.

"The butterflies and the lady buried here," Mary replied solemnly.

"Do you know who lies here?" Elsie was intrigued.

Mary's forehead creased as she contemplated the question.

"I think it is Great Taunte Galina. It's hard to read the letters." Her fingers trailed across the engraved stone.

"That's right. Great Taunte Galina. What were you telling her?"

"I was asking her to take care of Anna and Blackie. Make sure they found each other in heaven. I know I shouldn't, but I do think dogs go to heaven." She rushed on before Elsie could dissuade her from the notion of dogs in heaven.

"I told her about the butterflies and the roses, how pretty they are and what a nice morning it is today."

"That's nice of you, Mary. How did you know who lies here?"

Mary looked around before she answered. "I come here sometimes, it's quiet and peaceful and I like it. I read the names and wonder about who they were, you know, what happened to make them leave their homes and come all the way across the sea to Manitoba."

"They each have their own stories and I know them all. I can share them with you if you'd like?" Elsie replied.

"Oh, Oma! I'd like that very much." Mary clapped her hands. "Can we start now?"

"Not right this instant, no." Elsie laughed and patted the girl's head. "But I promise, right after we finish our work I'll tell all of you some stories over our picnic. Will that suit you?"

Mary nodded. "I'll stop talking about butterflies and get to work."

Her face set in serious lines Mary got up from the newly tidied plot and moved to the next one. Elsie noted the child ran her fingers over the top of the stone as she went by.

The family cemetery was located behind the orchard and reached by a worn path in the grass under the spreading branches of the trees. At this time of year the boughs were hung with blossoms and the air heavy with the drone of bees. May snow, Elsie thought, with the promise of bounty for the winter months and a good harvest as the seasons wheeled around them.

Agnes called everyone together and with Elsie's help planted the young rose bush by Anna's headstone. It wasn't usual to have the bush by the grave, but Elsie believed Anna would approve and it certainly seemed to give Agnes comfort. There seemed to be no need for words, and none were said. Elsie fought back tears, her throat clogged with emotion. Agnes wiped her cheeks with the edge of her apron, making no apologies for exposing her pain.

The sun was at the zenith by the time the work was done. Elsie straightened up from the last plot and surveyed the now neatened area. Long grasses still waved along the edges by the rose bush hedge, but that was fine in her mind. The headstones were all neat and clear of weeds and long grasses, all was in order.

The children were playing hide and seek in the shade of the orchard, their laughter brightening the serious mood of the early afternoon. Elsie picked her way across the grass to where Hank's Frieda and Ed's Betty were laying out a large blanket on the soft turf. Susan and Helena knelt beside it unloading the picnic basket and setting out the food before calling the children from their game. Agnes lingered at the opening in the hedge, hands on her hips. Elsie thought to call her to come join them but changed her mind. Let the poor girl say a final goodbye in her own way. Some bluebirds and golden winged warblers spun and spiraled above the fields, their song trilling through the honeyed afternoon air.

"Mome, come and sit," Susan called from the shade of the big apple tree. Small pink and white petals fluttered down like confetti.

"We should collect these to sweeten Sadie's hope chest in a few weeks," Nettie teased.

"I'm not sure they'll last that long. Rose petals will do though," Betty said.

"I think the lavender and verbena sachets are more than adequate." Elsie settled on a corner of the blanket and accepted a glass of lemonade from Frieda.

"Should I go speak with her?" Helena nodded toward Agnes who was still lingering in the entry to the cemetery. "I haven't lost a daughter like Anna, but Ruth leaving is still a sore spot in my heart."

"Let her be," Elsie advised. "She'll come to terms with it in her own way and time."

"Time to eat," Betty called to the children.

"We can't come now, Neil's it and he'll find us," a tiny voice piped from behind the gnarled bark of a tree.

"Game's over for now. Now come," Betty replied.

Squeals and laughter accompanied the small figures emerging from the shade deeper in the grove of fruit trees. They came and sat sedately around the blanket while the food and drink was distributed. In what seemed like no time the food disappeared. A few of the littlest ones curled up for a nap. Tiny heads in their mother's lap or sprawled in boneless abandon in the way only a small child can sleep.

Elsie looked down at the hand tugging on her sleeve.

"Can you tell us one of your stories now, Oma?" Mary asked, eyes bright with interest.

"Of course. Let me think which one would be best." Elsie closed her eyes for a moment, going through the well-remembered names, casting around in her mind for the proper story. "Ah, I have it." She smiled at the family gathered around her.

"What do you have?" Pida pushed his corn silk hair back from his eyes, turning his sun browned six year old face up to her.

"A story, Pida. One about some of the people who are buried there." Elsie nodded toward the rose hedge and what was enclosed there.

"Honest? Did you really know them?" Five year old Nita asked, her blue-grey eyes wide with amazement.

"Some of them, yes. Others, the oldest ones, I have only their stories passed down to me by my grossmama."

"Whose story are you going to tell?" Mary fairly bounced with excitement.

"Her name was Sarah Buller and she was your great grossmama. Her friends and family called her Zara." She paused while the children settled around her before continuing. Her daughters had heard the stories when they were growing up, but they would be new to her sons' wives. Good, perhaps they could pass some of the stories on as well.

"To understand why our ancestors decided to leave everything they knew and make the long and sometimes dangerous journey to Canada you need to know something of the history. You'll have heard some of this in school, I suppose. But bear with me, for the sake of those who haven't. Our ancestors originally lived in northern Germany, but due to persecution they moved first to Prussia, and then in 1789 to Russia. They settled on land to the north west of the Sea of Azov where they established Chortitza on the Dnieper River.

"Ah, I see you recognize that name. Yes, you see we brought not only our language and religion with us, but our names from the old country as well. Now, where was I? Oh yes, After Chortitza, they went on to establish Molotschna in 1803, this was a larger colony than the original.

"Now, this is the important part to understand, and something our people have struggled many times. It is important for our religion and community to be able to govern ourselves without interference from the state or government. Our colonies were self-governing.

"Schools were taught by men of the colony, and although they were largely untrained in teaching, they did a very good job. Often they were craftsmen or herders and taught around the duties of those professions.

"Now we come to the impetus that prompted Great Grossmama Sarah and her family to come to Canada. In 1870 the Czar of Russia proposed a plan called Russification. It would end all special privileges enjoyed by the Mennonites, including the exclusion from military service and the right for our schools to teach and speak German. The Mennonite leaders sent delegations to meet with the Czar, but their petition was denied. So, in 1873 another delegation went to explore the idea of moving to North America. The men returned with glowing reports of good arable land available in Manitoba, Canada, and Minnesota, South Dakota, Nebraska and Kansas in the United States.

"In 1872 the Canadian government announced a program to help settle the western provinces, so this is why they went. It was called The Dominion Land Grant. Bloc settlements were encouraged under section thirty-seven of the Land Act and allowed groups of ten or more settlers to group their houses together and fulfill their cultivation obligations on their own quarter-section while living within a community hamlet. This arrangement suited us very well." Elsie paused to take a drink of lemonade.

"So Great Grossmama Sarah and her family left Russia because they weren't going to be allowed to speak German or teach it in school." Mary's eyebrows lowered as she struggled to process everything Elsie had said.

"Yes, that, and the fact they would be forced to take part in military service as well as losing other privileges that are essential to keeping true to our faith. It is a thing that has happened over and over in our history. It is actually part of the reason your grosspape and I went to Paraguay in the 1920's."

"Was it a very long way to come?" Pida asked.

"Yes, and it was a hard journey. First overland by rail on the *Nikolaivesk* train to Hamburg. From Hamburg they travelled to Hull, England and then Liverpool. There they boarded a ship, the *Austrian No. 40*, and set sail for Quebec Canada. The sea journey was horrible. The waves were high and tossed the vessel around mercilessly. Sarah was afraid they would all end up at the bottom of the sea. She was only a young girl at the time and she didn't know how to swim. Her brother, who later died of diphtheria, thought it was a wonderful adventure. She related later that the more the wind howled and the waves crashed over the side the more he laughed. Sarah, herself, was terrified most of the time. The sight of nothing but water all around made her feel like they were lost and she would never see land again. It took over a month to reach their destination. A huge storm blew them off course for a time. Sarah recalled how she cowered in her parent's berth, which was an upper bunk in steerage. The structure swayed alarmingly with the pitch of the ship and our Sara remembers clinging to the bed clothes and the rail of the bed to avoid being tossed about too much.

"She was homesick, they sold almost everything before leaving Russia and Sarah didn't even have her dolls for comfort.

"When they landed at Quebec City on July 17, 1874, it was raining and very hot and humid. Everything was confusion and shouting with people pushing to get a place in the straggly line, eager to set foot on solid ground. Strange languages assailed Sarah and she could understand none of them. Tears flooded her eyes and with nothing else to hand she wiped them on her mother's skirt which she clung to. They were herded into a great hall that echoed with voices pleading and asking questions.

A man met with her father and they went off together to take care of the necessary paperwork. At least that's what Sarah's mother told her. Sarah was so tired she just wanted to lay down and sleep. Eventually, they boarded a train. It was again very cramped and Sarah sat squeezed between her mother and father while her brother sat on the floor between their feet, knees drawn up to his chin as far as he could. Of the journey from Quebec to Winnipeg she said all she remembered was feeling sick to her stomach from the swaying of the train and the incessant noise of the wheels on the iron rails. Once they got off the train, and boarded a steam ship called *The International* it was better. On August 1, 1874 they were put on shore at an uninhabited place on the river bank. It was just north of what is today Sainte Agathe. From there they made their way to the Jacob Shantz reception houses which were near Niverville. They loaded everything they had managed to bring onto an ox cart.

"The trail from the landing to the reception houses on the East Reserve—"

"Why is it called the East Reserve?" Willy wanted to know.

"Don't interrupt your grossmama," Agnes hushed her son.

"It's good to ask questions." Elsie smiled at him. "It is called the East Reserve simply because it is on the east side of the Red River, so of course, the West Reserve is on the west side of the river."

"Oh." Willy nodded and chewed on a stalk of grass he'd pulled.

"Now, where was I? Oh yes. The trip from landing place to here. The trail was little more than a track through the low marshy ground. It didn't help that it was a rainy year and the ground was a quagmire of gumbo mud. It stuck to the wheels of the ox cart and was slippery as ice when everyone, except Sarah who too small, put a shoulder to the wheels to help the oxen. Another vexation was the swarms of mosquitoes. Big as swallows, Sarah often said. Just like they do now, they plagued the people slogging through the mud. Even at night they came into the tents and gave no one any peace."

"Why did they keep going if it was so horrible? Couldn't they go to Winnipeg?" Doris asked.

"There was no choice. The land they were given was in the East Reserve, and what was there for them in Winnipeg? Not the freedoms they'd come so far to enjoy, and they were and still are, farmers not merchants or fur traders. Winnipeg wasn't a bit city then either. It was little more than a general store at Portage and Main and some ramshackle houses."

"I guess." Doris didn't look convinced but wisely said nothing more.

"When they finally reached the land they were allotted, it was nothing but bare prairie. Some of the land was stony and not easily cultivated, and some low and too wet to get a plough through, but before they could even think of that there were shelters to be built."

"Houses? Like your house? Is that the one Great Grossmama Sara's family built?" Frank, Ed's eldest son asked.

"No. Nothing so grand as that for quite a while. My father built the house your grosspape and I live in. What Sara's people built were sod houses, *semlins*. They dug into the ground about three feet down, then everyone helped cut sod blocks out of the prairie grasses. Even Sarah helped carry the blocks to the house site. They were piled on top of each other to form walls at least two feet thick, the blocks were firmly wedged together and packed with mud mixed with dung to fill any gaps that were found. Once the walls were high enough, poles from trees cut down by the rivers and creeks were put across to form a solid base for more sods. The roof had a slight peak and a gentle slope to the side. A space was left for a chimney pipe and once that was installed, the hole was chinked with mud to make it as weather tight as possible. Inside the area was divided into two parts that first winter. There was no time to build another shelter for the few animals they brought with them, so they occupied the back part of the semlin. It served two purposes. The arrangement offered shelter for the livestock and also provided heat to the house.

"The inside walls of the semlin were lined with shiplap boards which they had to buy in Emerson, but the trip and expense was worth it."

"They kept the oxen in the house?" Helena was incredulous.

"They did. Those animals were essential to the family's survival. How could they plant in the spring without the oxen to pull the plough? The goats gave milk, the few sheep were a source of both food and wool, the chickens provided eggs, and meat if needed. Now, I've talked on long enough. I will leave you with one more small thing Sarah passed down to us. When the first crops of wheat were in the milk stage in the fields the birds would come in the thousands to feed on it. The men and sometimes the children if they were old enough had to ride or run around the fields all day banging pots and singing and shouting to keep the birds from stealing the immature grain. Sara thought it was great fun, it wasn't until she was much older she understood how devastating it would have been if the birds had stripped the field bare."

"We still have to do that, don't we?" Frank piped up.

"Somethings never change," Elsie said with a smile in her voice.

"Thank you for the story, Oma," Mary said. "I'll remember it and pass it on to my children."

Her little face was so earnest it tugged at Elsie's heart. "When we have time I'll tell you more stories." She patted Mary's head. "But now," she addressed everyone, "I think it's time we cleared up and headed back to the house. The cows will need milking and there are eggs to check for."

Elsie got slowly to her feet. Goodness, she was getting too old to sit on the grass anymore. Mary's arms hugging her waist surprised her and she glanced down with a smile.

"Thank you again. That story makes Great Grossmama Sara more than just a name on the headstone. It makes her real."

"You're very welcome. Run along now and help your mother, that's a good girl."

It didn't take long to gather up the picnic things. Elsie lingered in the fragrant shade of the orchard after the others left. The afternoon sun slanted across the small cemetery holding her relatives who had been called home to God. *Such a peaceful scene, may it stay that way forever undisturbed by war and persecution.*

Agnes' appearance in the gap in hedge startled her. Elsie hadn't realized her daughter had returned to the graveyard. She waited for her to join her under the trees.

Agnes wiped moisture from her cheeks and took Elsie's hand. "There was some left over water so I took it to the rose bush." She paused. "I don't know why, but I just had to go back and say goodbye again. To feel close to my daughter somehow. I know she's with God and Jesus, but somehow talking to her there seems to help the hurt in my heart."

Elsie nodded and in silence the two women made their way back to the house through the golden May afternoon bright with birdsong.

Chapter Eleven

A Wedding and A Farewell

The month of May seemed to have no more than just started when Elsie woke up one morning beside a snoring Ike and realized the month was almost over. Where did the time go? Over four weeks since Sarah and Arnold left, and no word from them yet. Please let them be safe and happy, she offered a brief prayer before rolling over and shoving her legs from the covers.

It was early still, the pale pearl of sky telling her dawn wasn't far off. The sun came early and set late at this time of year. Good for offering long hours of daylight for planting and other chores, but hard on getting enough sleep.

Elsie yawned and stretched. The older she got, the harder it seemed to keep up with the steady stream of duties and chores. She blessed the fact Agnes and Walter lived with them and considerably lightened her load. Ike sat up, rubbing sleep from his eyes. She regarded him in the mirror of the dresser while gathering her clothes for the day. Iron grey hair spiked with sleep stuck up on the crown of his head.

He wasn't getting any younger, either, Elsie realized with a jolt. The years of their union spread out between them, odd and disjointed images flashed across her mind. Happy and sad mixed together, and she wouldn't change any of them. A pang of sorrow speared her heart, well maybe a couple. Sarah's troubles, and the blizzard that took Anna, for a start. Still, it was a good life they'd had.

"Why are you looking at me like that?" Ike's reflection frowned at her as he got out of bed.

"Just remembering. Just remembering." She patted her hair into place and secured it with some hair pins. Smoothing her skirt, she turned toward him with a smile. "Don't be long, I'll have coffee on and breakfast started by the time you get down."

Ike grunted and stumped over to the wash basin. "I'll be down as soon as I've dressed."

Agnes was already in the kitchen when Elsie came through the door. The newly risen sun shone hot and red through the open back door. The room was already hot and humid. This time of year it seemed the heat never ended, the nights almost as sultry as the days. In many ways the weather sometimes reminded Elsie of the heat of Paraguay. It wasn't a pleasant memory to be sure.

"I've started the stove in the summer kitchen for breakfast. No sense making the house any hotter than it is. I just came in to fill the sugar container." Agnes lifted the clear glass canister to emphasis her words.

"It is warm already, isn't it?" Elsie swiped at a bead of sweat trickling down her cheek. "Do we have everything else we need out there?"

"I believe so, Mome. Can you take this out for me? I need to tend to the twins. Walter's already out doing the milking."

"Of course." Elsie took the canister of sugar. "Walter's got an early start today."

"Well, you know how it is this time of year. Even with the long days there never seems to be enough hours to get done what needs doing."

Chuckling, Elsie pushed open the screen door, the scent of the pansies and geraniums lining the short path to the summer kitchen redolent in the sun spangled air. The mosquitoes hovered in the shadows along the way, but were thankfully avoiding the already strong sunlight. A few steps brought her to the door of the small building. Colourful curtains hung at the windows, the glass clear and sparkling. Checkered oilcloth covered the wooden table. Elsie set the sugar on the shelf with the other supplies and checked the fire in the stove. Satisfied it was well caught, she scooped some water out of the big cauldron kettle on the side of the stove and started the coffee. By the time Ike arrived, Walter was back from the milking. The voices of Agnes and the twins heralded their arrival.

Bacon she'd sliced from the side in the ice box sizzled in the fry pan scenting the air with its smoky fragrance. Toast lay in a napkin covered basket in the centre of the table, along with a butter dish covered against the flies. No matter how carefully the screens were mended the flies always seemed to be able to find a way in. Idly, she shooed one away from the jar of jam beside Ike's plate.

Breakfast was over quickly and the twins sent off to look for eggs in the new hen house. Agnes left Elsie to wash up while she went out to start weeding the large garden. It was a never ending task, she thought watching her daughter's back bent in the relentless sunlight. When the dishes were done, she turned her hand to separating the morning's milking, pouring the thick rich cream into cream cans. There was butter to be churned once this task was done and the majority of the milk to be put away in the cool milk house. Ike or Walter would make the trip to New Bothwell with the surplus milk to be delivered to the cheese factory.

* * *

The family gathered for the evening meal in the summer kitchen. The sun was still high in the sky and the men were planning to be back out on the land once their bellies were filled. The twins were quarrelling, cranky from the heat and being tired. It was a chore to get to sleep when the sky was still light and the upstairs of the house was like an oven in spite of the windows being opened to create a cross breeze and catch whatever coolness was available. The high pitched song of cicadas rang across the now shaded garden. Please don't let the grasshoppers come through this year, Elsie prayed. The insects could strip a field bare in a matter of hours once they descended, and short of firing the crop, there was nothing to be done. Either way, the crop was lost.

"I'm going to take the twins down to the creek to cool off. Do you want to come with us?" Agnes folded the dish towel and hung it on the rack to dry.

"That sounds wonderful, but Sadie is coming over to study her catechism. She's having issues with a few things," Elsie replied hanging up her own damp towel.

"Why?" Agnes leaned a hip on the counter. "She not questioning the faith is she? I can't imagine that."

"No, I think it's more the other way. She doesn't feel the pastor really cares about her personal thoughts, only that she knows the answers to his questions by rote."

"I guess I can understand that," Agnes replied.

"I keep telling her to focus on the fact she needs to know her catechism and be baptized before they get married so they can forge their new lives based on a spiritual foundation. And the girl does want to be married very badly." Elsie moved toward the door. "I'm going to go get my Bible before she gets here. I think we'll sit out under the big trees if the mosquitoes aren't too vicious."

"All done here. I'm off to take the twins for a paddle. We'll be back soon." Agnes let Elsie precede her and pulled the screen door shut behind them, catching the hook in the latch. Otherwise the dogs would be in there in a flash.

Elsie went into the main house, passing through the kitchen she carried on to the living room and picked up her well-worn Bible from the small table by her chair. With it tucked under her arm she went back out to sit under the shade of the Manitoba maples and wait for Sadie. A flash of yellow caught her eye just before Sadie joined her on the wide bench.

"Am I late? I hope I didn't keep you waiting." Sadie was a bit breathless. "Abram gave me a ride over, he had to stop at Onkel Jake's to pick up that wheel spanner thing Grosspape wants to borrow. I left them working on the old truck over by the barn."

"No, not late. I just got here myself. So," Elsie settled more comfortably on the bench, "have you been studying?"

"I have." Sadie nodded, a small furrow of concern marring her smooth brow.

"What's bothering you?" Elsie patted her granddaughter's hand. "Still the same thing?"

"I can't help it. It just seems like the pastor isn't concerned about whether I actually believe what I'm saying, only that I can repeat the information back to him word for word."

“Do you believe?” Elsie waited for Sadie to answer.

“Of course, I do,” Sadie declared.

“That is what matters. It is between you and God, Sadie. I’m sure the pastor is concerned with your faith, but your relationship with God is a personal thing. Do you remember that verse in the Bible where Jesus speaks about belief to Thomas the doubter? John Twenty Verse twenty-nine Jesus said *Thomas, because thou has seen me, thou hast believed; blessed are they that have not seen, and yet have believed.* A person’s choice to believe or not is a personal one and one that cannot be forced and should not be. If the love of the Lord and His Word is not in a person’s heart, then they are only mouthing empty words. Your love of Him shines in you, and you have always been dutiful and sincere in your worship and in how you live your life. Now, shall we get started?”

“Thanks, Oma. You always know what to say to make me feel better.” Sadie leaned across and hugged Elsie.

“Now, where can the church of God be found?” Elsie laid her Bible open in her lap.

Sadie folded her hands in her lap and dropped her head. “The church can be found around the globe. Mathew 18:20 *Where two or three are gathered in my name, there am I in the midst of them.*”

“Good. Why is it important that Mennonites adhere to the teachings and traditions that are passed down from generation to generation?”

Sadie cleared her throat. "It is important that we keep to the traditional ways. We should not follow the ideals of the world rather than those of God. Do no harm is an important tenet of our faith which is why our men can't serve in the military. We must teach our children in our own language in our schools so the heritage won't be lost. Language is an integral part of our faith."

Elsie nodded. "What is the first article of faith?"

Sadie was quiet for a moment, pleating a fold of her skirt between her fingers. She looked up at Elsie. "God is the Creator of all things. We believe that God created heaven and earth and all things visible and invisible as it is written in Genesis One. He sustains, rules over, and keeps all things in motion with His Almighty word. He is a holy and mysterious Spirit. John Chapter Four, Verse twenty-four, and Acts Chapter Eleven, Verse twenty-five."

"Go on," Elsie encouraged.

"He alone is God and all of mankind will one day kneel before Him. We should abide in our Lord and God with a living and everlasting faith," she paused and took a breath, "we should be obedient to Him, love Him and serve Him with our whole heart and soul and mind. The third Psalm , Verse nine, Isaiah Chapter Forty-five Verse twenty-three to twenty-four and Mathew Chapter Twenty-two."

"Well done, Sadie. Now the second article?"

"Jesus is the Son of God. We believe Jesus Christ, who is called the Word and has been with God since the beginning, is the true Son of God. Colossians Chapter one verse sixteen and Ephesians Chapter three verse nine. There is no other salvation by which we can be saved. I confess that he is the true God, and the eternal life, my own Lord, Saviour, Redeemer, and our salvation. John Chapter Twenty and Acts Chapter Four Verse twelve."

Elsie tapped the Bible with her finger. "And the third article?"

Sadie took a deep breath and released it before replying. "The Holy Spirit. I believe in the Holy Spirit, 'the Spirit of truth, which proceeds from the Father. The Holy Spirit leads us in all truth, and all He guides are His children. John Fifteen and Luke Twenty-four." Without waiting for Elsie to prompt her, Sadie plunged on. "The fourth article of faith is the Holy Trinity. I believe that God the Father, God the Son and God the Holy Spirit are one almighty and sovereign God."

"Very good, you've been practicing a lot since last time." Elsie smiled in approval.

"Oh, I have. I want to be baptised and able to marry Corny as soon as possible. It's only a little time before we leave for Paraguay."

Her words cast a pall over Elsie's heart although she took care not to let it show and dampen the brilliant joy on Sadie's face. She cleared her throat. "The fifth article of faith?"

The younger woman opened her mouth and then closed it, an expression consternation on her pretty face. "The Church of God…? No, that's not right. I can't remember." Frustration coloured her voice.

"The Birth," Elsie prompted.

Sadie's face lit up. "The Birth of Jesus Christ. I remember now." She sighed in relief. "I believe, as the entirety of the Scriptures testifies, that Jesus Christ came from eternity with God, and was born of God. At the preordained time chosen for the salvation of the world, God sent his Son, conceived through the Holy Spirit and the Virgin Mary. Isaiah Chapter Seven Verse fourteen and Luke Chapter One Verse thirty-five. He came from heaven to earth as God in human form. First Corinthians Chapter Fifteen, John Chapter One, John Chapter Six and Timothy Chapter Three Verse sixteen. Jesus was pure and without sin. Hebrews Four. He remained the true God and human in one entity and has saved us through His sacrificial blood, His suffering and His death on the cross. Only through belief in Jesus do we attain heaven. Colossians Chapter Two Verse one, First Corinthians Chapter One Verse thirty and Philippians Chapter Two Verses ten to eleven.

"Next is The Church of God," Sadie continued. "We believe that God has had, from the very beginning, a visible church or people, whom He loves. Acts Chapter One."

"Teachers and Servants of the church?" Elsie prompted her to go on.

Sadie nodded, more confident now. "Teachers and servants of the church. We believe the Lord Jesus has ordained shepherds, teachers and deacons to lead the church of God with exemplary teaching and conduct. Mathew Ten and Second Timothy Chapter Two Verse one." She paused. "The Holy Baptism. We believe Jesus Christ instituted baptism upon confession of faith. Mathew Twenty-eight and Mark Sixteen. The Lord's Supper. We believe our Lord Jesus ordained a communion of bread and wine for his followers in remembrance of His great innocence, suffering and death, done for sinful mankind. It was out of His true love that He allowed Himself to be sacrificed on the cross and gave His life as a willing Lamb to carry the sins of the world. First John Chapter One and Colossians Chapter One."

"You have been studying," Elsie declared. "Do you want to take a break? I can go bring some lemonade from the house."

"Let me do it. I need to stretch my legs." Sadie rose with fluid grace. "I'll be back in a moment."

Elsie watched the tall slim young woman cross the shade and sunlight spangled grass. She got up herself and arched her back, holding the heels of her hands to the small of her back. The achiness and twinges of pain were the result of weeding and transferring the tomato plants from the cold frames to the garden. Things she'd been doing for years and now gradually the small tasks were becoming more and more arduous. Old age creeping up on her, she supposed. Elsie held her hands out in front of her, the wrists were slim, the fingers tapered and pleasing to look at still. She ran her hands over her waist and hips, still trim and only a tiny bit larger than when she was a younger woman. It pleased her to realize she had aged well and kept her looks intact over the years.

"Here we are, Oma." Sadie returned with two glasses of lemonade. "I didn't bring the pitcher in case the sweetness attracted the flies." She handed Elsie a glass and sat down on the bench.

Elsie joined her and they sat sipping companionably for a few minutes while the birds sang and flitted through the spreading branches overhead. Wiping the condensation from the glass with a handkerchief, Elsie set the glass down beside her.

"Shall we carry on? Agnes will be back from the creek with the twins any time now."

"Of course. The Washing of Feet is next, right?" Sadie asked.

Elsie nodded.

"The Washing of Feet. We believe the Lord Jesus Christ, our Savour, lay his robe aside and washed His disciples' feet as a symbol of servanthood, whereby, He saved us and purified us from all sins. Therefore, as His followers, we should also serve one another with the same humility and love. John Thirteen." She stopped and grinned. “Now, the one closest to my heart at the moment. Marriage. We believe God ordained marriage when He placed Adam and Eve in the Garden of Eden and blessed them. Jesus also spoke various words regarding marriage. Genesis Chapter One Verse twenty-eight, Mathew Nineteen, First Corinthians Chapter Seven Verse thrity-nine, First Timothy Chapter Two Verse fifteen and Mathew Chapter Nineteen Verse six.

“The next one is a little dry, and I can see also how it may have gotten us Mennonites into tight situations in the past. But we have to stay true to the Word of God. Am I right, Oma?” Sadie raised an eyebrow in question.

Elsie nodded. “Yes, we must stay true to the tenets of our faith, even when that means going against government wishes and laws. We follow only God’s laws. Go on.”

Sadie frowned and thought for a moment, taking a sip of her drink. “The Government and Authority. We believe God has ordained the government and placed it in power, and all that oppose the government also oppose God’s ordination. However, in matters that go against the scriptures, we are to obey God rather than men. First Peter Two Verse fourteen, Romans Thirteen Verse four and Acts Five Verse twenty-nine.

“It’s kind of conflicted isn’t it? We need to obey the government, but then, only if their laws don’t contravene our beliefs and faith.”

"I agree. It does kind of say two things at once, but what we must remember is that, as Mennonites, we must always follow the Word of God and God's laws."

"Yes, Oma. I just had to puzzle over it for a while to come to truly understand what it was saying. Okay. Now. Revenge, Enmity and Non-resistance."

"Yes," Elsie prompted her. "Go on. We're almost done."

"Revenge, Enmity and Non-resistance. We believe Christians who have died to the world and were born again in God should not exercise revenge, but repay their enemies good for evil. Matthew Five Verse thirty-eight and Romans Twelve Verse nineteen to twenty-one."

"The last one?" Elsie asked.

"Man's Freewill." Sadie nodded decisively. "We believe everyone has free will with which to choose between good and evil and death or life in Christ, for him or herself. Deuteronomy Chapter Thirty Verse fifteen and Jeremiah Chapter Twenty-one Verse eight. God will judge the world. The righteous will be rewarded and the unrighteous, who have not accepted Christ, will perish eternally. Titus Chapter Two Verse twelve and Matthew Twenty-five."

"Very good, Sadie. I don't think you'll have any trouble when the pastor quizzes you."

"There might be another question, one they asked your mother when it was her turn. 'Is it necessary, then, to be born again, to be a true

Christian?" Do you know how to answer that one?"

"I think so. Yes, without regeneration no one can see the kingdom of God. Is that correct?"

"Yes, that answer should do nicely." Elsie patted her hand.

"Thanks, Oma. Oh, I hear the twins!" She laughed and got up to turn toward the house.

Elsie stood up as well gathering up the lemonade glasses. Agnes and the wet bedraggled twins came into sight through the gap in the caragana hedge. It was a pretty picture, Elsie thought, the bushes just starting to go golden with blossoms and the sun highlighting the shining faces flush with youth energy and happiness. "Oh, the innocence of childhood," she whispered too low for anyone to hear.

"Sadie! Are you around here somewhere? I'm ready to go home," Abram, Sadie's brother, called from by the barn.

"Coming!" she answered.

Elsie accompanied her to the barn yard, stopping to kiss the twins on the head as she passed. "Hello, Abram," she greeted her grandson. "Did you and Opa get the truck fixed?"

"Hi, Oma. Yes, I think we've got it in working order." Her tall dark haired grandson kissed her cheek. "We need to get going. I still have the milking to do when I get back."

"You run along then. Sadie and I are done now, too."

"I'm going to run into Landmark to get some fuel and pick up the mail. Do you want to ride along?" Ike arrived, wiping his hands on an oily rag. "Right after I wash up." He gave her that devilish grin that even after all these years turned her heart over.

"I have some things that need doing, go on without me. I do hope there's a letter from Sarah and Arnold. They should be in Mexico by now, don't you think?"

"Depends on a lot of things, Elsie. You know that. Worrying over something never made it happen any faster. There'll either be a letter or there won't." Ike walked away, stuffing the rag in his overall pocket as he went.

* * *

The house was quiet when the crunch of wagon wheels announced Ike's return. He had taken the horse and buggy into town in order to save fuel. Fuel that could be put to better use in the farm equipment, although when times were a bit tight, the horse powered equipment was still used. The racket of magpies arguing over something in the yard brought a sigh to her lips. With the calendar turning from May to June in a week or so the early wheat would be entering the milk stage when the all-important kernel of grain would be developing. Then it would be a daily struggle to keep the flocks of marauding birds away. Most of the children were old enough now to help with that which would save the men precious time away from the myriad of other tasks which required their attention in the long summer days.

She got up to pour a cup of coffee for Ike at the sound of him scraping his boots at the back door. Opening the ice box Elsie took out the newly churned butter and set it on the table. The bread baked fresh this morning was in the wooden box, she took it out and sliced a few thick pieces, setting them on a plate and adding a small jar of last year's Saskatoon jam. Which reminded her she needed to keep an eye on the strawberry patch. The first pale green berries were starting to blush pinkish red and soon it would be time to harvest the sweet fruits. There was nothing nicer than opening a jar of strawberry preserves in the dead of winter and eating a mouthful of summer while the winter winds raged outside.

"Let me take that. You sit and have your coffee." Elsie took the handful of mail from Ike as he came through the door.

Ike handed it over without speaking. After sitting and taking a drink he slathered the brown bread with a thick layer of butter and jam. Elsie caught the amused look on his face out of the corner of her eye as she shuffled though the envelopes. After so many years together there was no chance she could fool him. She knew, he knew, she was anxious to see if the much anticipated letter from Sarah was in the bundle, but didn't dare mention it and let her thoughts be known in case her hopes were dashed.

Elsie sorted the flyers from the other correspondence with trembling fingers. The letter had to be here, it just had to. Her heart leapt in her throat and a rush of excitement and relief flooded her when she came to the last envelope. From Sarah! Praise the Lord. Postmarked in some strange sounding place so they must have reached their destination and be settling in. For some unexplainable reason Elsie was reluctant to open the letter. While she held it in her hand unopened and unexplored, all things were possible both good and disappointing. Kind of like the idea Erwin Schrodinger talked about in 1935 with the theoretical cat in a box. Ike and Walter had discussed the paradox over the course on a long cold winter a few years ago. Heavens only knew why it stuck in her head. All Elsie had ever thought about was the poor cat. She sighed; even though there supposedly hadn't really been any cat in a box with poison it still bothered her.

"Are you going to open that letter or just look at it?" Ike's amused voice brought Elsie out of her wool gathering.

"Open it, of course. It's just I'm both excited and scared to know what it says. What if Sarah's sad and thinks she's made a mistake? What if—"

"What if she's happy and everything is wonderful?" Ike interrupted her. "Sit down and let's open it together. You can read it to me."

Seeing the doubtful look on her face he added. "Or I can read it to you if you like?"

Elsie stroked the paper with her fingers and made a decision. "You read it. But wait until I go and get Agnes and Walter. They'll want to hear the news too."

"Fair enough." Ike went back to finishing his coffee and snack, the letter lying by his plate.

By the time he was done everyone was gathered at the table. Taking his pocket knife Ike slit the envelope and took out the folded sheets of paper. Glancing around the table, he met Elsie's gaze and lingered there a moment before taking the reading glasses out of his shirt pocket and perching them on his nose.

"Ready?" His gaze swept the occupants of the table one more time. When everyone nodded he unfolded the letter. "It's dated May 7, 1947 and written someplace called Cuauhtemoc, Chihuahua, Mexico in the Manitoba Colony. Now that's surely a mouthful isn't it?" He paused and looked up.

"It all sounds so odd and strange. It doesn't seem possible our Sarah could be living there," Elsie said.

"Your parents most likely felt the same way when we went off to Paraguay and wrote home to them," Ike replied.

"You're probably right, but they never said a word about it to me, or to you." Elsie frowned.

"Nor will we, to Sarah and Arnold. This is their decision and their life, and I'm sure God has a plan for them and this is part of it." Ike resettled the spectacles on his nose. "I'll read it straight through first, and then we can go back and read the parts any of you want to hear over again. So here's what it says…

May 7, 1947
Manitoba Colony
Cuauhtemoc, Chihuahua, Mexico

Dear Mome and Pape and family,

We have made it to our new home! I must admit the journey was not as exciting as I thought it would be. At first it was, of course, but then it just seemed to take a very long time get to where we were going. I don't mean to sound like I'm complaining, just trying to give you an idea of how long and hot the travel was. Even though it is only May the temperature hovers in the mid 80s. I can't begin to imagine what it will be like in July and August. Mary assures me we'll get accustomed to the heat. Right now I'm not so sure. It's wonderful to see Mary and her family again, it makes missing all of you a little easier.

We have our own small place, not much yet, just a couple of rooms but it is all ours and Mary is helping me make it more homey. We haven't been allotted any land yet, but Arnold assures me it is only a matter of time. So far everyone has been very welcoming and we seem to be accepted quite willingly by the community. Some of rules are more strict than what they are at home in Manitoba and that will take some getting used to. But I'm sure in time I will not find any of the restrictions onerous.

Arnold and I saw some amazing things on our trip down here. We traveled from Winnipeg to St. Paul, Minnesota and honestly it didn't look any different than Manitoba. I wasn't fond of the train, too much jerking and the sound of the wheels on the iron rails made me grit my teeth. Some of the others found the clatter soothing, but it's beyond me how that could be so. As we went further south the landscape became much different than what we were used to. We stopped briefly at some place called Topeka in the state of Kansas to change trains. It was a time of much upheaval and confusion getting everyone organized and all our belongings from one train to the next. Arnold made sure our few possessions were transferred without any problem, but some of the women complained later that boxes of theirs were missing. I must count myself lucky that Arnold took control of our things. The next leg of our trip took us out of Kansas with its flat landscape and into Oklahoma.

I must tell you about what happened as we crossed through Oklahoma. It was unbearably hot and the humidity was terrible. Then out of a clear blue sky these huge thunderheads appeared. They were beautiful, all white on top and darker belo,w silhouetted against that brilliant blue sky. But then the wind whipped up and there was so much dust and dirt blowing around a person couldn't see out the windows. It howled and whined around the train and actually rocked the cars on the tracks. The children were crying and some of the women were weeping, the rest of us were praying. A few women wanted to stop the train and get off. They were sure the storm was a message from God that they should go home. Of course, the train couldn't be halted and we carried on into the teeth of the storm. Then the rain came, sheets and sheets of it. The land on either side of the tracks ran with water. The thunder was deafening, even over the roar of the wind and the sound of the train. And the hail! I have never seen anything like it. One instant the rain was sluicing down and the next the world outside my window turned white and huge balls of ice hammered on the roof making communicating impossible. Everything outside was smashed and flattened by the hail. Lightning was the only illumination as the world was dark as night except for the lightning and the balls of ice bouncing off the car. I'm not ashamed to say I was afraid and prayed for our deliverance. I clung to Arnold and although I could tell he was frightened as well, he was very brave and it made me feel a bit safer."

Ike paused to look around at her audience. "They must have made it through safely or Sarah wouldn't be writing us about it, but it sounds like a horrible storm. Now, where were we? Ah yes…

"Some of the coach windows were actually smashed by the hail. I didn't think it could get any worse, but it did. The sky was a strange black-blue colour and the clouds looked like they were touching the ground. Everything had a weird greenish cast when the hail finally stopped. At first I thought the worst was over. It was still raining very hard and the wind hadn't let up a bit, but the noise was less. It was still thundering and lightning and then, oh it was the most strange and terrifying thing I've ever seen, a thick finger of cloud poked down out of the bottom of this huge low cloud that took up the entire sky, and then the finger seemed to twist around itself, getting longer and shorter and then lengthening again. Suddenly it seemed to make up its mind and it reached out and made contact with the earth. Later the conductor told us it had been a least a mile away from the tracks, but at the time it looked like it was very close. The wind swirled around the angry looking cloud finger and picked up all sorts of things that got in its way. It ripped up a whole fence line of barbwire and flung it around like a child's toy. The posts and wire tangling itself like a skein of wool. Small trees, of which there weren't many where we were at the time, got plucked out of the ground and shot way up into the air before being carried away or dropped like matchsticks.

Everyone was terrified. I was certain the train was going to be carried away and us with it. Finally we left the funnel behind us still tearing up the land. Then the rain lessened and the sun came out. It was a glorious sight, pale blue sky peeking through the dark clouds and the most magnificent rainbow. It reached from one side to the other, intact, not a partial one like we so often see. And the glory of it! The colours were so vivid and there were actually two rainbows, one inside the arch of the other. Of course, we've all heard about tornadoes, I just never thought I'd ever get to see one. As I said before, both awe inspiring and terrifying.

I believe, and I told Arnold this as well, that the storm and then the rainbows were a sign that we were doing the right thing and God approved of our decision to move to Mexico. The storm was like the hard times we've been through, but we've left that all behind us now and the rainbows are a promise of better things to come. It's all in God's hands and I trust Him.

We finally crossed into Texas and arrived in Austin. I don't know what I expected Austin to be like, but it was nothing like what I imagined it would be. Enough said about that for now. I'll write more later. Then we changed trains again, leaving Austin for Presidio, Texas which is right across the border from Ojinaga, Mexico. Finally, we crossed into the country that would be our new home.

The heat was like an oven. Hot and dry and the air seemed to suck the moisture out of my skin. My face felt like it would crack if I smiled or talked. The sun burned me even through my clothes and I was very glad I had brought more than a few bonnets as it didn't take long for them to become wet with sweat.

When we arrived there was a delegation at the station in Cuauhlemoc to meet us and Mary was there as well. I was so happy to see her. I can't tell you how it felt to see a familiar face in that sea of strangers. I quite embarrassed myself by laughing and hugging her. Not at all like a mature married lady should act, but I couldn't help myself. I soon got myself under control as there was much to organize regarding getting our belongings from the train and packing them into the vehicles brought to meet us. I found out that they don't often use the vehicles except for farming and special occasions like this. Mostly it is horse and buggy or walking. I'm sure I'll get used to things in short order.

I must thank you, Mome, for insisting I learn Spanish. The form they speak here is a bit different than what you learned in Paraguay, but it helps immensely. It's only when dealing with people outside of the colony that language is an issue at all since we mostly communicate in Low German amongst ourselves.

I will close now and promise to write again soon. I'm very happy to be here finally, but I miss you all very much. Please give Sadie a hug for me on her wedding day and give her our best wishes for a happy life. You can write to me at the address on the top of this letter.

God bless you and keep you safe.

Your loving daughter, Sarah.

That's the end of it." Ike folded the sheets and handed them to Elsie who slid the paper back into the envelope and propped it against the sugar bowl.

"She sounds happy," Agnes offered. "I just can't imagine being that far away from everyone here, but I'm glad for her if it's truly what she wants."

"We all wish her happiness," Ike said. He pushed his chair back and got to his feet, snugging his cap down on his iron grey hair as he stepped into the mud room. "Still some things that need tending to before supper."

Walter followed him out. Elsie started to work on supper while Agnes went to check on the twins. It was all too quiet which usually meant there was some devilment in the works. Elsie allowed herself a small smile at the trouble those two could get into. Doris reminded her sharply of Anna sometimes which sent a spear of loss through her heart. Hopefully the younger girl learned something from her sister's death. Such a tragedy, she shook her head while her hands were busy making coleslaw. Just that morning she'd walked out to the hill where Blackie was buried to tend the small rose bush Anna had so lovingly planted. Anna and her animals…

* * *

Sunday June 1st, 1947 was bright and clear with the promise of heat later in the day. Elsie took longer than usual getting ready. She paid special attention to her hair, still thick and shining. Tipping her head this way and that to catch the beams of light coming in the bedroom window she admired the way the pure silver streaks of age served to highlight rather than detract from the over-all affect. Unlike Ike, whose hair was a stronger iron grey, Elsie was pleased her blond hair had faded to a silver that shimmered in the light. Like angel hair, Ike often told her.

The dress she selected was new, bought at Eaton's in Winnipeg for just this occasion. The pale rose colour suited her, she thought eyeing herself critically in the mirror. Smoothing the material over her hips Elsie smiled at her image in the looking glass. Satisfied all was in order, she picked up the matching hat and sat it on her head at a jaunty angle. She almost forgot her purse lying on the chair by the bed, but remembered it just in time before she left the room.

Ike was already outside with the big touring car he'd borrowed from one of his onkels. Elsie really preferred to take the horse and buggy to church. There was something about the slow pace and the rhythm of Polly's hooves on the road. God seemed all around her in the golden morning sunlight streaming across the land, the heady scent of roses blooming by the side of the road and later the sweet heavenly perfume of large clumps of milkweed where butterflies and bees flitted to and fro going about their business. She had to admit the vehicles were better on days when the weather was less than cooperative, but the horse and buggy would always own a small piece of her heart.

No time for wool gathering, she reminded herself taking the last few risers of the stairs and halting in the dim coolness of the hall. Agnes came down the stairs behind her mother herding the twins before her. They were dressed in their new clothes bought for Easter on the same shopping trip Elsie bought the dress she was wearing. The shining innocence on their small faces brought a smile to Elsie's face even while a surge of protectiveness engulfed her. What she wouldn't do keep the little ones from losing that uninhibited joy and belief the world was a kind and loving place. *Goodness, I'm indulging in odd thoughts today when all I should be thinking of is Sadie and Corny getting married.*

"Are we ready?" Elsie bent to adjust the tiny hat on Doris's fair hair.

"I think so. All we have to do is get these two in the car without getting a speck of dirt on them." Agnes gave a rueful smile. "Walter's already gone out, he's waiting with Pape."

"We'd best get out there too then." Elsie led the way through the living room and out the front door.

The big car purred in the drive, the back doors open. Walter swooped in and picked up Willy before he could kick his newly polished black shoes in the dust. He deposited the boy in the back of the car and turned to assist Doris who was daintily picking her way toward him. Elsie and Agnes settled on the back seat, one on either side of the twins. Walter and Ike got in the front and Ike put the car in gear.

"Roll your window up, Ike. The wind is going to ruin my hair," Elsie complained.

"It's hot, Elsie."

"My hair, Ike. And the dust is coming in. I don't want to show up at church all gritty and dirty."

"Please, Pape? It's hard enough getting these two cleaned up and harder keeping them that way." Agnes wiped a smudge of dirt off Willy's cheek with a handkerchief.

"Fine." Both men rolled up the front windows except for a tiny crack at the top. The action was accompanied by long suffering sighs.

It was hot, Elsie allowed. But a little heat was preferably to windblown hair and dusty clothes. Mercifully, the journey to church was quick in the fancy car. She stroked the material of the seat. It truly was a nice vehicle and very kind of Ike's onkel to lend it to them so everyone could make the trip up to St. Vital to see the newlyweds off. A spurt of panic made her lean forward and tap Ike on the shoulder.

"You did put the picnic basket in the trunk, didn't you? I left it on the kitchen table and totally forgot to check before I came out."

"Yes, Elsie. It's safely tucked away in the back, along with the going away present you want to give Sadie." Ike caught her gaze in the rear view mirror for a moment, amusement crinkling the corners of his blue eyes.

"Thank you for that." She settled back and tried to ignore the way her dress stuck to her back.

Ike parked the big sedan with a flourish under the shade of the line of Manitoba maples. A blessed breeze wafted over Elsie's skin when she opened the door. After getting out, she straightened her dress, smoothing the creases out and shaking the skirt so it fell softly around her. Taking a handkerchief she leaned down and wiped Doris's smudged face while Agnes ministered to Willy. Agnes took the twins' hands and started toward the church. Ike and Walter wandered off to speak with the other men gathered in the shade by the side of the building.

Elsie surveyed the people gathered, searching for Sadie and Susan in the small crowd. She spied them in the midst of a small group of women. Recognizing her daughters and daughters-in-law she hurried toward them. Sadie looked radiant, blond hair shining golden in the sun. A luminous string of pearls encircled her throat and small pearl studs adorned her ears. A gift from Susan and Martin to commemorate her baptism, the occasion of her joining the church, and her wedding day. Elsie thought of the small gift still in the trunk of the car. There would be plenty of time later for her to give it to Sadie.

"You look wonderful." Elsie hugged her granddaughter as she joined the group.

"Thank you, Oma."

"How did your catechism go?" She smiled already knowing the answer.

"I did well. Poor Corny struggled a bit with some of it, but the pastor was pleased enough, so nothing stands in the way of our marriage. There were some other instructions for the baptism candidates and then we were baptised on our confession of faith in the name of the Father, the Son and the Holy Ghost." Sadie's smile was brilliant.

"Let me borrow my granddaughter for a moment." Elsie took Sadie's gloved hand and led her a short way away from the group. "Now Sadie, did Susan have a chance to speak with you about your duty to your husband?"

Sadie's cheeks flushed pink and a dimple appeared in her cheek at the corner of her mouth. "She did, yes. I realize that living together as man and wife there will have to be some adjustments and compromises made. Mome has impressed on me the importance of respecting my husband and his wishes."

"That's good, then. A wife should look to her husband for guidance and protection. She should defer to his wisdom in all things. You realize that, don't you?" Elsie raised an eyebrow at her.

Sadie threw her head back in peals of laughter. "Oh Oma. If you could see your face!" She giggled again. "You look so serious. Of course I realize that. Haven't I watched my parents, and you and Opa, while I've been growing up? Please don't worry about me. Mome was very thorough in her explanation and instructions." She hugged Elsie close. "I love you, Oma. And I'm going to miss you very much."

"And I you, Sadie." Elsie released her granddaughter and smoothed her dress again.

"It's time! Hurry along, Sadie," Susan called from the church steps where the congregation was starting to file into the dim interior.

Grasping her hand Sadie pulled Elsie toward the church. The pale peach dress she wore was simple and suited her youthfulness. The matching shawl had small cream flowers in the pattern which highlighted the delicate flush on her cheeks. Elsie's heart swelled with pride at the picture her granddaughter made, laughing in the June sunlight.

The inside smelled of beeswax and lemon along with the peculiar scent of books and onion paper when Elsie stepped into the cool of the interior. She took her place in the pew with the rest of the females in her family. Sadie squeezed her hand before releasing it. This would be the last time Sadie sat with the family during service. Elsie's vision blurred a little and she blinked back the moisture gathering on her lashes. Such a day of joy and of sadness. Just as in life, she supposed. Happiness and joy leavened with a dollop of sadness and duty. She pulled the well-thumbed *gesangbuch* out of her purse and opened it to the selection indicated by the *Vorsängers*.

The familiar service flowed around her. Elsie paid attention and joined her voice in the praise of the Lord, Sadie's clear soprano soaring to the rafters beside her. When the regular service came to a close, Susan opened the cardboard box she'd carried into the church and handed Sadie a small bouquet of wild flowers and roses. Small shooting stars nodded over the brilliant yellow of marsh marigold, along with the yellow throated purple spikes of wild iris. Delicate feathery fronds of yarrow draped artistically from the sides and bottom of the arrangement. The twins had wanted to include the last of the tiny purple violets that were so fragrant, but the sweet smelling blooms were far too delicate and tiny to last. The whole bouquet was tied together with wide pale yellow and cream ribbon. Sadie's eyes were shining as she went to join her husband to be.

Another couple were also being married at the same time. They were also part of the group leaving for Paraguay that afternoon. Memories flooded Elsie's mind as the couples pledged their faith and took their vows. Were her and Ike ever that young and full of excitement at the promise of adventure and new life? A sigh escaped her. It seemed a long time ago now, that thrill of thinking about the long journey on the ship and the time to just get to know her new husband better. She remembered the happiness and contentment of those long days and nights.

She joined in the hymns and songs praising God and his love and asking his blessing on the young couples.

After the ceremony the newly married couples left the church followed by the congregation. Family and friends were invited to Susan and Martin's farm for a lunch before the trek to St. Vital. Elsie pushed the knowledge of Sadie's imminent departure to the back of her mind and determined to enjoy the upcoming celebration. The long tables under the trees by the house were loaded with potato salads, cheese, pickles, soups, and different types of bread along with roasts of ham and chickens. A special treat of watermelon with follkuaken was also present Everyone had contributed to the feast. Ike had driven Elsie and Agnes' contributions over earlier that morning almost before the sun was up.

Elsie found a quiet time during the chaos to draw Sadie aside and present her with the small gift.

"Grossmama, it's lovely." Sadie stroked the pebbled leather cover of the Bible.

"I'm glad you like it. It's the Bible my mother gave me on my wedding day and just before your grosspape and I left for Paraguay. I want you to have it and you can pass it on to your children when the time comes. Your opa and I wish you and Corny every happiness, Mrs. Hildebrand."

"Mrs. Hidebrand. Do you think I'll ever get used to being called that? It sounds so grown up, and I don't feel that way at all. I'm all giddy and so full of happiness."

"That's exactly how you're supposed to feel on your wedding day, Sadie. Full of happiness and promises."

"Oh, Oma! I'm going to miss you most of all." Tears sprang to her eyes.

"Now, now. No tears. This is a happy day. Your past will always be with you, but the time has come to look forward, to your future. Yours and Corny's. You will always have a place here, Mrs. Hildebrand. Now, I think I see Hilda looking for you. You best go see what your new mother-in-law wants. I see Jacob over by the house speaking with Corny, looks like a father son talk, so I imagine Hilda wants to have a private conversation with her new daughter."

"I love you, Oma. And thank you." Sadie hugged her and kissed both cheeks before hurrying off across the grass toward where Hilda Hildebrand waited.

Before it seemed possible it was time for those who were accompanying the emigrants to St. Vital to depart. Agnes and Helena, along with Nettie, Betty and Frieda volunteered to take care of chores and clear up the remains of the celebration so Susan and Martin could ride with Ike and Elsie in the big Tudor sedan. Elsie hesitated with one foot already in the door of the car when she caught sight of Sadie standing off by herself under the big apple tree she used to love to climb as a child. She rested her hand on the smooth bark and seemed to be trying to commit the scene to memory. Elsie empathised with her. She'd done the same thing on her wedding day before leaving for what she thought was forever.

"Mome, come on. Get in, everyone's leaving," Susan urged Elsie from inside the car.

"Coming." Elsie eased through the open door, settling in the seat. Her feet hurt in the new shoes and there seemed to be grit inside the collar of the new dress irritating the back of her neck. With the evening the day would cool off, but at the moment the June sun was still high and hot in the afternoon sky.

"All set?" Ike put the car in gear and the engine purred as they pulled away. The windows were rolled partway down, but Elsie was more interested in being cool at the moment. She pulled the pins holding her hat from her hair and set it on her lap. Beside her Susan did the same, laying her head back on the seat and closing her eyes.

"It doesn't seem possible my Sadie is married. I swear it was only yesterday when she was running around chasing butterflies and learning to sew."

"It seems like only yesterday you were doing the same thing, and now you've got a married daughter going off to Paraguay." Elsie smiled at her.

Elsie must have dozed off in the heat, she didn't remember closing her eyes, but when she opened them they were pulling into the parking lot by the train station. A small picnic was laid out under some trees on a patch of grass and the more intimate goodbyes of immediate family were said. Baskets of sandwiches and snacks for the journey were brought out and given to the travellers, and before it seemed credible it was time for the emigrants to board the train cars. Elsie stood in the crush of well-wishers gathered to see the travellers off. Sadie and Corny leaned out the open window of their train car, calling goodbyes and waving. They looked so happy and sure of themselves, Elsie thought. *Please God, let all their dreams come true. Let them always be as happy with each other as they are today.*

The engine hissed and smoked and with a great release of steam screech of wheels the train slowly started to move. Elsie stood on her toes and waved her handkerchief, shouting well wishes with the rest of them. Sadie leaned out the window, hanky fluttering in her hand from the increasing wind caused by the train's movement.

Elsie kept on waving until the train was out of sight. Sinking back off her toes, she tucked the handkerchief into her pocket and smoothed the wrinkled dress with her palms. Beside her, Susan wiped tears from her cheeks. Martin came and stood beside her, slipping an arm around her waist. Together they turned and walked toward the car. Ike appeared at Elsie's elbow and smiled down at her.

"Well, they're off. Do you remember what it was like?" His gaze was warm on hers.

"I do. I think it was easier to be the ones leaving than the ones left behind."

"I think you might be right." Ike took her arm and they moved toward the parking lot.

Elsie paused to look down the track where the east bound train had disappeared around a curve. "I hope she doesn't regret it and things turn out exactly the way those young people want it to."

"It will be as God wills it," Ike said, turning her back toward the car and home. "It worked out just fine for us, didn't it?"

Elsie glanced up at him with a tremulous smile. "It did, didn't it?" Her step was lighter as she accompanied her husband to the borrowed car and the trip home.

Epilogue

June 1948

Elsie stepped into the cool dimness of the kitchen with a sigh of relief. Placing the full pail of strawberries on the table, she wet a cloth and wiped her overheated face. Only the second week of June and it was as hot as the height of summer. Ike was worried about the hay and grain crop. They needed rain badly, and not the deluge a thunder storm would produce, but a nice steady down pour that could soak into the thirsty earth.

Wringing the damp cloth out she hung it on the towel rail to dry. Not that it would dry quickly in the close humid air, she thought wryly. Elsie reached up to take the big butterscotch coloured pottery bowl from the top of the cupboards. She sat down and prepared to clean the berries. Her gaze fell on the small pile of mail propped against the sugar container in the middle of the table.

She was surprised she hadn't seen it until she sat down. Her hand trembled a bit when she picked up the sheaf of envelopes and started to sort through. Ike must have run into Landmark for something for the tractor and decided to pick up the mail at the same time. Her assumption was borne out by the dirty thumb print that smudged the last envelope. Elsie's heart leaped in anticipation at the sight of the foreign post mark. *Mexico!* She pressed the unopened envelope to her breast and closed her eyes to give thanks to the Lord.

News from Sarah had been brief and sparse. In the months since she and Arnold had emigrated there had been only a few letters and the last one almost nine months ago. Even though the mails could be slow, the lack of communication worried Elsie. There must be trouble, or something Sarah didn't want to share. That had to be the reason. Sadie was a better correspondent that her Taunte Sarah, sending letters regularly every month. They were of course out dated before they arrived, but it was a pleasant feeling to still be part of Sadie and Corny's lives.

Sarah on the other hand had been positively miserly with her news. Taking a breath, Elsie slit the envelope open and pulled out the thin sheaf of folder paper. She should wait and read it with Ike and the rest of the family, but she couldn't wait. If there was bad news, Elsie needed time to process it and come to terms with whatever it was. She took another deep breath and closed her eyes, offering a silent prayer before starting to read.

April 30, 1948

Manitoba Colony

Cuauhtemoc, Chihuahua, Mexico

Dear Mome, Pape and Family,

I must apologize for not writing more often. We have been very busy here getting settled and arranging for our own portion of land. It hasn't been as cut and dried as it was made to sound before we got here, but I'm sure Arnold will get it all worked out.

Mary and her family are well. The weather here is unendingly hot. Sometimes hot and dry, then hot and wet. I almost find myself missing the cold of a Manitoba winter. I know I sent a letter to Agnes after Anna's death, but honestly I still find it hard to realize she's really gone. I can't imagine how Agnes must feel, but I'm sure the Lord will lend her and Walter the strength they need.

But enough about that. I do have some good news and once you hear it you'll understand why I've been such a bad correspondent these last few months.

Elsie quit reading for a moment and wiped her eyes. Her heart hammered in her chest. What was the girl going to say next? She did say it was good news…Elsie pressed a hand to her heart and turned back to the letter.

There's a photograph taped to the last page of the letter, but don't peek at it yet.

Elsie's fingers tested the papers in her hand and indeed the last page was a tiny bit thicker than the rest. Resisting the urge to flip to it immediately, she read on.

I hope you didn't peek. I want to tell you this myself first. Mexico has been everything I thought it would be for Arnold and I, the land issue notwithstanding. I feel wonderful and happy, maybe because there aren't any old memories waiting around every corner to haunt me. The climate seems to suit me and there is a doctor here who came from Paraguay and he knows some different things to keep my malaria from flaring up. It's called Rimijia and he gets packets of it sent up from South America. It tastes quite strong, but it seems to work better than anything I've tried.

So, now for the good news. I became pregnant late last summer, near as I can tell sometime near the end of August. It's hard to tell, as you know I've never been regular. (Don't read that part to Pape or Walter or anyone). I was quite sick for a time, not with malaria thank goodness, but with morning sickness that lasted all day and more than the three months everyone else seemed to endure. I didn't want to write and tell you about this because I was afraid it would end like all the others before. Somehow, if you didn't know I thought I would find it easier to bear. So I waited until I was sure everything was going to be okay.

On Friday April 16th, 1948 I gave birth to a baby boy! There, I never thought I'd get to say that! I'm a mother and Arnold is a pape. He's *so thrilled it's funny to see. You'll most likely hear from his mome about this as he sent off a letter to them the same day I mailed this one. We've decided to name our son Isaac Arnold, after both our fathers. We'll call him Ike for short. Mary's mome told me that Ike means 'He laughs' or 'laughter'. I didn't know that. Arnold and I liked the name Ike not only because of Pape but because he was the only son of Abraham and Sarah in the Old Testament.*

The doctor isn't sure I'll be able to have any more children, so our Ike may be our only child as well. Are you crying, Mome? I am as I write this. I can't describe how much love I feel for this tiny perfect person. It is overwhelming. Sometimes I get up in the middle of the night and just watch him sleep. I'm sure you will think that's silly of me and I can't see how you would ever have had time to do something so silly with all of us underfoot. But Ike is my one and only, and I don't think I'll ever get enough of looking at him and holding him.

So, now, if you haven't already, take a look at the photograph. Mary took it for me right after Ike was born. Look at the grin on Arnold's face! I've never seen him so excited about anything in my life.

I'll be sure to write more often now and send photographs when I can get them taken. I love you all and I miss you, but now I know I was right in coming to Mexico. I'm sure Arnold will be able to get the land we were promised soon. Right now we're working some common land with other couples waiting to be allotted a spot of their own.

With much love,
Sarah, Arnold and Baby Ike
Oxoxo

Elsie flipped the last page and stared at the grainy black and white photograph with the scalloped edges. Sarah's face fairly beamed out of the frame and Arnold had the silliest expression on his face as they held the tiny bundle between them. Elsie peered closer and could make out the tiny face of her newest grandson, his eyes wide open, seemed to look right at her as if he was saying hello.

Clutching the papers in her hand she almost ran out of the house toward the machine shed where Ike was clanging away on the old tractor.

"Ike, Ike!" she called. "You'll never guess what's in the letter from Sarah and Arnold. Oh, Ike! It's such good news."

The End

Glossary

Danksheen, Mutti Thank you, Mom

Dominion Land Grant This act allowed each applicant 160 acres of land, which is 65 hectares, at no cost except for a ten dollar fee to cover administrative costs. The applicant had to be a man of at least twenty-one years and he had to agree to cultivate at least forty acres of his land and build a permanent dwelling within three years. It was referred to as 'proving up the homestead'.

Gesangbuch Mennonite hymn book

Groottaunte great aunt

Grootonkle great uncle

Grosspape Grandfather/Grandpa

Grossmama Grandmother/Grandma

Kjinja children

Mome Mom

Oberschulze overseerer of Mennonite colony in Mexico

Oma grandmother

Onkle Uncle

Opa grandfather

Pape Dad

Shiplap fit (boards) together by halving so that each overlaps the one below.

"shiplapped pine used as facing for the first floor"

Taunte Aunt

Vorsängers men who lead the hymns in church, also called choristers

Author's Note

This novel could not have been written without the help of Margaret Kyle, Helena Hiebert, Peter S. Hiebert and Lynda Hiebert. A great deal of research has gone into this book and any errors are mine, so many people have helped bring this story to fruition and it is immensely better for their contributions.

I thought a brief history of the Mennonites and their journey to Manitoba might be helpful here.

In the early-to-mid 16th century Mennonites began to move from the Low Countries, Friesland and Flanders to the Vistula delta regions. They were seeking religious freedom and exemption from military service. At this time they gradually replaced the Dutch and Frisian languages with the Plaudietsch or (Low German) spoken in the area and blended it with their native tongues. Today that language is recognized as the distinct Mennonite language. The difference between Low and High German is that Low German developed in what were referred to as the 'low countries."

In 1772 most of the Mennonites' land in the Vistula region became part of Prussia in the first of the Partitions of Poland. When Frederick William II of Prussia took the throne in 1786 he imposed heavy fees on the Mennonites in exchange for the right to military exemption,

In 1763 Catherine the Great of Russia issued a Manifesto inviting Europeans to settle various parts of Russia, particularly in the Volga River region. For various reasons this appealed to the Mennonites. A delegation from the Vistula delta region of Prussia went to negotiate an extension to her Manifesto. Crown Prince Paul signed a new agreement in 1789. The migration to Russia from Prussia was led by Johann Bartsch and Jacob Hoeppner. They were given land northwest of the Sea of Azov. Most of the Mennonites in Prussia accepted the invitation and established the colony of Chortitsa on the Dnieper River in 1789. A second colony named Molotschna was founded in 1803.

When the Prussian government removed the elimination from military service on religious grounds, the Mennonites remaining there emigrated to Russia and settled along the Volga River in Samara. They were promised an exemption from military service for twenty years, after that they would be required to pay a special tax for the privilege.

Nationalism became stronger in central Europe and the Russian government chose to no longer uphold the special status of the German colonists. In 1870 Russia announced a "Russification plan" that ended all special privileges by 1880. The Mennonites were most upset at the thought of being forced to participate in the military, and losing the right to use German as the language in their schools. Both these things were deemed necessary to maintain their culture and religion.

In 1871 a delegation went to Petersburg to meet with the czar to appeal on religious grounds. They failed and another attempt was made the following year. They weren't successful, but the Tsar's brother Grand Duke Konstantin promised them a new law would offer a way to for Mennonites to be only involved in non-combatant military service.

Many conscientious Mennonites refused to accept that. So, 1873 twelve delegates went to North America looking for large tracts of farmland. The group returned with reports of good land available in Manitoba, Minnesota, South Dakota, Nebraska and Kansas.

The more conservative groups from Kleine Gemeinde, Bergthal and Chortitza came to Canada and settled in Manitoba. The more liberal groups chose to go to the United States. Between 1874 and 1880 eight thousand Mennonites moved to Manitoba, while forty-five thousand went to the States.

The Mennonites settled in Manitoba in two Reserves, the East and the West, which fell on the east and west side of the Red River. They formed villages with German names like Blumenort, Steinbach and Gruthal. A more conservative group of the Mennonites who settled in Manitoba near the Landmark, Niverville and Bothwell areas chose to move to

Mexico after World War I. This was in protest against their childrens' compulsory attendance at public schools where English had to be spoken rather than the Mennonite ran ones where German was the first language. There were also anti-German sentiments which played into their decisions. In the 1920s and late 1940s there was also an exodus to South America, Paraguay in particular for much the same reasons. Some emigrants returned to Manitoba after finding the new lands they had chosen didn't live up to their expectations.

There are different groups under the Mennonite umbrella, some more conservative and some more liberal than others. The group I have chosen for this story are more liberal, dressing in a mainstream style and not shunning mechanical means of farming or transportation.

With regards to the Blizzard of 1947, this was a real event that paralyzed the prairie provinces for well over two weeks, the storm itself lasting ten days. There are many articles and historical accounts and photographs of the event. You can find links to some of them in my Bibliography.

Anna's death in the blizzard is a purely fictional event, but based on facts. Some people did become lost in the storm and perished. It is further recorded that during the first winter the Mennonites were in Manitoba and living in semlins, one of the leader's young children passed away from a fever. It was impossible to go out and bury her, so they swaddled her and placed her in a cradle which they hung from the rood of the semlin until the storm passed and they could clear the snow and hack a grave out of the frozen prairie. I had this example in mind when I put Anna's body in her cold bedroom until the storm passed and there could be a funeral and burial.

I hope you have enjoyed this story. If you find you are interested in learning more about the Manitoba Mennonites, please visit Steinbach, Manitoba where the Mennonite Heritage Village is located. It is a wonderful place full of authentic historical artifacts including a semlin which you can enter and admire the ingenious way the walls were made of slabs of sod and the roof attached by poles and covered with more sods.

Other Books by Nancy M Bell

Canadian Historical Brides Series
His Brother's Bride ~ Ontario
On a Stormy Primal Shore ~ New Brunswick
Second author with Diane Scott Lewis
Landmark Roses ~ Manitoba
Lead author writing as Marie Rafter with
Margaret Kyle

The Cornwall Adventures
Laurel's Quest ~ Book One
A Step Beyond ~ Book Two
Go Gently ~ Book Three

Romance
Storm's Refuge A Longview Romance Book One
Come Hell or High Water A Longview Romance Book Two
A Longview Wedding
A Longview Christmas Seasonal Novella

Arabella's Secret Series
The Selkie's Song ~ Book One
Arabella Dreams ~ Book Two

Co-Authored with Pat Dale

The Last Cowboy
Henrietta's Heart
The Teddy Dialogues
She's Driving Me Crazy

Historical Horror
By N.M. Bell
No Absolution

Nancy M Bell, writing as Marie Rafter here, has publishing credits in poetry, fiction and non-fiction. Nancy has presented at the Surrey International Writers Conference and the Writers Guild of Alberta Conference. She loves writing fiction and poetry and following wherever her muse takes her.

Please visit her webpage
http://www.nancymbell.ca

She posts on the Books We Love Blog on the 18th of every month

http://bwlauthors.blogspot.ca/
You can find her on Facebook at
http://facebook.com/NancyMBell
Follow on twitter: @emilypikkasso

About the Author ~ Margaret Kyle

Margaret Kyle was born in Colony Bergthal, Caaguazú, Paraguay and moved to Manitoba, Canada in 1968 at the age of six. She grew up in Niverville and lives there with her husband. She has four children and three grandchildren. She works at the local school with special needs and EAL (English as an additional language) students. She has an interest in Mennonite history and she is proud of her rich heritage that she was born into. She, along with her sister and 91 year old mom are currently editing an autobiography that her father wrote for his family before he passed away. She has her Bachelor of Fine Arts. As a student she wrote an illustrated children's book about her parents' life in South America from 1948-1968.

Bibliography

The unpublished autobiography of Peter S. Hiebert.

http://manitobia.ca/resources/books/local_histories/096.pdfHistorical Atlas of the East Reserve: Illustrated. East Reserve Historical Series. Braun, Ernest N., Klassen, Glen R. (2015), Winnipeg, Manitoba by the Manitoba Mennonite Historical Society ISBN 9780973687750

Research Sites

https://en.wikipedia.org/wiki/Landmark,_Manitoba

http://cmbs.mennonitebrethren.ca/inst_records/halbstadt-mennonite-brethren-church-landmark-mb/

https://archives.mhsc.ca/seventh-annual-conference-of-evangelical

http://tipnut.com/mustard-plaster/

http://www.encognitive.com/node/14650

https://en.wikipedia.org/wiki/Timothy_Eaton_statue

http://www.thedepartmentstoremuseum.org/2010/06/t-eaton-co-ltd-winnipeg-manitoba-canada.html

http://www.plettfoundation.org/articles/cemeteries-and-country-cafes-where-old-friends-meet/

http://www.borealbirds.org/blog/2012/10/10/the-birds-of-manitoba

http://www.thecanadianencyclopedia.ca/en/article/mennonites/

https://en.wikipedia.org/wiki/Russian_Mennonite

http://www.mhsc.ca/index.php?content=http://www.mhsc.ca/mennos/hcanada.html

https://en.wikipedia.org/wiki/Dominion_Lands_Act

http://www.plettfoundation.org/articles/something-we-had-not-seen-nor-heard/

http://www.mennonitegenealogy.com/canada/quebec/quebec7480.htm

http://www.thecanadianencyclopedia.ca/en/article/winnipeg/

http://www.threshermensmuseum.com/old-stuff/heritage-buildings/100-sodhouse

https://mennoniteheritagevillage.com/heritage/tour/semlin

http://mennoniteeducation.weebly.com/faith.html

https://en.wikipedia.org/wiki/Ciudad_Cuauht%C3%A9moc,_Chihuahua

https://www.mapsofworld.com/usa/usa-rail-map.html

http://www.mennonitegenealogy.com/canada/quebec/quebec7480.htm

http://www.waymarking.com/waymarks/WMFD2W_MHM_Mennonite_Memorial_Landing_Site

Manufactured by Amazon.ca
Acheson, AB

10873516R00164